BROND

Frederic Lindsay is one of Scotland's most prolific and respected crime writers. He was born and brought up in Glasgow, and now lives near Edinburgh. After graduating with first-class honours in English Literature and Language he worked as a library assistant, a teacher and a lecturer before becoming a full-time writer. He has written for the theatre, radio, television and film, and is the author of over ten highly acclaimed novels, including *Jill Rips*, *A Charm Against Drowning*, *Kissing Judas*, *Death Knock*, *The Endings Man*, *My Life as a Man* and *Tremor of Demons*.

C153213770

Brond

FREDERIC LINDSAY

Polygon

First published in 1984 by Macdonald Publishers Ltd.
This edition first published in
Great Britain in 2007 by
Polygon, an imprint of Birlinn Ltd
West Newington House
10 Newington Road
Edinburgh
EH9 1QS

9 8 7 6 5 4 3 2 1

www.birlinn.co.uk

ISBN 10: 1 84697 032 6
ISBN 13: 978 1 84697 032 0

British Library Cataloguing-in-Publication Data
A catalogue record for this book is available on
request from the British Library

For Shirley

ONE

Something was wrong with the light. I could not get him into focus as he stood above me on the steps of the Union. The white shapeless flesh of his face stretched in the strange brightness, not a sharply turned corner from chins to hairline, and cool also and unsweated despite the fact he will be wearing, hidden under the denim suit, a set of woollen underwear down to his ankles. Hidden not secret – he wears them all the time; and asks strangers, as an introduction, if they do as well, plucking sometimes slyly at a loose fold of trouser. It is one of his obsessions.

The Union, the University straggling schizophrenic over the hill in Gothic stone and peeling concrete, the blackened church opposite, all of it was one dimension short: a film set discarded by the profit makers. Hard clear sunlight flooded down, pinning everything by a corner of solid shadow.

'I am moving to the climax of a story.' The high withdrawn voice has the Highland trick of lengthening some words into a plaintive tune.

'The teuchter Tolstoy,' I said.

The adjective coming from my own mouth surprised me. It was a word my father used to describe a Highlander. He was not a man of informed sympathies. Everything that was ever any good in Scotland, he would say, came out of the Lowlands. He had never heard of the Race Relations Board; like the rest of the world, it had never heard of him.

'Everyone interests me,' the teller of tales said with a characteristic wriggle of his shoulders.

Under the grubby shirt, torn scars ridge the flesh of his back. Each one made, if they are there and if he is to be believed at all, by soldiers in a camp for conscientious objectors. In anybody's book, he is a very old student indeed.

'Even you,' he said. 'Even you interest me.'

I move away as his spittle falls on me like an unintended benediction. At the corner I hesitated about walking through to Great Western Road, but turned instead into Gibson Street. In a city of a million people, it was nice to be in a quiet street in the afternoon just before work stopped. As I came on to the bridge, I passed a boy who was pulling himself up to get a view. His behind stuck out as he hung by his elbows from the narrow parapet of iron. In the hot stillness his feet made loud scrabbling noises as he struggled for purchase against the stone base. The noise irritated me. Children of that age risked death too casually. I wanted to lift him down, but if anyone saw me I would feel foolish.

When I stopped in the middle of the bridge, the view wasn't worth risking anything for: a smear of bleached grass along one bank, water that turned the blue sky grey, a whisky advertisement on the gable end of a warehouse where the river curved out of sight. The light hurt my eyes. I looked back at the boy in time to see a man put the flat of his hand under the little wriggling behind and give one good heave in passing that lifted him over the parapet. It looked effortless but then the boy had been drawing his weight up high.

There was nothing so explicable as a scream. Perhaps there was no time. When the noise came, it was sticks being broken on a drum. It had nothing in it of water for the boy had fallen on the edge of a pier built out from the blank wall. One arm and a leg trailed out over that platform; he did not look much better balanced than he had on the bridge, but down there it did not matter since the soiled water flowed near his outstretched fingers. There was red on the planks where his head had opened. Nothing could matter to him now or make a difference. At that moment I had no doubt that he was dead.

I looked round for support and all the million people were somewhere else. The other side of the bridge was buildings – a blank factory front and a brown tenement, its smooth stones stranger than a cliff wall, with not a face at any window to share what I felt.

If the man had stopped to look over, I still think I would have done something, but it was not like that. At school I had learned the game of chess and that a pawn can be taken by a move that is made in passing. I hadn't played the game much, and I could not remember the rank of the piece that made that capture. The man was big and grew bigger as he hobbled nearer. Held in the hot still light he was a cripple. With every second step his body, deep chested in expensive grey cloth, dipped and turned from me. His eyes were bent on the swaying ground, but not evasively or with any other emotion I was able to read in the powdered mask of a stranger's face. Plump on the jaws but with high cheekbones, rimless glasses, a blue sheen of cropped hair on the cheeks but the complexion pink and fresh. Powdered? I was not sure. Almost past me, he glanced up and one eyelid flickered shut.

I saw the stranger's eye almost close and the fine hairs of the lashes suspended trembling. Perhaps it was because it was magnified by the glasses that I saw it so clearly and for what seemed such a long time. Under the heavy white flesh of the lid, there was a line of white as if the eyeball had rolled up. At the last moment, a faint smile acknowledged me. Fixed on every muscular fold and tightening, I did not miss a detail but had no idea what any of it meant. Meeting him at another time, another place, I would have thought his smile was too . . . friendly. I have always been suspicious of people who wanted to be nice to me.

Confused by his smile, I let him go by, yet if I had doubted what I had seen I only had to look again over the parapet. Instead, I followed him. He did not look back. Our shadows moved along the blank wall of the factory. The ground beat up under my feet too painfully for me to hurry. His shadow ducked and beckoned ahead of me, but when I came to the corner the narrow side street was empty. There were half a

3

dozen cars parked. He was not in any of them. A door opened on to a yard and I crossed and looked inside the factory. It was abandoned, derelict, a vacancy of echoing concrete. I began to shake, but that was only because it was so cold out of the sun.

Back on the bridge, a man was leaning against the parapet looking down at the river. He wasn't old, maybe about fifty, but he looked as if he had all the time in the world and nothing to fill it. As I came near, he took a pipe from his mouth and with a fat plop of pursed lips spat over the side. The stream of brown juice splashed on the wood of a pier built out from the wall. There was nothing else on it, not even a stain of red on the planks as far as I could see. It was hard to be sure though because of the strangeness of the light.

The issue settled like strings of clover honey in the frying water. Saul had slain his thousands and David his ten thousands but I gave myself the name mass-murderer, true man of the twentieth century. It was not something I usually did in the bath. Desperate ills, unusual remedies. At least to my credit sex had been the last thing on my mind.

The door handle shook above my head. Miracle that I had been left in peace so long. Everybody would be out eating. The couple that ran the place lived on the bottom floor and let out the other two and the attic where Muldoon roosted. They only provided breakfast, or rather he did before he went to work. Heavy food, but plenty of it, fried eggs, bacon, sausages, fried pancakes, seas of strong tea: more a labourer's feed than a student's. He was from Coleraine in Northern Ireland and apparently they ate that way there. His name was Kennedy, a melancholy man looking older than his wife, who was blonde, very small made, with a bright silly face that got unexpectedly shrewd if you claimed an overcharge on the electric. In the house they called her Jackie, which she seemed to like, taking the joke as a compliment. He worked as a clerk in a bookie's so he was in and out of the house at odd times.

After a pause, the handle rattled, cracking on the release like a frosty morning rifle behind the farm at home. I didn't feel like struggling out for Willie Clarke or foxy-faced Muldoon the failed seminarist, who had jumped over the wall into personnel in Marks or somewhere; and if it was Kilpatrick I'd hang on till he gave up, not wanting to find myself in a fight. By this time, though, he'd have been kicking the door. I stirred the water with my hand and ran in more hot.

At the sound of the water, the door was shaken violently.

'All right. I'm coming!'

I lay back comfortably. Although in so long, I hadn't soaped and so the water was clear. The settled honey wove in the hair above my left ankle. I lifted my leg out of the water and rolled hard rubbery pellets of life between my thumb and forefinger. It was tough stuff, tenacious and remarkably abundant. I thought about the people I knew, and wondered why, with so much choice, chance should make such a hash of things.

'Would you mind hurrying, please?'

Not Kilpatrick or Muldoon. It was Jackie Kennedy and her sharp Belfast tone broke on a sweet note of desperation. There was a lavatory as well as a bath and toilet basin in here but the need hadn't occurred to me since there was another downstairs. Now I wondered about a plumbing crisis.

Not knowing what to say, I yanked the plug with my big toe and landed myself flailing as the water circled away.

I opened the door with my shirt squeaking on my sides. To my surprise she didn't explode in, bundle me out and, slamming the door, enter on the movements of Handel's *Water Music*. Instead, as I edged awkwardly round, resisting the temptation to gesture her in, she, cold-bloodedly enough, turned with me.

'You're a hell of a man,' she said at last. 'Don't you know it's weakening?'

'—?' I said, or even, '—?!' while my left ankle hid behind the right.

'Ba-athing. You must have been in near an hour and you look not much cleaner. Apart from being as red as a boiled lobster.'

5

Random Flahertyisms from 'Man of Aran' flickered on memory's back projection screen – certainly we had never seen lobsters as a delicacy on the à la carte here; fried pancakes now . . .

'In Belgium,' I said, 'they charge you for the water you use.'

'Dirty devils!' she exclaimed, making past me at last and closing the door in my face. I hesitated and heard noises of her settling down, muttering with fearful clarity, 'In Belgium, for God's sake!'

That nettle prick of foolishness must have been what brought Jackie Kennedy back to my mind hours later when Professor Gracemount tilted forward and asked Margaret Briody in his gentle malevolent fashion, 'Ah . . . ah, yes . . . would you care for cheese?' I was, you see, empathising with her – though her seeming foolish was not in my opinion his prime intention. At that time, I was a great admirer of the Professor's and saw the offered platter of cheese as an admirably civilised attempt to take her out of the line of combat. In any case, Miss Briody blinking her violet eyes was not it seemed violable by embarrassment.

We had come to the Professor's from an uncomfortable room at the University where we had been listening to a talk on the Modern American Novel. Vonnegut, Ken Kesey, Richard Brautigan – all the great names were there. When the speaker had answered the last question, the chairman said something and people applauded.

'The only American novel worth reading post-1945,' I said then to Margaret Briody, 'is *Across the River and into the Trees*.'

I was trying to catch her interest. Those were the first words I ever addressed to her. By a happy chance, she had been seated next to me, and for more than an hour I had been deluding myself I could feel her warmth spread between us and lap around my thigh.

Only moving around unobtrusively had kept me comfortable.

She looked at me seriously as if she were judging what I had said against some long perspective.

'I'm sure that can't be so,' she said, an atavistic music of peat water rippling under her Glasgow articulation. (God protect you from a teachers' training college, prayed I in passing, and the inanities of a speech department.) 'Although to be honest, I've never read any Faulkner,' and as I wasted the moment on loving astonishment at her ignorance, she turned to some chatterer on her other side.

The lecturer, a Liverpool voice with American back vowels as souvenirs of all those sabbatical leaves, was crying, 'Drinkies time, Dennis? Hell, I could certainly use a drink. We leaving for your place now, Dennis?'

'The Professor's actually. But yes now, we're going now, Jerry,' and a set towards the door began as Dennis Harland, lecturer in Old English, six feet topped by a narrow skull and the blue eyes of a Midshipman Ready – if not Old certainly standard English – stopped in front of me. 'Would you care to? A chance to talk over all Jerry's given us to think about. At the Professor's.'

I was flattered.

'Yes. Thanks very much.'

'Fine. See you there then.'

Bobbing on the tide, I was more pleased than suprised to see Margaret Briody by divine right of those long legs join the group around Jerry, who was still audible later as I drank my second glass of the Professor's sour economy wine.

' "God, Lord David," Jack told me he said to him, "haven't you ever wakened up and yelled, Christ! I'm in love, I've possessed this woman?" and Lord David hesitated, gave him that look, you know? and replied, "Well, my dear chap, I am maw-wied." '

Haw! haw! deep then and masculine from this son of the new world of exchange lectureships.

'He gave me this book of his poems.'

Held up, bashful, proud, a slim volume with, yellow on

green, *Cocksuck*, but he was opening it to give the Professor so it might have been Slowworm or Coachtrip. Cockroach?

'Dedicated it to me actually. Well, not the book, of course, but this . . . this copy. He's written here at the front.'

Impassive, the Professor studied the dedication and then held it up to give us a glimpse of the hasty slanted scrawl – 'To Jerry, one of the gang – I think.'

'I really value that. It's the highlight of my last trip. I mean, it made the trip – I did feel that.'

'Has Mr . . .' the Professor wafted the volume in decreasing circles, 'has— has he written anything else?'

As if he had been away long enough to mistake that kind of careful stammer for nothing more than diffidence, Jerry expanded: 'Anything else! Jesus, *everything* else would describe it better – but then I'm an enthusiast.' He grinned boyishly. 'After putting up with me all evening, you won't need to be told *that*. He's simply covered the whole American experience. Past and present. Future too, possibly – that is if you believe Dexroth. He called the Epsilon sonnet sequence "science fiction made over into prophecy". Wasn't that good?'

'When I listen to remarks like that,' someone said, 'I get the feeling we're being asked to pay a high price for the privilege of the Americans protecting us.'

The Professor laughed, and Jerry cried, 'Christ! isn't that typically English? Isn't it time we stopped pretending to some kind of cultural superiority that hasn't existed for fifty years?'

'Is that what I was doing?' the same someone pondered ironically. The voice was deep but soft. I envied its certainty that everyone would listen. From where I perched on the windowseat, I could see only one shoulder and a hand very white against the black leather of the chair. ' "Science fiction made over into prophecy." Does that mean anything? Most science fiction tries to be some kind of prophecy anyway, doesn't it?'

'Like – ah – *Dr Who*,' the Professor volunteered.

'Who?' Jerry looked bewildered.

'It's a serial on television,' Margaret Briody said, laughing, intervening innocent in the arena to draw the Professor's offering of biscuits and cheese and embarrass me on her behalf into a hallucinatingly vivid, brief memory of Jackie Kennedy.

'Actually,' the Professor took up the definition with surprising amiability, 'it is by this time a series of serials. Do you see? Sets of episodes, each forming a story, and each leading into a new set while all the time featuring the same central character.'

The incorrigible Margaret rang out, 'We've discovered your secret vice – watching *Dr Who*.'

'My grand-niece is devoted to it. But I don't apologise for watching it. The format has some interesting conse— consequences. Take this latest episode. The Doctor is confronted by an alien intelligence, a splendid villain. For him to overcome it entirely would mean it couldn't crop up in a later serial of the series. So, at the moment he's about to obliterate it, his friends burst in with the best of intentions and inadvertently allow it to escape off into outer space. The intelligence which runs away, lives to fight another day – or aeon rather.'

'The point's a nice one, Tom.' The same deep soft voice sounded from the depths of the black leather chair. 'Take the parallel case of our local theology. God and the Devil are locked in perpetual conflict, but Dr God never manages to wipe Lucifer out. Just as well of course, or the world and all of us with it, moon too, sun and stars, would snuff out and be done.'

'I don't see why the world should do that,' Jerry grumbled. It was obvious he disapproved of this conversation but couldn't resist trying to retake the high ground. 'Get rid of the Devil and the world should turn back into Eden.'

'I seem to remember, Brond,' the Professor addressed the man hidden from me in the chair, 'you inclining to the opinion that Satan made the material universe in a series of feints, weavings and subterfuges as he defended himself against a vengeful Creator.'

'I've never been persuaded,' the hidden speaker said, 'that God would not dispose of evil at once – if He could.'

'Oh, great!' Jerry said harshly. 'So God's a loser as far as you're concerned. What happens then if Satan wins? Have you a theory for that?'

'That would be absurd,' the soft voice said dismissively.

'For a man who wants to limit the divine power, Brond,' the Professor said, 'it hardly seems sporting to argue its omnipotence in the next breath.'

'You misunderstand me,' the voice said pleasantly. I could not see his face, but I imagined somehow that he might be smiling. 'It's my idea that defeat is what Satan is after, not the destruction of souls and all that melodrama.'

'The Devil wants to be defeated? But you've already said that he has the power to prevent God from doing that. Isn't there a contradiction there somewhere?'

'Not really. Satan sets out to torment and so God, who is good, is compelled to encounter him – when required. God has no choice, however weary He may be of the game. Satan has to be defeated – but never is entirely. In which case, we owe roses and sunsets,' the white hand tapped upon the black leather of the chair, 'to Satan's pleasure in being mastered.'

'It's the wine Prof Gracemount serves that does the damage,' Donald Baxter said and belched. 'Cheap wine, cheap theology. If I could find a church that served Château Lafite for communion, I'd become a convert.'

He lifted his pint and took a long slurping draw on it. I had to lean forward to hear what he was saying; the downstairs bar of the Union was crowded and everybody was yelling over the Country and Western.

'You look awful,' he said. 'You're sweating like a pig. Gracemount's wine has poisoned you.'

'I didn't feel like going home.' My lips were thick and rubbery. 'My digs, I mean. Not home. Long way from home.'

'Are you all right?'

'I don't despise you,' I said. 'For being a conscientious objector. That's your business. And anyway the war's over a long time. That's the way I look at it. I don't believe in wars myself – or violence. I'm a pacifist.'

Baxter looked offended. 'I'm not a bloody pacifist,' he said. 'Never have been.'

I tried to get him into focus but his face ran like white fat melting against the smoke.

'What about – what about all that stuff about being in a camp? What about all that crap about getting beaten up by the guards?'

The oldest student in the world scowled at me. 'I refused to join the army. But it wasn't because I didn't believe in fighting for my country. Only I'll pick the country. Do you understand?'

I shook my head. The movement hurt; waves of pain came and went. 'I don't get a bloody word of what you're on about.'

'I could believe that,' Donald Baxter said. 'That's why I don't explain any more why I didn't let them call me up. Who would know what I was talking about? What's the use in this country?'

Before I left the Professor's, things became a little blurred. I seemed to remember Professor Gracemount talking about being in Czechoslovakia. He had been in charge of some examination – for the British Council? did that make sense? – and a young Czech girl had come to see him. My brother has to pass this exam, she had said to him. It's very important to the family. It's very important to me. We would do anything to make sure he passed. I personally would do anything to make sure he passed.

I could *see* that girl. She was wearing a long cotton skirt with the kind of bright pattern a peasant in a movie might wear. I could see the way she licked her tongue over her upper lip when she murmured 'personally'.

Had the Professor told that story? Was that the kind of story he would tell?

I wasn't sure.

Yet I could remember everything the Irish lecturer from Stirling had said. He had started just after the Professor finished. It had been a long speech, but he had delivered it with great gusto.

'What size was Shakespeare's London or Plato's Athens?' he had asked rhetorically in a rolling brogue. 'Or take Kierkegaard who was followed by jeering children through the streets of Copenhagen. Isn't it wonderful that a philosopher should be as public a figure as that? But it's not astonishing if you get the scale right. Those places weren't conurbations. They had nothing to do with the nightmare cities of twenty million inhabitants we'll have by the end of the century. Why, Stirling at the moment has more of a population than Oslo had when Ibsen was scribbling. Yet I don't expect to find some kilted Henry Gibson clutching a manuscript of *A Doll's Hoose* when I drive back tonight. Not a hope, not the measliest little chance of it. Why? Because you need not just a town – although you *do* need that – a town with its human scale – but a town that's also a capital with a capital's sense of bearing a place in the scheme of things. The human scale – Joyce going to George Russell's door at midnight to knock and talk philosophy at him as an introduction. Or encountering Yeats – and Joyce, remember, young and unknown – and telling him, 'You are too old. I have met you too late.' Dublin in 1903, you see, was a small town. But it was a capital too – and that's the point. In Europe's eyes, a provincial town; but in the eyes of a sufficiency of its citizens, a place where a nation's destiny was being reforged. In 1903 who would have imagined that Dublin might be of more significance than London or—'

At that, however, Jerry, who had given up showing people his copy of *Cocksuck* and grown morose, twanged loudly, 'Talking of Dublin reminds me of a joke. Do you know what happened to the Irishman who tried to blow up a bus? Do you, eh? Anybody? He burned his mouth . . . on the exhaust pipe, do you see?'

'In Ireland,' the Irishman said, 'we have Kerry jokes. If it's joke time, I'll tell you a Kerry joke. A Kerry man got on a boat and as they sailed across the blue blue sea there was a cry, "Man overboard! Man overboard!" And then the captain shouted, "Throw over a buoy!" So the Kerry man picked up a boy and threw him overboard. A two-legged boy that was, do you understand? a human boy. The captain rushed down from the bridge and shouted at him, "You damned fool, I meant a cork buoy!" "Alannah! captain dear," said the Kerry man, "and how was I to know which part of Ireland he was from?" '

He told the joke very slowly and in a flat monotone quite unlike the animation of his earlier manner, but when there was practically no response he didn't seem at all disturbed. Only as the pause lengthened uncomfortably, at last a little smile broke at the corners of his mouth.

'It is odd, isn't it,' Dennis Harland intervened, his Midshipman Ready blue eyes twinkling, 'how every community chooses a butt for its jokes? From a little piece of research I did recently, I discovered that most of the jokes about Scotch meanness were originally jokes told by other Scots against the Aberdonians.'

'Or the Poles in America,' someone else said. It was the man hidden from me in the black leather chair. The deep soft voice had the same effect as before. Effortlessly, it made you pay attention. 'The Irish joke and the Polish joke – when I was in America, I decided they were interchangeable.'

'Goofy Newfies – that's what they call us at home in Canada,' a big red-faced character leaning against the wall said.

Since I didn't recognise him, I took the excuse to lean forward and touch Margaret Briody on the arm. 'Who is he?'

'He's from the Institute for Defence Studies in Aberdeen.' Her voice though musical had a touch too much carefree volume. 'He's a friend of the Professor's.'

I subsided as the Professor looked in our direction.

'I'm not really per – persuaded by this seductive argument about Joyce and company,' the Professor stammered dismissively. 'It smacks more of ecology – of politics – "small is

13

beautiful", that kind of thing – rather than corresponding to any reality in the history of culture. As I recall, Joyce got out of Dublin as soon as the going was good, and Ibsen didn't spend much time in Oslo, you know.'

'I think that's absolutely true,' cried Dennis Harland loyally. 'The Dublin that inspired Joyce wasn't a capital, and since Southern Ireland has become independent I don't think there's been much cultural activity.'

'I wouldn't say that was entirely so,' the Irishman said reasonably.

'There are probably more writers and poets in Scotland just now,' cried Dennis, warming to the job. 'They don't seem to be handicapped by being a region of a larger country. It suits them perhaps. It's an interesting idea.'

This seemed to catch the Canadian's attention. He levered his weight up from the wall. 'I don't pretend to know anything about culture,' he said. 'But I'll tell you straight – the independence some people in Scotland claim to hanker after is just a no-go option from a strategic point of view. They want to forget about their poets and history and stuff and just get out a big map and catch up on the geography. This is a useful piece of real estate and if things hot up the Russians are going to grab it. And if they do, the Americans just aren't going to have any option. They're going to have to blow it away.'

Other people talked then, but that bit isn't clear. I am almost sure that most of them had Scots accents, and that there was a kind of competition among them to take the point. They were very reasonable people. They could see how this idea of their country being independent must be unwise or unnecessary. Some of them provided their own reasons why it was probably immoral. Certainly, it seemed unlikely. I didn't disagree with them. What the Canadian had said seemed sensible to me. It was just that, for some stupid reason, I felt embarrassed for them. They embarrassed me.

At that precise moment, in the way these things sometimes happen, everyone stopped talking. We looked at one another and listened to the silence. That is always a mistake; no one wants to be the one who breaks it. It was a relief when someone laughed.

'I can't think where else in the world I could enjoy such a conversation,' remarked the deep soft voice of the man hidden in the depths of the black leather chair. 'You don't appreciate how unique you are.' He chuckled. 'The only comparison which comes to mind is of those unfortunate monks in the Middle Ages who took melancholy to the excess of desperation and committed suicide. The medieval Christians disapproved of that very much. Not just of the suicide – but of the despair. The theologians called it *acedia,* the despair of salvation. Some of them believed that this was what was meant by the sin against the Holy Ghost. Isn't that right, Tom?'

Professor Gracemount nodded and laughed. In response, the man who had been sitting in the black leather chair got to his feet and, turning from the fire, stretched as casually as if he were in his own home.

'Tell me,' he asked holding us all in his glance, 'do you think it possible for a nation to be guilty of that sin against the Holy Ghost?'

Now I saw him plainly, the man whom the Professor had called Brond: the deep chest, the one-sided stance as if his weight were taken on the left foot. It was the man I had seen on the bridge. I heard in the stillness the crack of sticks breaking.

There is only one moment for denunciation. The possibility recedes at the speed of absurdity, twice that of light. Before Brond had finished lighting a cigarette, the identification had emptied like clothes dropped from a ventriloquist's dummy. I seem to remember my first clear thought was, It can't be him – he isn't even wearing glasses. Whatever the first thought, the one that mattered was – it can't be him; he's a friend of the Professor's.

How could I have any confidence that I had seen him once before?

'He wasn't even wearing glasses,' I mumbled.

'Who?' Donald Baxter asked, floating his moon face across the table at me. 'Are you going to be sick? If you're going to be sick, go away. What's this about glasses?'

All of that was too complicated to explain, and so I told him about the Canadian and his geography lesson, but heard myself adding, 'He's a friend of the Professor's too.'

'Gracemount has some strange friends,' Baxter said. 'It comes from having been a spy. Have you never read that all the bright students get recruited at Trinity Hall for one side or the other?' He laughed at the look on my face. 'Don't worry. M.I.— five or six and a half or something. He was on our side.'

I tried to tell him what the others had said after the Canadian but I couldn't remember it very well and my throat ached from talking against the noise in the bar. It didn't matter though. It seemed as if Donald Baxter had heard it before.

'What could happen in Scotland that would have any significance? Decisions are things that happen somewhere else. The nationalised industries moved all the R. and D. south and took the steam out of James Watt's kettle. Adam Smith got himself a transfer to Head Office in St Louis. Bright chap young Smith.' It was impossible to tell if he was angry or play-acting. 'Real things happen in the real world. Here in never-never land all you can do is beat your wife or batter a stranger senseless against a wall.'

'That sounds real enough to me,' I said. 'You'd think it was real enough if you were the guy against the wall.'

'What do you know? You're a country boy. A clown. You don't know anything. That stuff doesn't matter. It's only *personal*.'

I didn't know what he was talking about. To be sociable, I said, 'Happy is the country that has no history.'

'Don't be stupid,' he said.

I didn't have to stay there and be insulted. I started to get up, but lost my balance and staggered back. I turned to find a beefy face above a rugby tie glaring at me.

'You spilled my beer,' Beefy Face said.

It was true. I could see the back of his hand where it held the glass was wet, and some of the liquid had given a dark edge to the white cuff of his shirt.

'Sorry,' I said.

'That's not good enough.' Beefy Face had a nice voice. You could tell that Daddy had paid to send him to a good school.

'Can't say any better than sorry.' I wanted to go home and lie down and go to sleep. 'I'll buy you another pint. What is it you're drinking?'

'Tell you what. I'll let you have it. And you can guess.'

As he finished, he turned his wrist and poured what was left of the pint down the front of my jacket.

I don't often lose my temper. It frightens me. I must have hit him for he had fallen down. He collapsed so fast I went down too and landed on my knees beside him. That was all right. It made it easy to keep hitting him. Something in his face broke against my fist.

Hands grabbed me by the shoulders and I resisted until someone got a handful of my hair and dragged me backwards off him.

'You bloody madman!' someone panted in my ear. 'You'd better get out of here! Fast!'

Choking on my rage, I saw Donald Baxter staring down at me.

'My God!' he said. 'A homicidal pacifist!'

To the plaintive tune of his reproach, a white moon lost its shape on a drift of smoke.

Some uncertain time afterwards, the lock in the Kennedys' front door had turned upside down. Cunningly I upturned the key and marrying it with the lock brought things to order.

Foxy Muldoon, least favoured of my fellow lodgers, was on his head on the bottom step of the hall stairs. If this shape was delirium, it should waver and give to let me pass through. Closer, it resolved into a great arse in chorus girl's knickers and under it a face inverted yet too malignant not to be part of reality.

'You look awful,' Muldoon said. In some complicated manoeuvre, he reversed himself upright. He stared and exclaimed, 'Christ!'

'You called, my child?'

'You're sweating drunk. You look awful.'

'Father, I have sinned – or I would have if she'd given me the chance.'

'You shit!'

He began to crab up the stairs backwards, fixing his tiny malevolent eyes on me.

'What shop did you get your knickers in?'

'Double shit!'

'Whoo!' I made a poke towards the shadowy bulge of his trousers and then was lying on the stairs.

From this new angle, I saw the knickers went down to his ankles. Pyjamas! it was a revelation – pyjamas and his suit jacket on top! – and one I shared with him at once.

'Why are you creeping about, little Jesus, in your jammies? Has Jackie been giving you holy communion?'

There was a crepitation as of skull plates. Inevitably, when I rolled over, the bookie's clerk, Jackie's husband, muffled out of the night with his key in his hand hung over me chewing his cheeks. I found my eyes watering and looked away.

I caught Muldoon's exotic tail vanishing.

Behind me, a door closed and Kennedy was gone. Had he been there at all?

When I wakened, I struggled to get out of bed until I realised I was already on the floor. It was black dark; but then, if the curtains were drawn, they were of heavy velvet. Mornings I had lain in bed thinking it was the middle of the night, only when I had opened these curtains to be blinded by the sun. I crawled to check and when I came to the wall I felt a velvet hem and at full stretch stroked another. It was night. I erected myself. At first country dark, an accident of housebacks and the run of the hill, it sieved out into gable ends and a lightness of shifting cloud. To insult a man in his own house was a terrible thing. What right had I to call her Jackie? That had always been a bad joke. And 'holy communion' – if there was a God, I'd slipped up there.

The blasphemy decided it. I would go and apologise to the man, and had started to dress when I found I was, and the stairs ran under my feet as effortlessly as an escalator.

I knocked on the closed door, and then leant my head against it for coolness.

'Ohahah!' Jackie Kennedy cried on a sweet apprehensive note as my poor head fell through the open door into the cloven warmth of her bosom.

'Are you an entire eejit?' she asked, with something more than an idle curiosity.

I stared sadly at her as she removed herself from me.

'Are you all right? You're a hideous colour.'

'Oh, I'm well. I'm fine. Would you call my landlord, please?'

'Dear God! Your landlord? It's five o'clock in the morning.'

'It would only take a minute.'

Suddenly tired beyond tiredness, I nodded forward on to her breast. Upright, I might have slept in its musty comfort like a baby if one hand needing support had not fallen astray just as the inner door opened. The restful glow of the lamp was split by a white finger stretched from Kennedy to our tableau of innocence.

Terrified by the muscles of his cheeks in profile, I called out, 'Don't be upset, dada, it's only me your own little gossoon Oedipus,' and fell backwards out of my own poor mimicry of a Belfast accent, overtaken until I could feel falling no more.

TWO

Not that I had ever been in anything you could call doubt about the nature of my own true father. Careering in slow motion up in bed, on impulse I checked to see if he had changed out of his boots before coming to town to visit me.

'Whit's up? Ye're no tender still?'

'Not at all. I was just easing myself.'

He stared down at his feet as if he had been reading my thoughts. If he had been wearing his boots, they would have carried an edge of dried sharn in each welt as a souvenir from the byres of Trailtrow.

'Aye . . .' he said without looking up. 'Ye're over it then?'

'Fine. I'm fine.'

There was a pause.

'Well. That's fine.'

He sighed.

'Looking after you all right?'

'Oh, sure. They're . . . fine. No problem. If you have to be in hospital, this must be as good as you'll get. On the National Health at least.'

'I've never been in hospital,' he said, changing the subject. It was a rule of my father's not to discuss politics. I had never asked him why he had that rule. There had been a time when I had been wee and you did not question your father's rules; and a time when I had been older and learned to keep the questions to myself; and there had been a time when I did not care why he had made one rule or another for himself. Shifting up in one piece to hold straight the clamp of stitches on my belly, it occurred to me the time I was in now was the one where I wouldn't ask in case he told me politics were not for the likes of him.

'Lying in your bed at this time o day's no for the like o me,' he said grinning companionably.

'Oh, Christ!' I groaned.

'Whit's up?' he cried in alarm, starting out of his seat.

Visitors all around looked at us. The man in the next bed, a saturnine barber with varicose veins, said something out of the side of his mouth. A girl laughed, but she was at the far end of the ward and it must have been about something else.

'For God's sake, faither, sit down!'

He subsided without altering his unmasked concern.

'Something's wrang wi ye or ye widnae hae made that noise. I've heard a pig dee happier. Ye'd a pain that time, tell the truth.'

'A wee pull on the stitches when I moved. Nothing to worry about.'

'I wouldnae just take that for granted.' He leaned closer and lowered his voice. 'Times they're careless devils in hospitals. They wouldnae hae left one o the wee dichtan cloots in ye?'

'A swab!'

'Just that. One o the wee cloots. I've heard o that. It could be inside ye festeran away.'

'Come on, faither, don't be daft.'

He gave me an offended look and sat back pretending to study the bottle and glasses on the bedside cupboard. For an idiot second, it seemed to me his eyes had filled with tears. I must have been more ill than I had realised.

'I've had a shake,' I explained.

'What was it they cried it? Not just your appendix . . .'

'Peritonitis. Without any pain until it happened. No pain no warning, so I should be dead.'

'You were lucky wi your landlady.'

I thought about that.

'Everybody said I looked terrible. I remember everybody saying I'd gone a terrible colour. It was still luck, though, that they called a doctor who put me in an ambulance instead of giving me four aspirin.'

Somewhere in the middle of that my father lost interest.

'I've never been in a place like this in my life,' he said looking round. 'It's the work like. Out in the open in all weathers.'

I had a rough idea of my father's age, and an exact one that he appeared ten years older than he should. He had been serving a sentence to hard labour since he was born; eighth child of a farm worker and a serving lassie in one of the two rooms plus outside lavatory of a tied cottage half way up a dirt road. I imagined it as looking more or less like the house my sister and I were born in – less than half way up the dead-end road to Trailtrow home farm.

'You've had your share o fresh air,' I said.

'And never a day's illness.'

We spent a while looking around. Only two visitors were allowed at each bed and there was an occasional bustle of folk changing place. The barber's fat wife went out and a young woman came in instead, bringing a small boy. She sat just behind my father and I stared at her crossed legs until the barber stopped grinning and talking. She would be his daughter, I guessed.

Abruptly, my father made the dry noise I recognised as his chuckle.

'That fool Thomson!' My mind went blank then cleared. Thomson had come as dairyman. He had got the cottage my father had been wanting for years. It wasn't an enormous ambition, but the in-comer Thomson was due the better house being a skilled man where my father was the general labourer, what they called in some parts of the country an orra-man – a do-everything man. 'That Thomson! I saw him on the other side of the road last Saturday. I was in the town. He didnae see me mind, but I spotted him. Ye couldnae hae missed him wi his gloves an his driving jacket up tae his bum. Ye'd hae thought he'd never seen a farm end aa his days. I waited till he stopped at a corner an just roared over, Hey, then, Jacky, did ye mind tae muck oot the byre the morn? He pretended no tae hear but his lugs lit up like traffic lamps.'

It was a relief when the bell went. My father jumped up at once, not waiting to be chivvied away by the nurses.

At the bed end he hesitated. 'I'll tell your mother you're looking fine then.'

'Sure.'

'She was right sorry she couldnae manage. She, eh, she . . . couldnae.'

'Tell her I'm fine.'

'Aye.'

There was no danger of loving my mother to excess; and I could not imagine anyone ever being impressed enough by my father to hate him.

If I had a problem, it was only that this pale thing I felt for my father might be what other people called love.

There was no reason for me to expect anyone at the evening visit. I had scrounged something to read from the fat man on the other side of the barber. 'Are you getting up to help?' he had asked me after the afternoon visitors had left. He was pushing a trolley of teacups. 'Up? Me?' 'They're very short of staff. It helps if we all muck in.' 'I don't take sugar,' I said. He seemed to be a cheerful lunatic, and I borrowed a bundle of his paperbacks, sagebrush and gunplay on grey paper.

I was hiding on the range from the barber and his visitors back for the evening when I saw Kennedy pass between the swing doors. It was horrible luck that he had somebody to visit in this ward. I slumped low in the bed and read the same sentence twice over: ' "If any durnfool foreigner ever invades into these parts," Paps said, "I just reckon the boys'll take their rifles and head for those mountains back there." ' As the white man said to the Indian, I reckon this treaty ain't big enough for both of us.

Kennedy loomed into the corner of my eye. Would my stitches burst if I jumped out of bed and made a hobble for it?

'I've brought you a bottle,' he said, sounding very Belfast and aggrieved.

'A bottle?'

If he hit me with it, dear God, let it be on the head.

'It's a bottle of squash. You get thirsty after an operation.'

He took the chair from the bed and pulled it up beside me.

'It's the anaesthetic,' he explained, sitting down. 'It dries you up.'

'Thanks for the squash. Are you sure?'

'Sure of what?'

'That it's all right. I mean if you meant it for someone else – I wouldn't mind. Were you surprised to see me in here?'

'You're not still delirious, are you?'

'No. I'm fine. They took it out.'

I gestured ambiguously towards my middle.

'You're still sweating.'

I dabbed and a line of sweat streaked my fingers.

'You were sweating that night surely.'

'I wasn't well.'

'You were not. Another three hours, the doctor told us, and you'd have been dead. The poison was pouring through you though you knew nothing about it.'

'I had no pain at all. No pain, no warning – the surgeon said that on his rounds. I was lucky.'

We looked at one another. I owed my life to them. I wanted to thank him, but I couldn't remember Jackie's proper name.

'I was lucky you realised I was ill.'

'That was easily told. Unconsciously you must have known you were bad. It was help you were after . . . unconsciously.'

'I can see that.' I tried to match his seriousness. 'I only remember that whole day in bits. I don't suppose some of it happened at all. I was at a . . . party.'

'You've been to plenty of those.'

He said it dourly. I wondered why he had come if he disapproved of me. Was it possible that Jackie had insisted that he come? The compliant husband; my stitches throbbed.

'Fooling around is all right until you fail your exams, then

24

the easy companions disappear. You're on your own. Fellowship is all right, if you choose the fellows.'

Kennedy as Polonius. Later when I woke, I lay thinking the poison might still be running like acid in my head.

The place was quiet. The lights were shaded. Behind Brond's head, I could make out the humped and muffled shape of the barber. Being right under the blankets must have made him feel safe. Brond's shirt was white with faint yellow markings. As a child at Trailtrow, I had seen new drawn milk turning in a buttery churn. The barber lay dreamlessly still in the hot tent of his breath.

'You were almost dead,' Brond said. 'They tell me you are making a good recovery.'

A tall nurse in the uniform I now recognised as a sister's passed between the beds. She didn't seem surprised to see Brond, but glanced our way and went softly by.

'It's not the visiting hour.'

My dry tongue filled my mouth.

'That doesn't matter.'

'Are you a doctor?'

His nose and mouth took on the coarse practicality of a surgeon, but he smiled and shook his head. I didn't want to think of any other reason why he should be here at this time of night. He was a distinguished looking man – he might have a Nobel Prize for medicine. Perhaps he had invented a bedpan that would let you piss without embarrassment. I couldn't use the ones they had in here. More poison to fester inside me.

My thoughts chattered above an attentive stillness which was fear.

'You don't remember where you saw me before?' Brond asked.

I shook my head. I denied it. That had been part of a dream when I was sick.

'That interesting evening at Professor Gracemount's—,' he began.

The breath I had been holding sighed out.

'It comes back to you.' It was not a question. 'We had a long talk.'

'I don't remember.'

'Oh, yes. You told me your ambitions. So, hearing you were ill . . .'

My ambitions? How could I believe that? I had never put them into words even for myself.

'I found you interesting.' He spread the bundle of paper-backs on the locker and picked one up. 'I hoped for something more interesting than this.' By one corner, he shook it gently at me. 'This is commonplace.'

Even studied in this shadow-pooled light, it couldn't be mistaken for the cover of a cowboy story. I had taken the paperbacks too much at first glance and face value, and wasted an afternoon on sagebrush that could have been spent on more intriguing stuff. Inside the blubber, the fat man had hidden shallows.

'Pornography,' Brond said, setting the book aside on a note of dismissal. 'That's a natural interest at your age, but even in such things there is a hierarchy. I read something once in that line which struck me very much. The man who wrote it was clever and impecunious and young. Like his friends then in Paris, he put that side of his imaginings on paper for money. They pretended to themselves it was done cynically. The truth was not so simple.'

At the far end of the ward, a hard painful effort of coughing began. Like a stone in a pond, it rippled to us in a muted disturbance of sleep mutterings and sighs.

'He wrote of a man and a woman facing one another across a table. Now and then, she reaches out with a finger and gently strokes him. Their only expression is a certain placidity. They are very tranquil, but then they are drugged. Perhaps something in the eyes if you were able to look very closely. He is a masochist and she is torturing and degrading him. When it is over, there is no blood, no business for the police, no hospital bills to meet. It struck me as an improvement on this world.'

He nodded thoughtfully, 'They shake hands very correctly, or perhaps they go off together and have tiny cream cakes with black sweet coffee.'

I looked at the books I had got from the fat man on the far side of the barber. Both of them had nagged me to get up; no doubt so that my wound could tear and get adhesions like the ones they bore as veterans.

'It's not mine,' I said. 'That book. I borrowed it.'

'You are right,' he said briskly. 'You are right. It is better to live in the real world.' He didn't say it as if he believed me, but as if it didn't matter. 'A student needs books – and money. A student needs time to think about what he needs. He needs to travel. It's possible for a young man of your . . . background not to understand how important that is.'

'I have my grant,' I said. My side had begun to ache; the warnings the surgeon had spoken of, coming too late to be useful. 'And I'll get a job in the summer vacation.'

'I will help you. I will find something for you,' Brond said.

'No! . . . I can get something for myself.'

'You have determination. That's good. Character achieves more than brains, if one has to choose. Finish your degree and I'll find work for you to do. I might have a career in mind.'

'I know what I'm going to do,' I lied in fright.

'Don't be too determined – that's a false pride. I'm not such a stranger as you imagine. I have a friend in the place where you lodge. People's lives become connected. Take help where it's offered and be a successful man.' He laughed quietly. 'That young man in Paris . . . When he was twenty, he had never slept with a woman. One day he stripped himself naked, beat his flesh with a leather belt and felt such joy! At last this is something real, he told himself. Now I join the real world.'

When he had gone, all the sounds came back, chiming glass and a voice scolding out of a bad dream. The barber was awake. Round his eyes the olive skin furrowed as he watched me from his ambush of pillows.

Yet hours later as I started awake, it was Kennedy who had

disturbed my dreams, one hand on the chair as he tick-tacked some mysterious emotion.

'It's long years since I've stood in a hospital. It must be . . .' Down the length of the ward, evening visitors were streaming to the door. It was surely time for him to go. 'We'd been married a year and Val was going to have a child. She had to come in for rest because she had high blood pressure. We lost the baby. I was sure it was a son, but I never asked.' All the visitors were gone. Kennedy hesitated in isolation. I disowned him. 'She was in a side room because she was on the danger list. She had a tube into her arm. After that we couldn't have children.'

I closed my eyes as if in pain; overcome by weakness – though, naturally, not unsympathetic.

'I can see you're done with tiredness.'

I heard him move away and opened my eyes. He had stopped at the end of the bed.

'Take care of yourself,' he said.

In the middle of the night, sweating out of sleep, it seemed to me his story about Jackie – he was the only one who ever called her Val – had been a kind of blackmail intended to make me see her crotch as out of bounds forever to my hand. When I woke up in the morning I saw things differently. He had opened the door when I was sick and resting my head in the shelter of her breast.

Prostrate at seven in the convalescent morning, avoiding the barber's eye, all I needed was a father.

THREE

That summer jobs were hard to come by, but I was so lucky I could turn one down. Dennis Harland described it to me. It would take me out of the country for the whole vacation, and the pay was good. Yet I turned it down. 'Professor Gracemount mentioned your name,' Dennis twinkled. And later, 'I know you've never had the chance to be abroad. You'll find it an invaluable experience.' Something bloody-minded in me made me refuse. I regretted it at leisure, of course.

When the goalkeeper of the amateur team I played for had his appendix out, he was back fumbling crosses inside three weeks. They wrote a story about him in the local paper. I reckoned I was at least as fit as that and a lot stronger, so to prove something I got myself a summer job as a removal man.

It is important to be in charge of your own life.

We wore aprons with the company's name and went in and out with chairs and children's trikes and washing machines. There were old machines plumbed into the kitchens of tenement flats all four of us lifted together. Andy the driver organised – if you felt underneath there were handgrips.

'I've been at this game thirty years,' Andy said more than once. 'You'll get young guys like you built like bulls and half the time they're knackered. Don't know how to lift. It's a knack.'

And he would hold up a kitchen chair balanced by one leg and grin at me through the bars. He was a small man, white headed though he wasn't more than fifty. As the driver, he organised where stuff went in the van, and packed in extraordinary amounts for he was good – although after a while I got it into my head that his knack ran too much to steering clear of the heaviest work. Of course, I was only the student who would walk away at the end of the summer. Why not pile it on to me? They were probably all at it, and I worried about the ache in my side. I began to match cunning with a bit of cunning – seeming to be busy but avoiding as much of the awkward stuff as I could. That went on until the second man, Davie, spoke to me. He was married and moody tempered.

'Look ya young bastard,' he said. We were at the back of the van waiting for Andy to come out of the office. 'See if you keep this up? Ye'll get hurt.'

'What are you on about?'

He was about half my size and not much older than me. He wore what looked like the same green dirty pullover all the time and had a cold most days. I couldn't see him giving me any trouble.

'Ye know all right. You're hell of a fly right enough.'

'No idea what you're talking about.'

He squinted at me in the sunlight. A long drop of water sparkled from the end of his nose.

'Fine. Ye'll no be bothered about Andy watchan ye then.'

'That's up to him, isn't it? He's old enough to speak for himself. Till he has a complaint I'll reckon he's satisfied.'

Across the sunlight in the yard, we could see him on the other side of the glass chatting up the counter girl. She was blonde and shiny and miniature.

'He's taking his time.'

'Wasting it more like,' I said. 'Daft at his age.'

'Oh, Christ!' He hawked up a gob of disgusted green slime. 'You've got it all weighed up. That's a wee ram in there. Magic wi women. He's had his candle in more candlesticks than you've had wet dreams.'

Andy turned away and came out into the yard. Through the glass the little blonde watched him. He winked at us and started over.

Like a rattle of peas, words were spat in my ear as we watched him strut towards us at his leisure.

'Last chance. He'll no *tell* ye tae buck up. Ah've seen him put folk oot the game. Never prove a thing.' His voice dropped appreciatively. 'It's a knack.'

We were to pick up the fourth man on the way to the job.

'Told Primo to wait at his corner,' Andy said.

Primo wasn't tall but he was broad, broader than anybody I had ever seen in real life. If Andy was not there, he would snatch up one of the monstrous machines all four of us usually handled and take it out on his own. He had arms like a gorilla and never rose to Andy's baiting, which went on more or less non-stop. I had a theory this was based on professional jealousy – if you were as uncannily strong as that, knack played second fiddle. Primo, Andy called him, or the man mountain.

'He'd better be there,' Andy said.

He swung the van out into the traffic. In the cabin you were high up, above the roofs of the cars. A horn brayed under our wheels.

'He's no happy,' I said. 'You made him stand on his brakes.'

'Tough.' He grinned at me. 'If any of these mugs hit us, they'll fold like a box o cream buns. And this big sweetheart'll no even dent.'

He patted the wheel, pleased with himself. He had a very pleasant open manner. I wondered about the four of us on a heavy lift and Andy's knack telling him when to let go. Racked muscles would be getting off lightly. Broken bones would be likelier.

'I'm feeling a lot better this morning,' I said.

'Oh, aye.'

'I was feeling rough the last couple of days.'

'Oh? Keep your eyes peeled, Davie, for the man mountain. He might be hanging oot a window peeling a banana.'

The morose Davie grunted. We were in a street of dilapidated tenements and bricked up windows. Chunks of broken glass glittered light up at the gang slogans. I tried again.

'I had an operation for my appendix. I thought my side was playing me up.'

31

'Stupid job tae take,' Davie said.

'I felt good. I suppose I was proving something.'

'Proving you're away wi it.'

'Don't be hard on the boy,' Andy said with the same pleasant grin. 'You were young yourself. Pay him no heed, son. He has his bad days wi being married. She no let you in last night, Davie?'

Davie sniffed the loose water back up his nose.

'It's a rotten feeling when ye cannae find the door key. The boy here doesnae know about door keys coming in all sizes. He's too young. No use taking a yale key tae a big lock.'

'Give it a rest. Do you never get tired listening to yourself?' Andy laughed delightedly.

'There's Primo,' I said. 'At the close mouth.'

'Typical,' Andy said. 'I say the corner so he waits at the close. When they were dishing out brains, he was hiding behind the door.'

The van pulled up on the road side of a row of cars.

'For God's sake,' Andy said, 'what's keeping him?'

From the cabin, bright sun shining across the dirty glass, the close beyond Primo was a black tunnel. He looked into it with his back to us, then turned as if at a word and came over.

'Whit kept ye? What were ye lookan at?' Andy nagged.

Primo stared at him peaceably.

'Would you like me tae get a bigger van? This one too wee for ye tae see?'

I had not once heard Primo answer in anger. For Andy and Davie that confirmed him as stupid, but I could not get rid of the image of him trotting down a flight of stairs with a machine two other men would have struggled to lift. He was such a quiet man, though, that you lost sight of that great difference, that gap – and Andy helped, if that was the right way to put it.

'I don't know how Primo sticks it,' I said to Davie. The job was in an old tenement; open stairs with awkward turns and stone steps worn in the centre with a hundred years of trudging down.

'Bet you the bugger'll be on the top floor,' Davie said cheerlessly. Andy had gone up to check.

I lowered my voice. Primo was hunkered down against the wall by the close, easy in the warm sun.

'I don't know why he doesn't tell Andy tae can it.'

'You frightened of Andy?'

'Me? He's been okay wi me.'

He took a watery pull at his nose.

'Should be.'

'What? Should be what?'

'Nothing. Long as you're happy.'

'Are you still on about me taking my share of the work?'

A stir of temper gave me an unwelcome surprise. I very rarely got angry but it would come on me without warning. Sometimes afterwards I could hardly understand why I had reacted so badly.

'I do my share,' I said. 'But I'm not doing more than my share. I'm not a mug.'

Davie snorted.

'Talk sense, ya young clown.'

The dangerous movement of temper coiled tighter. I was no good at arguing with words. I couldn't find them, and when that happened the anger pressed inside me. At school in my fourth year it had pressed too hard. I broke the prefect's cheekbone and they wanted to expel me but the evidence came out of how I had been provoked. The headmaster was sympathetic: I was one of the bright boys who was going to do the school credit.

Desperately I tried to sidetrack what was happening.

'You lot have been at this game for years. And you're a team. Know one another.'

Any words would do.

'Not at all,' Davie said. 'Years! Jesus! This is a fly by night outfit. I've been wi them three months. And the monkey,' he moved his eyes in the direction of Primo, 'he joined up the day before you came.'

The miracle happened. The tension washed out of me – and only because he had dropped his voice on 'monkey', careful against even the outside chance of being overheard. I had been taken off the hook.

As if he realised there had been a change, he harked back to where we had started.

'Why should the monkey tell Andy tae chuck it? He's too stupid to ken he's being kidded.'

'I wouldn't bet on it. If he did take exception, Andy would have to run for it.'

'Oh, the Uni teaches ye to be smart.'

I had not realised he had a grudge against students. 'Yooni,' he said, dragging it out like one of the gobs of slime that parted so affectionately from his lips.

'Don't need to be smart to know Primo could hammer Andy into the ground wi one hand stuck up his jumper.'

I had gone through my life making resolutions to keep my mouth shut. The empty pot rattles loudest: that was the kind of proverb my mother had branded into me; I told myself, a still tongue and keep your ears open. It had never worked so far. I was a strong silent man who liked to gossip.

Behind me Andy's voice crackled, 'Gentlemen o leisure, are ye?' and Davie sneered discreetly as I twitched like a frog's hind leg. 'Top floor – right hand side – auld party name o Morrison.'

If he had heard me, he gave no sign, but pantomimed a kick at the big man resting against the wall.

'Shift your arse, jumbo. You're no paid tae get a tan.'

Primo opened one eye and smiled peaceably.

It was a two-room and kitchen flat. Morrison was old and tremulous. He explained that most of his furniture was going into store.

'Ye'll be careful with that,' he kept saying.

'No sweat, grandpa,' the cheerful Andy repeated with never a sign of being ruffled or getting impatient. The reassurance came automatically, 'No sweat, grandpa.' Davie sniffed steadily as we worked.

'My wife had beautiful taste,' the old man explained. 'Bought at the auctions.'

Everything we lugged out was old and solid: oak tables and dutch dressers, everything wood without a veneer or plyboard from front to back. Sweat ran down my chest and my side niggled. Too many years had polished the stairs smooth. I groped for every step and wished I had toes that would grip like a monkey on a branch. Using my operation as an excuse to Andy, I had brought a curse on myself.

When we had emptied the flat, except for one wardrobe, the old man produced a six-pack of lager.

'Would you care for a refreshment?'

We drank and studied the monstrous wardrobe. It came to within inches of the ceiling and hid most of that wall.

'My wife was very proud of it.' He was drinking tea from a tumbler. I'm a teetotaller myself, he had said, producing the beer, but I don't object in others. His thin old man's hand curled blue around the glass. 'She'd be sad to see this day. Not that I blame my daughter. With a young family she has no room for my furniture. But I'll not see it sold.'

Andy opened the doors and peered inside.

'Unbelievable,' his voice came muffled from inside. 'It's in one piece. I was sure it would split up. Here, get it out frae the wall till I check.'

Before we could work it out, Primo took one end and flexed it out a couple of feet. Andy squinted along the back.

'Bloody solid,' he reported. 'They must have had a hell of a job getting it in here.'

'We were very lucky,' Mr Morrison said seriously. 'The outside door and this room being in line. It wouldn't have been possible otherwise.'

'That was right lucky,' Davie said grimly. He had finished one can and was opening one of the two that was left. He walked the length of the wardrobe, then came to the middle and leaned on it with one hand. Apart from his face getting red, nothing happened. 'Come on!' he said. 'I'm no paid enough tae

shift something like this. It's out o order. Ye'd need a block and
bloody tackle.'

'Oh, no.' Morrison looked alarmed. 'They had no equip-
ment when they brought it.'

'How many did it take tae bring it up?' Davie demanded.

As the old man blinked, I had the eerie impression he looked
cunning.

'Oh, I can't remember that. It was such a long time since.
Four like yourselves – or maybe three.'

'And the rest,' Davie said.

'We'll do it,' Andy said. 'It just takes a bit o thinking. No
sweat, grandpa.'

'Join the professionals,' Davie said and gathered stuff into
the back of his throat audibly.

Andy began lifting out drawers and stacking them neatly out
of the way. The wardrobe was furnished on both sides with tie
racks and shirt drawers, drawers for socks and little drawers for
bits and pieces. They were all empty except one of the small
drawers that had three cufflinks in it. Old Morrison fished
them out apologetically, wrapping them in his handkerchief
and tucking the lot into his breast pocket.

'This should have gone earlier,' Davie said.

'Not at all,' Andy said. I had never thought to see a fifty-year-
old furniture remover bridle. 'It's all planned. Don't you worry.
There's a place for it.'

'Once it's down.'

'Don't give me that. The flaming boy here would give ye a
showing up.'

Davie disconcerted me with a look of snot-green venom.

'He's too educated tae know there's something tae worry
about.'

The wardrobe doors were closed and locked with a little
brass key produced by Mr Morrison, who winced as we bound
a rope round the brute.

'Make it two,' Andy said.

After that there didn't seem to be any excuse for not starting.

36

We managed it to the first landing and put it down for a rest. Primo had taken the front end by himself with Andy at the back and Davie and me in the middle. The weight was incredible. I leaned across the bannister to get privacy while I gasped for air. Behind my thighs the long muscles jerked and twitched.

'You could die doing this.' I said.

'Not you, boy,' Andy said. I could see the sweat starting out under the grey line of his hair. 'You're a horse.' He grinned. 'You've earned your corn too for a change.'

'No way!' Davie's nose had gone as sharp as a bacon slicer. He was a rickety monument to a life's diet of cream buns and chips. I couldn't imagine how he survived this job. He sobbed at me, 'Ah don't think you're lifting the bastard at all.'

'You're a boring little prick,' I said.

When he came at me I watched his hands, which was a country boy's mistake. A good footballer when he heads the ball bangs it with the hard bone at the ridge of the forehead. That's where Davie – who must have been a handy player, at school, or even among the juniors – and often outside the dancing when the boys lined up for trouble – was going to connect, not with a leather ball but across my nose and teeth.

During the winter since I had come to the city, I had seen it done. Stumps and fragments of teeth spat out in sprays of blood from between burst flesh and then a gush of vomit.

I heard the suck of his breath as if he was drawing up liquid through a straw and then his head came at me like a bullet. I had no chance to get out of the way. It happened too fast for me to move and I would feel it, see my own blood, hear the blurt of teeth and sour liquid vomited out; and in the same second Davie's head struck the flat palm of Primo's hand held before me. There was no give in it at all. Davie seemed to be stunned. As for me, I was in shock.

Minutes later we were reorganised and heaving at the brute wardrobe. If there was a knack, Andy must have had it. Or maybe it was the only way out we had left ourselves – to get that monstrous burden down. Primo and I took the front for the awkward turn of the stair. Again the weight crushing down put everything out of my head except the pride that wouldn't admit it was too much for me.

My mouth stretched wide, a yell of protest in silence.

'Steady as you go . . .' Andy's voice sounded extraordinarily controlled. 'Together . . . Let her come.'

I watched it come and it dipped down at me. It was like Davie's greasy skull, inevitable. I tried to hold it but it tipped and I watched it go down on my foot. The pain was white like going into ice. I fell on one knee, twisted half under the weight. I was held between the wood and the worn stone. I was helpless against every particle of the weight. A mountain of wood moved and leaned out over me.

I knew I was going to die.

At a distance Andy was shouting and then Primo made an animal noise and his arm came round above me. Against nature, the mountain rose. I fell away to one side, crouched tight against the bannister like a child refusing to be born, and the great side hurtled down before me endlessly.

There was an avalanching uproar and when I could look everything was smashed and the wall sliced with crazy gaps as if it had been bombed.

Into the silence like reverence Andy said, 'Christ! What a disaster!'

Primo was pressed against the wall. I could see the thick cords of his neck black and swollen. He was staring up at them.

'You were pushing,' he said not loudly. 'I wasn't just holding that weight – I was taking you pushing it down on me.'

God help Andy! I thought; but it was Davie who whimpered and started to back up the steps. He did not get far. I had never seen a man being punched in that way – professionally, even after he was unconscious and falling.

'Can you walk?'

Before I could answer, he picked me up. Above us Mr Morrison squealed like an old nanny goat and Andy shouted about *Police, police,* and more faintly *bloody maniac* and as we wound down the old stairs I felt the calm thunder of his heart.

'In you go!'

As I slumped in the seat, deciding I wouldn't go unconscious after all, the ramp door slammed up and then there was the noise of bolts going in with an iron, final *chunk! chunk!*

Primo came in at the driver's side. Without paying any attention to me, he started her up and we pulled away – another job done: satisfaction our motto. I was too big to cry so I giggled, but that didn't sound too good either so I sat and watched the dogs foul the pavements.

'Foot bad?' Primo asked.

When I put my leg up on the bench seat, I was astonished.

'Bloody hell!' I said. 'The toe of the shoe's squeezed in.'

'Shoe? It's your foot being squeezed in you should be worried about.'

I unpicked the laces and eased my foot out. When I felt inside, there was a gap left under the steel toecap: not much but I sweated to think how lucky I'd been.

'I had them from my father. They're – like factory shoes. I nearly didn't wear them. It's just that I've only got one other pair and I wanted them kept decent. I nearly wore an old pair of trainers.'

I was babbling. The thought of what might have happened kept down the pain of what had.

The van stopped.

'I thought we were going back to the yard,' I said.

'Why?'

It was a good question. I couldn't imagine our welcome back, not once Mr Morrison contacted them.

'Well, we've a vanload of furniture. The old guy'll go crazy.'

Without answering, Primo got out of the van. He left his door swung open and the keys dangling from the ignition. I scrambled out, wincing, but could not refrain from closing the door on my side. As he walked away from the van, I followed him, not wanting to be left with the responsibility for the load.

39

It was a bad street; but although it reminded me of the one Andy collected Primo from every morning – hundred year old tenements, gouged and broken down, smelling of piss and rotted wood – I was sure I had never been here before. He led the way into what seemed to be an alley between streets, but it took us into an enclosed space. The black stone backs of the tenements reared up like the boundaries of a prison yard. I followed him as he began to cross to the other side. There were iron railings that should have separated the back courts but they were partially destroyed. In the middle there was a cluster of brick wash-houses and near them we waded through rubbish spilled and scattered from bins set in alcoves at their sides. A thin boy about five with bright red hair stretched down by his hands from the edge of a wash-house roof as if trying to find the courage to let go. Suddenly, convulsing out from the wall, he fell and rolled from us, his feet scrabbling among the rubbish. Despite the windows open for the heat, it was quiet. I could make out the words as a woman somewhere above started to scold. In a thin wail like a knife edge she made a weapon of her misery.

Primo swung round to me. The broad face with the splayed nose was thrust into mine.

'Sometimes you're ordered to do a thing,' he said, 'and it doesn't matter if it sticks in your craw. You're a soldier. You can't plan the battle.' He glared round. 'I don't know how to get rid of all this shit.'

I hadn't realised he could be angry. Even when he had been punching Davie to the ground, it had seemed more like an execution than something done in anger. It came out of him like something you could touch, but it wasn't aimed at me.

'Come on,' he said, 'but remember I didn't ask you to follow me.'

I didn't feel like arguing with him. We crossed at an angle and went side by side into a rear close entry. After the sunlight it was very dark. I limped up the stair after Primo. Old man Morrison's close had been several cuts of respectability above this. There the walls had been tiled; here it was dull maroon paint and whitewash peeling from shoulder height. On the first landing it was too dark to read the names on the brass name-plates. The sash window on the half landing was boarded up apart from a slot of light where a plank had been torn away. When I peered up the stair, I couldn't see him though I had the impression he was there.

'That you, Primo?'

My voice sounded thin and young. I took a breath and deepened it.

'Anybody there?'

He was hunkered down between the doors like a bull in a June heatwave. The doors looked like the others I'd passed coming up, only instead of a brass nameplate or a clan tartan one in plastic from Woolworth's, each of these, one on either side of the landing, had a white card pinned in the middle of the upper panel. The one beside me had the word ANDERS printed on it like a business card.

'Is this where you live?' I asked.

I did not know his real name but only the joke nickname the driver Andy had given him out of malice.

'I don't live anywhere any more,' he said.

As he stood up, I backed down a step. He reached out and prised the white cardboard nameplate from the door. He held it out to me and I snatched it from him because I was afraid he would grab my hand. I had seen people pulled into a punch that way. I kept backing down one step at a time.

'Take your chance,' he said from above me. 'You should go away.'

I groped my way down. The light was dim like a church but the walls smelled of evil and too much poverty. It was a bad church. One afternoon in a close like this, when I was looking for digs, I had surprised two boys holding a cat out of a third floor window. They had tied a string to its hind legs and it swung sobbing hate high above the stones of the back court. This is the city, I had thought, I'm in the city.

I came out of the front of the close into another street of desolate tenements and walked out of it into a hallucination of green fields. They had demolished streets of buildings and sown the vacant places with grass. These dazzling plots glowed like jewellery in the vivid light. On the far side, with the dirt of a hundred years cleaned away, it turned out that tenements were built of brown stone and cream stone. They shone like summer castles, but there were no banners.

A bus came and I took a seat at the front which was a mistake. When the driver swerved to avoid a dog, my bad foot slammed into the partition. I swallowed vomit and thought either you were the kind of driver who could run over a dog or you weren't. Children were being killed all the time by drivers like this bastard who swerved.

Waiting on the bench outside the X-ray department, I found the card Primo had given me in my pocket. It had a puncture in each corner where it had been tacked to the door.

On the back of it in the same neat print as 'Anders' on the front, someone had lettered the word BROND.

FOUR

There was something wrong about Kennedy. He would come in and sit with me for half an hour and then get up and go off to work. I had never asked to be any more than his lodger. He was always working, but now he had time as well for these communions. It was not as if he was a great conversationalist.

'A strange thing . . .'

Pause till he had gathered the last modicum of my attention. I glazed over with the effort of attention he required.

'In Ulster now they've had these killings, knee-cappings, that bombing.' He paid out his insight slowly like a fisherman with a length of line. 'Would you credit it that sex crimes are not one iota higher than they ever were?'

He was drinking the last of a mug of tea. Lately he had taken to joining me with his last cup before he went out.

'I'm not sure,' he said, 'but that they're not lower than they ever were, though it's hard to get the truth of it.'

'The legendary purity of the Irish.'

'How's that?'

I was sorry I had mentioned it.

'Nothing. It was just something I read in a book . . . It was a book about Chicago or somewhere in the States. One chapter was about this gang of bankrobbers and killers – public enemies one to seven – "mad dogs" the papers called them. And the guy who wrote the book had this great bit where he said: "There is no record of irregularity in their sex life; in that they preserved the legendary purity of the Irish."'

'What would their names be then?' Kennedy asked.

'Names?' Anybody I had told that story to had laughed.

Nobody had ever asked for their names. 'It's a while since I read it. I don't know. O'Bannion probably.'

For a second I thought I had offended him, but he said innocently, 'Ah. There's a lot of them RCs in crime.'

On the other hand, since being confined to the house I had seen less of Jackie. Not that I should have been confined to it – or was particularly since whenever boredom overtook me I swung out between my sticks with an old Chirnside Amateurs sock pulled on over the bandaging. Still, I spent most of my time about the place. I didn't much want to meet Brond or the mysterious Anders – in fact the way I was feeling I didn't even want to meet Mr Morrison. When I thought of that behemoth of nostalgia butted into firewood against the tenement wall, the person I least wanted to see again was the old gentleman.

At the beginning, though, I used the excuse to hang about the house because I had the notion that with everyone else out of the way – gone home for the summer or at work – Jackie and I would get to know one another better. Like the song said: Getting – to – know – all a – bout you.

'God bless all here!' I said hopefully, limping into the kitchen the morning after they'd put on the plaster.

'Have you nothing to do?'

She rattled greasy breakfast dishes into the basin.

'I'll dry for you, if you like.'

'I can manage.'

My backside rested comfortably on the edge of the table. It was nice to get the weight off my foot.

'How long are you going to be like that?' she asked in a tone less kind than interested.

'Not long. I'm a quick healer. I lost three of the toenails,' I added, trying to strike a balance between being brave and being honest.

'Not meaning to be uncivil,' she said knocking one plate on another, 'but since when did your lodging money buy you the use of the kitchen?'

That had been the first day and after it Jackie cooled as

Kennedy warmed to me. I was surprised one morning when she put her head round the door of the lodgers' sitting room and smiled at me.

'There's a lady to see you.'

I thought of my mother, but it was Margaret Briody who came and stood just inside the door. She was wearing jeans and my head was level with her crotch because she was taller than I remembered. Over it the cloth was frayed, faded blue and stretched.

'It's nice to see you,' I said.

Jackie offered us tea and she refused and then Jackie told her to sit down which I should have done and all the time I was looking at her and wondering what beautiful chance had brought her.

'Burst toes sounds horrible,' Margaret said wincing.

Half the winter we had kept benches warm in the same two Ordinary classes, but apart from the night of the Professor's party all she had ever said to me was, 'Thank God, that's over,' after an exam at Easter.

'I've been very brave,' I said. 'How did you hear I was out of commission?'

'I met Peter. He told me.'

The only Peter I could think of was Peter Thomson, the dairyman my father laughed at and envied because he dressed like a townie and put the farmer's back up by refusing to do odd jobs when he wasn't tending the herd.

'Peter Kilpatrick,' Margaret said widening her blue eyes at me.

'I didn't know you knew . . . Peter.' In my head I usually thought of my fellow lodger as that loud-mouthed bastard Kilpatrick.

'Well, I'd be bound to,' she said. 'Since I'm in the club.'

'Club?'

'Moirhill Harriers. I joined when I was fourteen. Peter was their star then – particularly for us girls.' She had a dark brown laugh like peat water pouring off a hill. 'He has marvellous thighs.'

45

'What about you? I mean – do you still do the running bit?'

'I won the four hundred metres at the Inter-Universities,' she said.

'I didn't know.'

'I wouldn't worry about it. The world's full of people who haven't heard the news yet.'

'You must be pretty good all the same,' I said.

Under the circumstances, it seemed reasonable to have a look at her legs. Neither jeans nor running to be first could spoil them.

'I'm thinking of taking up athletics next session myself,' I said.

The way things were going I could train for the stitched-up one-legged events.

As if reading my thoughts, she asked, 'Will your foot be all right by then?'

'That's no problem.' Round the perimeter, I pictured us jogging gently. Would a poll of fourteen-year-old harriers – girls only, please – rate my thighs as marvellous? 'When I go back to the hospital in a fortnight, they're going to amputate. That gives me plenty of time to get used to the tin foot before classes start. I wouldn't go in for the sprints, of course, and the marathon might be a bit hard on the join. Something in between.'

I had forgotten her response to wit. She bit her lip and both lovely eyes brimmed with tears. 'Oh, that's just awful,' she said in that marvellous voice like rippling water. And then forced by concern and honesty added, 'But though it's brave of you, I don't think it would be possible for you to be a miler like Peter – not with an— an impediment.'

How could you help loving anyone as obtuse as that – given youth, naturally, and beauty?

'I was joking.' Plunging in and admitting it seemed best, particularly since I had this temptation to go on and see how much she would believe. 'I've a stupid sense of humour. It hangs over me like the custard pie of Damocles.'

I had a glorious hallucination of her saying, 'Should that not be sword?'

'You were joking,' she said instead.

'Yes.'

Together we looked at my joke: it fell sick and died.

'I'm glad you're not going to lose your foot,' she said.

She rearranged her body on the sofa and my unmanly doubts fell away.

'It was great of you to come. I mean it's not as if . . .' my mind which had been going, went, 'as if we know one another . . . really well.'

'I had to come,' she explained.

I lurched up and joined her on the sofa. If she was going to make a declaration, it seemed as well to get closer.

'Peter asked me to give you this.'

She dumped a thing like a postman's sack between us. From it she pulled crumpled paper handkerchiefs, a bunch of keys, a pack of cigarettes and finally a parcel.

'You've to keep it for Brond,' she said. 'He'll send for it.'

'Who?'

I gave it back to her.

'It's for you,' she said and pressed it firmly into my lap. It was a sign of my distress that the contact was no more than a subliminal distraction. I sketched a return of the parcel, which was fended off.

'How would you like to keep it?' she asked laughing. 'I think the music's stopped.'

Blow after blow – now she was making jokes.

'You really are weird,' she said kindly. 'I had heard you were.'

'I don't know anybody called Brond,' I said.

'Yes, you do. He was at the Professor's, when we had the party after Jerry's talk.'

'I don't think that adds up to knowing somebody. I don't even know Peter Kilpatrick come to that.'

'Oh, but he lives here.' She showed alarm. 'I'm sure this is the right house.'

I thought she might ask if there was someone with a bandaged foot next door – a lookalike who went to listen to Jerry and go on to the Professor's and a party.

'*Know* him, I mean. I'm not a post office.'

Her eyes went watery.

'If you don't want to do it— I never thought—'

She moved her crossed legs in a little upheaval of emotion; as if hypnotised I matched it sympathetically: our knees touched. She moved away.

'I didn't mean that the way it sounded.'

'I should hope not,' she said. 'You do a favour and it's like a crime.'

'It's just that I don't see why he's sent it to me. What is it?' I hefted the parcel.

'I don't know. He gave me it and asked would you keep it. He said to tell you he'd be at his uncle's for a visit.'

'Why would I want to know where he is?'

'If Brond asked,' she said, 'that's what you were to tell him.'

'Tell Brond?' I was supposed to be crazy?

'His uncle in the country,' she added, proud of her accuracy.

'In the country . . . I can see that would make a difference.'

'I'll have to go,' she said. 'I'm supposed to be out finding a job for the rest of the vacation. I'd have one now, but I went to Greece after the exams.'

'Nice to be rich,' I said in envy.

To my surprise she blushed. I wondered if that meant she really was rich. Maybe her mother owned a chain of fruit barrows or her father was a bookie. Or maybe it was nothing to do with money; maybe she had a convent girl's bad conscience because she had gone off, after that night of the lecture, on a literary excursion with Jerry to talk about the Great American Novel while he did the grand tour of that magnificent body. Except that Jerry wa 'one of the gang, I think' – and I thought he probably was at that.

'The weather was lovely there,' she said, getting up and hanging the postman outfit over her shoulder.

'It would be an act of charity to come back and see me,' I coaxed. 'Being stuck in the house is pretty boring.'

'Are you sure you need to stay indoors? With crutches—'

'I wouldn't like to risk having to get that amputation.'

After a thoughful pause, she laughed. The jackpot spun round all oranges.

'If you won't forget to do what I asked you, I'll come,' she said.

'If I can manage,' she cautioned.

'Depending on whether I find that job.'

And she was gone – leaving me with the parcel.

'It's for Kilpatrick,' I told Jackie. 'How about you taking it? Someone's to call for it.'

'Why shouldn't he keep it himself until someone comes?' she asked.

I had re-invaded the kitchen and leaned at my old post watching her stir grated cheese into a bowl she was holding under her breasts like a painting 'Girl with Fruit': oranges no doubt.

'Because he isn't here. He's gone off. Didn't you know that?'

'Gone off?'

The question came so sharply I stared at her in surprise.

'He has an uncle in the country.' I tried to see her face, but her head was bent in concentration over the bowl. 'So I'm told. Anyway, that's where he is apparently.'

'It was that girl,' she said, without looking up. 'I thought it was you she was interested in – but she came for Peter, didn't she?'

'Peter' she had called him. It came to me with a kind of shock that I might have found another member of the Kilpatrick Thighs Fan Club. She wasn't fourteen though, and that let me feel prim and disapproving.

'Whoever she's interested in,' I said 'according to her he's off to the country.'

'Why should I care where he is?' She banged the bowl down. 'But he is due his rent. Not that he would—'

When she came back, she looked puzzled but, it seemed to me, relieved as well.

'If he is gone,' she said, 'he went in a hurry for he's taken nothing. That fancy jacket he's so taken with is there. His pyjamas over the bed – even his toothbrush. If he's gone to live with her, he hasn't taken much with him.'

'Live with— with Margaret Briody? No,' I said, and then less confidently, 'she's just a friend.' I didn't like the sudden image I had of loudmouth Kilpatrick on top of Margaret. 'I suppose even Kilpatrick is entitled to one friend.'

'Not you though. It wouldn't be you. You don't like him. He doesn't like you. Yet he sends you that parcel.'

I had known that it didn't make sense, but put into words menace took a shape that couldn't be ignored. It was as if she had put a curse on me.

'Peter's so thick with that fellow Muldoon,' she said. 'He would have sent it to him. I can't see how it can be from Peter at all.'

'Well, suppose . . . suppose he was in a hurry and he met Margaret – she's a student and knows me – but she wouldn't have known Muldoon.'

Putting back her hair from her cheek, she looked at me thoughtfully. I could see in her gaze a judgement on the feebleness of what I had just said. It didn't follow that because someone was blonde and small built that she was a fluff brain. I was learning something new every day.

'What's in the parcel?' she asked.

'I don't know.'

It sat on the table between us: about the length of a watchman's torch, wrapped in brown paper that was taped and bound with fat hairy string.

'It's heavy.' She shook it, holding it to her ear. 'Doesn't rattle. Who did she say was to call for it?'

I told her and she repeated the name after me. 'He'll be a foreigner.'

'I don't think so,' I said. 'But I'm not sure of anything about him.'

'You know him?'

'In a way. After a lecture one of the Professors invited us back to his house. Brond was there.'

'Oh.' She relaxed. 'If he was at your Professor's. I suppose it's all right then.'

'It was the night I was ill. When I—'

'I remember the night you were ill,' she said.

'Well, will you keep it for me then? After all, I might be out – if he came for it.'

'You're very eager to get rid of it. Or is it that you don't want to meet this man Brond?'

'No,' I lied. 'When I was ill, he came to see me in the hospital. He said he would get me a job in the summer.'

'I don't see why he would do that.' For the second time, her steady gaze disconcerted me. 'Why would he do that if he'd only met you the once?'

Twice. I had met him twice. Only the first time didn't happen: it was a lie, a delirium. I had been sick.

'I don't like any of this,' she said.

She turned to chop vegetables on the board. I had the crazy notion that I wanted to rest my head against her and tell her about the boy Brond had pushed over the bridge. It didn't happen, I would tell her; it's an impossible thing that never happened. Only, I would say to her, I don't understand why every detail gets clearer. For something that couldn't have happened, that didn't seem fair. *Chunk! Chunk! Chunk!* Jackie hammered down the knife.

'You take your parcel,' she said. 'If someone comes when you're out, I'll tell them to come back.'

With the parcel under my arm, I had the door open to go.

The blows came down on the chopping board and she raised her voice over them, 'I don't like your friend Margaret or her parcel. Give it to Muldoon! Get rid of it somehow. Give it back to the girl.'

'But why?'

In my excitement, I went over to her and when she ignored

me took her arm and held it to stop the stupid pounding. Pieces of vegetable were scattered off the edge of the board. She pulled from me.

'Why must I get rid of it?' I asked her. It was senseless expecting that she could know. Senselessly, I wanted someone to help me. 'What's wrong with it?'

There had to be something wrong, since Brond had come into my life again.

FIVE

To give the parcel back to Margaret Briody I had first to find her. I didn't know where she lived, but she had still to get fixed up with a summer job so it was possible she might be in the Queen Margaret Union.

The entry hall looked forlorn in the morning. I went upstairs to the coffee room. There was no one in it or behind the counter. Going back down, I noticed how the light peeled back broken tiles and drew dirty brown scuffs on the concrete walls.

The hall that had been empty was filled by a tall girl who looked as much at home as if her father had bought the University as a coming of age gift.

'I'm looking for somebody,' I said to her.

'Aren't we all?'

It was no time for philosophy. The parcel stuck under my wet armpit like a limpet mine.

'Her name's Margaret Briody. She's just finished her first year.'

'So has everybody else. Finished the year, I mean. There aren't many people about.'

She showed signs of moving on.

'Isn't there any way of checking if she's in the building?'

'Hold on.'

She disappeared behind a frosted glass door. When she closed it behind her, I saw there was a notice taped to the glass: Keep Out – This Means You. Music from a transistor started on the floor above and then turned off. Time passed.

'Margaret Briody!'

I felt my ears twitch like a rabbit's. There was a tannoy just above me.

'Margaret Briody. Wanted in the hall, please. Margaret Briody in the hall, please.'

The tall girl came out.

'If she's about, that should fetch her.'

'Will she hear that upstairs?'

She laughed.

'You can't get away from it. Even the loos are wired.'

When it had become pointless to wait any longer, I wandered down the hill to the Men's Union. It was another hot day. A small wind lifted dust from the gutters and blew it round the wheels of parked cars.

After the empty spaces in QM, the Men's Union seemed busy. A group were talking on the steps; I heard voices from the billiard room; in the lounge a scatter of figures nested in the deep shabby armchairs.

'Have you broken anyone's jaw since I saw you last, dear pacifist?'

He is wearing a tartan waistcoat louder than a pipe band in a phone booth. Even in this heat he looks cool, despite the fact I know he's wearing woollen underwear down to his ankles – he always does and has a theory about it. He is a very old student in anybody's book.

'What's wrong with you?' he asks. 'Are you ill?'

I sat down and the room settled steady again.

'I just remembered when I last saw you.'

He stared at me suspiciously.

'I suppose there's a joke there I'm missing for some reason.'

I shook my head. I didn't have the strength to explain. He nibbled a biscuit with large yellow teeth; there was a plateful of them in front of him, round small ones sparkling with crusted sugar.

'It's annoying,' he complained, swivelling his big head and spraying as he chewed. 'The people in this place get more ridiculously juvenile every year.'

'There's a reason for that, isn't there?' I responded automatically.

He had to be in his fifties, if those scars he claimed from the rifle butts of patriots were anything to go by. A life member of the Union, there was no good reason why he shouldn't be sitting in that chair twenty years from now senilely sucking on sweet biscuits.

'Just before you came in,' he said breaking the biscuit with a sad little snap, 'I was thinking of my fiancée. She was torpedoed in '43, you know.'

The last time I had heard him say that, someone in the group had snarled, 'Torpedoed in the middle of the Mediterranean like?' and he had looked puzzled while everyone laughed.

'As a writer,' he said, 'I live in my memories.'

'The last time I saw you,' I said, 'I was ill.'

'It's wretchedly true,' he said, not listening as usual, 'that here in Scotland we have this difficulty in finding our voice. I imagine at Oxford or Cambridge every fledgling can strike off an effect because he pulls on the teat of tradition. We, on the other hand, have to invent our manner as well as our matter. The Americans used to be the same – everyone having to begin all over again each time – but I suppose all those PhD theses helped to cure that – very self-conscious people, Americans. Unfortunately, not being English or Americans, for us that's neither here,' he broke his biscuit in two, 'nor there,' and popped the smaller piece into his mouth.

'I was ill.'

He blinked slowly and moved his lips like a goldfish surfacing.

'You look disgustingly healthy.'

'The last time we met I was ill. I was on the operating table the next day. My system was full of poison.'

'But now you're healthy.'

'I heal fast.'

'Show me your stitching,' he said and smiled disquietingly.

'I wanted to ask you about— a dream I had.'

'The afternoon's improving.' He edged up the collapsing slope of chair; the struggle producing inches of grey underwear over the belt of his trousers. 'I love dreams – and people so rarely offer them now.'

'I was walking over the bridge in Gibson Street and I saw a boy being killed.'

'By a red Jaguar.'

'No. He was lifted over. He fell on the wooden pier. A man lifted him over.'

'Can you describe the man?'

'No. It was a dream. Only . . . it's stupid – I heard his bones breaking.'

He settled back with a cheated look.

'I've heard more lurid adventures of the unconscious. I'd put it down to a presumptuous little cheese for last night's supper.'

'Not last night. I told you – the last time I met you. On the steps outside. It was the night I . . . fell ill.'

'You remember your suppers uncommon clearly. Was it the cheese put you in hospital?'

When he laughed, the black spaces showed where soldier guards were supposed to have knocked out his teeth. I wondered if it might be true. Perhaps it was that night which had beached him among these easy chairs.

'I'm not sure it was a dream,' I said.

He took that calmly enough.

'Pretty serious if it wasn't,' he said.

'It would be murder.'

'Probably yours.'

'The boy's,' I said stupidly.

'If you got a look at the man, yours too I should imagine. Assuming he ever comes across you. You would be the missing witness – in better days you might have been the death of him. Still he could feel strongly enough about these modern effete reproofs to return the compliment in the old style.'

He drew a finger across his neck. Above the collar, flesh sagged like a bag of soiled crepe. He was obscene and omniscient. I heeded the oracle.

He spoiled it by guffawing, wriggling as he settled into the depths of the chair.

'I've heard better but you told it well.' He patted his breasts in congratulation. 'Mind you, I doubt it would be hard to decide which of us had the other one going there.'

'Was a boy killed that night?'

'Naughty,' he said. 'Know when to stop. That's a mark of the artist too.'

Yet, outside I felt better. He was a gossipy compendium of information about what happened in or near University. No boy, no death. He had taken it as a joke. No death then. That night I must have been as sick as hell. Without bravado I stopped in the middle of the bridge.

It was another hot, still afternoon. The shadow of the bridge was black on the oily polluted water. Somebody had dropped a mattress over the parapet on to the wooden pier; its stuffing leaked out between beer cans and a jagged rubble of broken glass.

The footsteps coming from the far end of the bridge were very clear since the afternoon was so still. They limped light and heavy. On the whisky sign, painted on the gable end of the warehouse up river, a white letter hung like a swollen ladder, one rung to heaven. I was no sacrificial victim.

As the limping man came level with my shoulder, I spun round, and almost knocked the woman leading a child by the hand.

'Drunk! drunk!' she mouthed at me. 'Drunk' as a talisman against violence, not because the staring shock in her eyes believed it.

Their mingled footsteps faded as I lay against the parapet, more helpless than any of her children.

In the Kennedys' hall, it was a silly technical scruple that made me hesitate about using their phone to make a call. I was sure the house was empty. It felt empty, settling in the heat, old timbers complaining. I put the parcel by the phone and looked up my diary for the date I'd taken ill.

I gave the date and asked, 'Was there a report of a boy being killed that day?'

'Would you give me your name and address, please, sir?'

'It might have looked like an accident.'

I told him where the body had lain.

'And your name is?'

Would they insist on that if you phoned to say you were bleeding to death? Probably. How else would they know it was you when they got there – apart from the blood?

'You don't need my name to give me a piece of information. It's your district. A boy who died that day. By the river.'

I realised I was not alone. Kennedy stood in the doorway of the back sitting room. When he saw I was looking, he shook his head.

I put the phone down.

'You shouldn't make such a racket. I was well away to sleep.'

It seemed to be true: he was in bare feet, braces dangling from his hips. He yawned and ran two hands through his hair until it stood up in a bush. At the uncovered roots, there was a streak of what must be white hair that looked blond against the black.

'Sorry. It was a bad line. I didn't know anybody was at home.'

A bad line. Did anyone die, please, sir? All the time. Every minute of every day behind those stone tenement walls. Neighbours found them, the old solitaries, the unburied dead, like the old woman's corpse her daughter had kept secret until the soft corruption dried into a shape on the bed.

'I'm awake now anyway. Come through into the front parlour.'

As I followed him, I wondered if I should offer at once to pay for the phone call.

'It's the kind of day a drink is forgiveable. There's only Guinness mind. Not that it needs an apology. The only good thing the Irish ever made, eh?'

By this time I had learned that Kennedy was that odd kind of Ulsterman who thought that Irish was whatever he was not.

From the sideboard he fetched two glasses. It was another milestone, I could see by the careful ritual he made of it, that I should be given a drink by him. I would have sworn there was no alcohol in the house. With his dour northern look, I had taken him for a sabbatarian and a teetotaller.

'Better days!' he said and drank in a long hungry swallow.

I followed his example though it wasn't a drink I liked. The stupid idea came into my head as I drank that the dark bitter liquid tasted of death and the ambiguous lights on a city river.

Kennedy watched me with pleasure.

'There's nourishment in that. You could live off it.' His face crinkled at some private thought. 'I've known men who lived off it.'

I was astonished by the look of the room. I had been in it once before – the day I came in search of my new lodgings; that had been after my father's only visit, when he had taken one look at the old tenement where cats fell like fruit from windows and asked me to find somewhere else. That day this room had been like the rest of the house, neat, clean, nothing new but everything polished. Now it smelt stale. There was an over-turned glass on the sideboard; on the arm of my chair an ashtray balanced dangerously full of stubs.

'Put it on the floor,' Kennedy said, rubbing his hand over his face. 'Filthy habit.'

I had seen Jackie smoking but so fastidiously I could not imagine her building that mash of blackened ends.

'You've a grip like death on that. Is it University stuff?'

He tapped a finger in the direction of the parcel. I was holding it on my knee with one hand cupped over it protec-tively.

'It's not mine. I'm supposed to be keeping it for Peter Kilpatrick.'

'You'd better let him have it then.'

That sounded simple.

'I would if I knew where he was.'

'Upstairs snoring if he's on form.'

'Didn't you know either? He's gone off to some uncle in the country.'

'Either?'

'Jackie.' I was so involved I used her joke name without thinking; but he paid no heed. He must have been used to us calling her that. 'She hadn't heard either. She thought he might have skipped his rent.'

'She wouldn't like that. It's a big upkeep this place. Still, I wouldn't worry. He seems honest enough. Bit impulsive maybe – but then he's young.'

He irritated me blethering on without an idea in his head.

'Impulsive isn't the name for it. Jackie checked his room and he hasn't even taken a toothbrush with him.'

He seemed hardly interested, heavy sleep weighting him down as he drank.

'Just what I said – impulsive. The country'll do him good. There's more important things in life than washing your teeth.'

Like getting rid of this damned parcel before Brond came asking. I had sat too long. I could go to the library and check the back numbers of newspapers to see if the death of a boy had been reported that night.

'I'll have to be off.'

I stood up, putting the parcel familiarly under my arm again.

'Already?' Kennedy widened both eyes. 'I thought we would have a wet and a talk. I don't often have a chance of a talk.'

He followed me out into the hall.

'Are you not leaving that thing here?'

I was tempted. But I didn't want Brond anywhere near the house. Anyway Jackie would throw me out if she found I'd palmed it off on him after all she'd said.

'I'm going to get rid of it. There's a girl who'll take it.'

He reached out and touched the parcel.

'Is that the girl Val was telling me about? What's her name . . .?'

'Margaret.'

Suddenly I wanted to get away.

'Margaret Bridie – was it?'

'Margaret Briody.'

'Ah, Val's no use at names.' He looked at me sadly. 'That's not a Protestant name.'

Tribally, in this city, you could tell.

'If I were you,' he tapped the parcel to mark each word, 'I'd think – twice – in – that – direction. I've seen many a lad ruined for life with a hasty marriage.'

Impulse being a funny business.

SIX

The Reading Room consists of a set of concentric circles, the lending counter at the centre, department sub-libraries in rooms round the gallery. The entire structure acts as a reflector of noise; a shuffle echoed round the place. It was such an atrocious drawback in a library I was sure the architects must have won a clutch of awards. On my second circuit, heads came up, signalling fury or hope. At night when everybody was bored or desperate with studying it was a good place to pick up a girl.

As it happened the one I wanted was not there.

I was leaving when I wondered about the department rooms in the gallery. What else had I to do? My first plan had been to go to check the newspapers. The lure of old newspapers was not strong; I was tired and did not want to find out more that night. I was not sure if I wanted to find out more any time or ever. I was walking with only one stick. Properly, they should have a rubber ferrule on the end. Mine did not. My heel came down with a bump; my stick tapped. As I circled the gallery, all the heads below swung up like blind moles sniffing the air.

She was in the history library, a room about fifteen feet long, books on the walls, a table and half a dozen chairs in the middle. I looked at her through the glass. As if feeling my eyes, she glanced up. Her look was not welcoming.

I pushed the door. When it shut behind me, we were alone. All the coughs and sighs from below were shut out. In this echoing house of glass, the department rooms felt deceptively private. A character in one of my classes had claimed that one night about ten to nine, just before the building closed, he had glanced into the theology library and seen a couple on the job under the table. I tended to disbelieve the bit about the theology library – no sense in spoiling a good story.

'History library,' I said, 'or English possibly. Sociology very likely. Theology too good to be true.'

'What?' she said looking frightened or maybe just bewildered.

'I was thinking of something a guy told me.'

Impulse again; or a defence against the look on her face when she had seen me.

The look came back – only worse – when she noticed the parcel. It was still under my free arm; a kind of fixture. I hefted it gently in the air – it was heavy as Jackie had said – and laid it on the table in front of her.

'Yours, I think.'

She pushed it back at me as if it was hot. Too hard, for it slid off and landed at my feet. I picked it up hoping it had ripped but its web of string and tape was intact. If it was to be opened, it wouldn't be by accident.

'I don't know what you think you're doing. I told you it would be collected. What's the point of carrying it around with you?'

'It started to tick.'

'What?'

'You know – tick. As in tick, tick, tock. Tick, tock. If it's going to explode, I thought I'd bring it along so we could share it together.'

To my astonishment, she went white. Like a rabbit from a conjuror's hat, instantly white, and ready to disappear. Shame and sympathy took me out of myself so that I went round the table to comfort her. She wrestled away from my arm and my hand took her breast which put me rapidly back into myself.

It was when she pressed back further from me that I realised I was holding the parcel by her head.

'Please!' I said. I put it back on the table and pushed it away from us. The memory of her breast's weight lingered on my palm and fingers. 'I was just being stupid.'

'Why would you say it was a bomb? What made you say that?'

Suddenly I was infected by her fright.

'Jesus! It isn't, is it? You wouldn't have—'

The passion of my cowardice persuaded her at once. In a blink, she went from terror to rage.

'I can't conceive of a mentality like yours. Do you ever read the papers or look at the television news? And it's not funny!' As usual when I was embarrassed, I was grinning. If I had been a puppy, I'd have rolled over to show her my belly. 'Babies in prams burned. And people all torn to bits. While fools like you make jokes. You'd think God would strike you down!'

I had thought of that myself – about people being struck down all the time and how you could hardly ever see it as God's work.

A shape moved past on the other side of the glass. If we went on like this a janitor would come up and throw us out. I sat down and tried to still her with my eye. It probably didn't work with tigers either. She was scrambling up out of her seat when I caught her by the upper arm. For an instant she resisted and I felt the strength of her body and caught its scent, sweet with powder and sweat.

'Sit down, you bitch!' I heard myself saying. 'Just hold everything for a minute.'

On the far side of the gallery, behind the closed doors of another library, a girl stared across for a long moment before she lowered her head. Perhaps she had decided it was all right; perhaps she had not even been aware of us, looking up unseeingly from the book she was studying. I wished I was across there beside her; we could worry together over some textual crux. After all, I had come to the city for the academic life.

'Go if you want,' I said without unclenching my fist from her arm. 'But take your bloody Christmas present with you.'

'You're hurting me,' she said.

At home, they always said I didn't know my own strength.

'I didn't mean to. Will you please sit down?'

She rubbed her arm, pushing up the sleeve of her sweatshirt.

'You can see the marks of your fingers.' She turned her arm round and craned to see. 'And your thumb. It'll be black and blue.'

By the time she had finished saying all that she sounded judicial, almost cheerful.

'See?' she said. 'I'm not running away.'

'That'll be a disappointment to her,' I said nodding towards the girl across the gallery. She had lifted her head again to watch us. Lots of people were not made for the academic life.

'She's getting her eyes filled,' Margaret said, original as ever.

'She thinks we're having a lovers' quarrel. She's bored with her book – Anglo-Saxon poetry or, I don't know, mercantile law, and she's looking at us and wishing somebody would push open the door and say, Come out of there, and I'll show you some life.'

'And she says, being a lawyer, *caveat emptor*.'

My mind went blank on the Latin tag then cleared. "Let the buyer beware." I didn't see the joke, but it sounded danger-ously close to being witty. Of course, Kennedy would have explained, the RCs did a lot of Latin at school.

I indicated the parcel, cautiously so as not to upset her.

'It's not a bomb and so why not take it back?'

'No one in his right mind would have thought it was so why don't you keep it?' she said.

It was a good question.

'I wouldn't mind. Why should I? Only I'm thinking of going back home. I can't get a job so I'll go home. No use Brond coming to collect it, if I'm not there. That's all I was thinking . . .'

I trailed off. It would have made a reasonable story if I had worked it out before seeing her. Now, after all the melodrama, my reasonableness sounded weirdly unreasonable.

'Why don't you leave it with the people in the house? I can't see why they'd mind.'

'I tried that. My landlady wouldn't touch it with a barge pole. To tell you the truth, she told me to get rid of it.'

Margaret had forgotten all about wanting to get away. She fixed those enormous eyes on my mouth as if she could read the words as well as hear them.

'That's terribly strange,' she said. 'What did you say that made her feel that way?'

'Nothing. I told her you'd met Peter Kilpatrick; he'd given you it and asked you to give it to me. And I told her somebody was to call for it.'

'Did you tell her Brond would send for it?'

I thought about that. I could remember Jackie's arm and the knife chopping down on to the wooden board. Funny, I had caught hold of Jackie by the arm too.

'Does it matter?'

'I can't see why it should.' She looked offended. 'It's just very strange that she should talk that way.'

'Maybe not. Since I was ill, they've decided to adopt me.' I appointed Jackie an honorary member in Kennedy's concern. 'She was just being protective.'

'Your landlady, you mean? Was that her that opened the door to me?'

'That's her. We call her Jackie. As a joke, you know . . . because her name's Kennedy. It's not very funny.'

As she showed no reaction, I thought it would be like her never to have heard of the ex-Mrs Onassis.

But when she did speak it was on a different track altogether.

'If you think she's old enough to be your mother, your eyes want tested. And another thing,' she went on without taking a breath – inadvertently I kept monitoring the extraordinary evidences of her taking one – 'where do you get off swearing at me?'

'Me?' I was astonished. 'When have I sworn at you?'

'Just now. You called me a— you know what you called me.'

We discussed lady dogs and then we found we were both ravenously hungry. Excitement does that to you. I had no money but she said it would be her treat. As we left, the girl in the other library watched us wistfully, which was a consolation although I still had the parcel under my arm.

SEVEN

The parcel lay on the bench seat between Primo and me. When it had occurred to me that it was still a fixture under my off-side arm, I had put it there between us as a gesture of goodwill. Looking at Primo's fingers on the steering wheel like a bunch of bananas, I felt goodwill was in season.

'Primo?'

'Uh–huh.'

'I never did thank you for getting between me and that maniac Davie.'

The car swung into the side and stopped as abruptly as that length of executive metal could.

'Don't whine,' Primo said seriously. 'You were beginning to whine there. Sometimes it's more dignified to say nothing. Believe me, that's sincere advice.'

That was a long speech for him. Even when he had appeared outside the restaurant, he had only grunted what amounted to an invitation to climb in. He hadn't explained why but then I hadn't asked him. I had sat in the passenger seat looking up at Margaret.

'Not you,' Primo said to her. 'Let's keep it simple.'

When I twisted to look back, she was alone on the pavement like a girl who had been stood up by her date.

Now, as we drove, curry and two glasses of wine rumbled in my stomach. 'My treat,' Margaret had said. 'I'm hungry too.' She even beat me to paying for the wine; which was easy since I only had the price of a coffee. I had begun to ask myself what my chances were of getting somewhere with her. Why else, I asked, tossing my head, should a girl ply me with wine? Well, two glasses. After that Primo appeared with an invitation to join him that only his size prevented me from refusing. He had been sitting in the car waiting for us to come out.

After a while, I recognised a street like the one where Andy had collected Primo in the mornings, then another one like it and another. We rolled across potholes in an alley like a cart track and came into a street surrounded by black space. Tenements had been knocked down and, as the main beam flicked on, light lanced out across a plain of rubble. The road took a long curve uphill and we were back among decayed tenements with bricked-over windows like old men's filmy eyes. When he switched off the ignition, it was very quiet. He came round the front of the car and opened the door on my side, which made it seem that he wanted me to get out. I got out.

'Don't forget the parcel,' he said.

I had left it on the seat. He was holding the door open with his hand folded over the top. With all my strength I kicked the door shut and in the same movement turned to run for it. A vice caught me by the shoulder and turned me back. The door swung juddering.

'Get your parcel,' he said.

His voice sounded the same, no louder than before. I scrabbled inside and reached out the package. Curry and wine came up at the back of my throat.

We climbed the stairs. On the first and second landings the bulbs were out, probably smashed. Primo's voice came out of the darkness.

'I'll say this for you,' he said. 'You can listen to advice.'

On the top landing, a gas jet flared blue. Primo laid the palm of his hand across the rough holes where a nameplate might have been torn out. He didn't knock. Across the fingers under the first knuckles a welt of black and purple flesh was rising. It didn't make him more human. I could hardly imagine how he had ignored the shock and pain or how fast he must have reacted to catch me. His voice had been level and low but as he bent his head, waiting, I saw sweat glitter on his cheeks.

In the flickering glare of the broken gas mantle, raw tears showed on the panels of the door. It looked as if it had been attacked with an axe. Squalor, poverty, I could imagine the flat behind the door. I was wrong though. Certainly the hall we entered, when the door had been opened by someone who went off too quickly for me to see him, was bare enough; but the first room into which Primo led me was comfortably furnished and the remnant of a meal showed where someone had eaten; wine glasses chimed as I brushed past the table. Primo nodded me towards the door into the next room.

Brond got up out of a deep armchair. He was wearing slippers and had the air of a man at home. There was a decanter on the little table beside the chair and he had a glass in his hand. He held out the other to me in what I thought was greeting until he tugged the parcel from under my arm.

'You've brought my little surprise at last.'

I felt an astonishing relief at parting with it.

'You're welcome,' I said. 'I'm glad to be shot of it.'

I assumed the demeanour of someone getting ready to leave, but he offered me a drink in a tone that didn't allow for refusal.

I sat in the chair facing his. My feet gave me messages about the depth of the carpet and between the curtained windows there was a tower system hi-fi deck flanked by tapes and records, lots of them. He seemed to be a man who was fond of music.

'Whisky?' he asked again patiently.

'Please.'

'You have a preference?'

I didn't understand.

'A favourite blend or a malt perhaps?'

'A malt,' I said.

He smiled.

I twisted in my chair to watch him. There were shelves of bottles.

'Water, soda . . .?'

'Water,' I said.

Usually when I drank whisky I filled up with lemonade – a very sound lemonade. Just recently I had discovered tonic water and liked better than anything the odd sharpness it added.

'Ideally,' Brond said, 'the water should be from the burn that feeds the distillery. I had business once with the managing director of— one of the malt whiskies, and he took a flask out of the safe in his office. It was water from the well in Ross-shire they used in reducing the malt for maturing.' As he spoke, he poured a little water from a tall beaker into each glass. 'Is that admirable or fanaticism? Either way we can only manage water from the tap here. Fortunately, it's the softest city water in the world.'

He held up his glass and smiled at me through its amber light.

'Here we are,' he said, 'in this warm room with a glass of Laphroaig. What can we have done to deserve it?'

Everything under my eye was clear and sharp-edged so that I knew about the grain of the table as well as the light changing in the glass and each of Brond's words separately like objects you could weigh in your hand. He sat opposite me. The table stood just at the height of my knees as I lay back in the deep chair. The parcel lay on the table between us.

'Slainte!' he said, grinning as if at a private joke.

The whisky plucked at my temples.

'So what's inside?'

'I don't know.'

'You've been carrying it around, quite reluctant to be parted from it and yet you weren't curious?'

'I didn't say I wasn't curious.'

'To take a peep inside must have been a temptation.' He turned the box and I saw the dent from its fall when Margaret pushed it away in the library. 'Was that how this happened?'

'The wrapper's still across it. There's no way of telling what's inside.'

He picked at the tape. It held firm and he eased place after place till it curled free. Once started it lifted off in one piece bringing with it a skin of brown paper. Unhurriedly, he picked at the tape until he had cleared the top. Gently then he started to tease out the knots on the string. I must have let out a breath for he smiled at me.

'Like sharpening pencils,' he said, 'one of the not quite mechanical tasks that soothes.'

'Wouldn't scissors be faster?'

Just then, though, another knot parted and he folded back the wrapping paper. I could have cursed to see the box inside was also taped.

'No need to be consistent,' Brond said and he pushed his fingers in under the edge and ripped off the lid. It tore and shredded against the tape and he brushed the wreckage aside until the opening was cleared.

I craned forward so that our heads almost touched. Brond sat back.

'Satisfy your curiosity.'

There was a towel folded round something. The cloth was stained, dull patches like fruit stains.

'Someone's been hurt,' Brond said. He lifted the bundle out and laid it beside the box. All down each side of the cloth was marked. 'Someone's been hurt badly.'

Using the tips of his fingers, he flipped the bundle open.

'Recognise that?'

'I've never seen it before,' I said.

'You know what it is though?'

'I'm not blind. It's a gun.'

His smile seemed genuinely amused.

'I suppose,' he said, 'you would have to drop this little box into the Brazilian jungle before there would be a chance of a finder who wouldn't recognise that much.'

'Has it been fired?' I looked uneasily at the stains on the cloth.

'More than once. Someone has been angry or frightened. I wonder which.'

The towelling would soak liquid up and there was so much

72

staining. I was afraid. I had done nothing but, as I had learned the shapes of guns without handling them, heard them fired in films, seen newsreel deaths, so I had learned being innocent was no excuse.

'I've never seen that thing before. It was a parcel I was trying to get rid of.'

Brond gathered the cloth round the grip and lifting the gun pointed it towards me.

I knew the function of a gun; its operations as a mechanism and their consequences. I understood what Brond was doing when he put his finger into a fold of the cloth and laid it on the trigger. I expected to die. I watched the slow pressure of his finger as he squeezed.

'You were telling the truth,' Brond said. 'You don't know anything about hand guns.'

'You must be bloody mad. I might have died of fright.'

'Young healthy man. You're not fragile.' He laid the gun down. 'Czechoslovakian. A favourite weapon of terrorists.'

He put more whisky into a glass and laid it beside the one I had only sipped.

'Neat this time, eh?'

I drank it off, choking a little, but the warmth ran down the centre of my body. I put my hand to my face and the index finger of my left hand touched my lips. They trembled and I willed them to be firm. Then as my upper lip pressed against my finger I felt the strong beating of my heart. I was alive.

'A gun, a cloth that tells its own story – though pages are missing. If it tells of an end, we should be even more anxious to hear the middle and the beginning.' He tipped up the box, stirred the wrappings with his hand. 'No letter, no cryptic message. Only yourself and the question what is to be made of you.'

'All this is nothing to do with me. I was asked to keep it—'

'For a friend.'

'No, for you.'

'I had asked you to keep this for me?'

73

'The girl who was with me in the restaurant. She brought it to my digs. She said she'd got it from Peter Kilpatrick.' I waited but he gave no sign of recognising the name. 'She told me Kilpatrick was going away and I was to keep the parcel. She told me you would collect it.'

'Why?'

'I don't know why. Jackie wouldn't keep it for me and I wanted her to but she wouldn't. And I—'

'You got suspicious.'

He sipped whisky and I looked down to avoid his eyes. He was a good listener; at least he hadn't interrupted me to ask who Jackie was. It was possible, of course, that he didn't need to ask. The shoe on his right foot had a raised platform sole. With a shoe like that, you would limp; the upper body dipping at each step. When I looked up, his eyes were on my face. It felt as if he was reading my thoughts.

'The girl interests me,' he said. 'Tell me about her.'

'Her name's Briody. Margaret Briody. She's a student – in her first year. I think – yes, it must be her first year, she's in two of my Ordinary classes. You know her. She was at the Professor's party.'

It tumbled out, whatever I knew; if I had known more, I would have told him. I had not thought of myself as being like that, but at the time I had no shame.

'"I want to be shot of it." You said that a moment ago.' Brond looked at me thoughtfully. 'It's an idiom, but an odd one. Yet you had no idea what was in the package?'

He picked up the gun again. My stomach clenched, but this time he pointed the muzzle at his own head.

'The package you want to be *shot* of.'

In the silence, I could hear the parts slide across each other as he squeezed the trigger for a second time.

'Russian roulette,' he said, 'devised in an obscenity of boredom. Your turn.'

'For God's sake!'

He put the barrel in his mouth and pulled the trigger, then

pointed it at my stomach. I had had enough. I clutched my
stick and headed for the door. Brond made no attempt to stop
me. I tore it open.

Primo was sitting astride a chair facing me. Without getting
up, he shook his head in warning. His hands rested on the chair
back. The flesh across his fingers was pulpy and liver-coloured.
It looked bad, as if one or more fingers might be broken.

I closed the door on him.

'You still have some of your drink left,' Brond said.

Slowly I went back and sat down. Since there was nothing
better to do, I drank the whisky. It was a taste in my mouth,
nothing more.

Brond brought the bottle and put it between us. We had a
still life – the whisky, a muddle of wrapping paper, a length of
marked towel, a gun.

'I don't want any more to drink.'

'Nonsense.' He poured into both glasses. 'You're what – six
feet? With a sound pair of kidneys, excited as you are, you could
finish the bottle and keep your wits.'

It was easier to drink than to argue.

'We'll have a longer chat another time. You're an interesting
young man. When I'm less pressed for time, you'll tell me all
about yourself.'

The absurd idea came into my head it was like a job
interview; only instead of a knife to see if you balanced peas
on it as a test there was malt whisky and a Czech gun.

'I'm a student,' I said. 'I was given a parcel to keep. I wish I'd
never seen it.'

Into the silence a clock behind me spaced sweet chimes.

'What an uncomplicated young man you make yourself
sound.'

He stood up and I followed him to the far door. With Brond
leading the way, we passed through another room, a passage,
another room. They were places we crossed – Brond in front,
Primo behind me. No one knew I was here. Perhaps Margaret
. . . No. She only knew I had gone away in a car.

We came into a small entrance hall. It looked very much like the one I had come in by, but smaller. When he opened the door, I saw across the landing the other door with its raw gouged panels.

I stepped over the threshold on to the dirty grey stone landing like a prisoner released.

'Wait!' Brond said. 'This won't do!'

Stopping me then was like a cruel joke. He touched my shoulder.

'Your stick,' he said. 'You've left it behind. It must be by the chair in the study.'

Primo turned back into the flat. I concentrated on keeping upright; I wanted my face to be without expression. Don't whine, had been Primo's advice; don't whine. On the door there was a piece of cardboard with a name printed on it: Anders.

'Not an alias,' Brond said following my glance. 'A simple forename. Anders Brond.'

'Anders,' I said. The name Anderson and its history came to my mind. 'That's a Swedish name.'

'Or you'll find it in Finland. The Swedes are the aristocrats of Finland.'

A door closed inside and Primo appeared again. I took the stick from him and felt the difference at once.

'It's not mine,' I said, and cursed my stupidity. Yes, it's mine. Let me take it and go. Any stick does to lean upon. To walk away.

'Never mind,' Brond said. 'I'll make you a present of it.'

For some reason, perhaps because I was exhausted, perhaps because I had been sitting for so long, walking was harder than it had been since my accident. I needed the stick. All my weight fell on it. With great labour, I crossed to the stairs.

'Wait!' Brond said for the second time.

I stopped. It seemed as if the cruel play was to be ended. As I waited, I saw a body, as if it had never been mine, lying by the side of a road with rain falling on it.

Brond came close.

'It's only fair to the Finns to add,' he said, 'that a time came when those proud Swedes lost their university posts and their comfortable places in the civil service.'

At what he had chosen to say or at the look on my face, he burst into laughter and tapped me on the chest. Even when the door closed behind him, the laughter hung with the echo of what he said last, 'Things change.' I was alone on the landing of an old tenement that smelled of a hundred and fifty years of betrayal.

As I stood, a child whimpered. The sound shocked out of the darkness below me. The bulb above my head lit the two doors and the boarded window at the turn of the stair. From somewhere beyond that, a child whimpered out of the dark.

At the second flight I stumbled, afraid of a fall. There was a rustling whisper in the dark. I slid one foot until I found a step then gripped the bannister edging my way down. In a field last summer a pheasant had sprung up from under my feet. It was like that: an uprising turbulence and I could see nothing and threw out my hands. There was a cry of pain and a child's voice, 'I'm sorry.'

Under my hand a thin shoulder. Without letting it go, I passed my other hand up to her face.

'Who are you? What do you want?'

I whispered the questions as if it were a trap. The child's voice wheedled at me out of the darkness.

'Don't hurt me,' she said.

'What do you want?'

'I live here.'

'For Christ's sake then, knock and go in.'

'My daddy put me out.'

Why did I have to meet her?

'I'll knock,' I said. 'You can't sit here alone in the dark.'

I had dropped my stick and now, holding her, I felt around my feet for it. I wanted it in my right hand when a father like hers opened the door to my knocking. The wood brushed my hand and I pulled it to me.

'What are you doing?' the child whispered.

'My stick. I wanted my stick.'

She moaned and took my hand from her shoulder and carried it in both of hers down between her legs. I felt the bone under the heel of my hand, and my fingers curled into her.

'Don't hit me,' she said.

And I pushed her away. I heard the thud of her hitting the wall but she made no sound. Flailing, crippled, stumbling in the dark, I fell from flight to flight until I reached the outer world.

I left that street and the next before I stopped. It was moonlight and I put a hand across my eyes and was weeping.

EIGHT

The last time I had been in a taxi had been at my Aunt Netta's funeral. Don't upset your Aunt, they'd told me when I was little, she won't have a breath to draw. I sat watching the dark streets go past, on my way to the Kennedys' house where I lived, remembering my Aunt's fat white arms and the noises that knocked in her chest when she got excited.

I had taken a taxi because one came past empty when I was tired. I began to look through my pockets for money. I reached into my breast pocket with two fingers and felt a fold of paper which I drew out between them. It seemed to be a note of some kind and I remembered Brond touching me there. At first I could not read it but when I angled it at the window, brief light caught Margaret Briody's name. Under it an address had been pencilled.

There was a sliding glass between the driver and passengers. I tapped on it and he pulled it back. I leaned forward until I was almost through it.

'Do you know this address?'

'What?'

'On this paper. If you know it.'

He reached with one hand and like me held it slanted to the street to catch the light.

'So?'

'Would you take me there?'

'You mean after or instead of?'

'I want to go there now.'

'You're paying.'

I wanted to know where Kilpatrick had gone, and why she had given me the parcel, and if she had known what it was. I wanted someone to talk to me. I wanted to see Margaret.

You're paying, he'd said. A gun had been pointed at me that night, the trigger pulled, and now I was sweating because I might not have the money to pay for a taxi ride. Very cautiously, I started to feel again through each pocket. It was hard to count. I got different totals and then I dropped a coin on the floor and it rolled and got lost though I scrabbled after it.

When I sat up, the driver was watching me in the mirror.

'What's up?'

I leaned forward again into the opening.

'Nothing . . . I was wondering. Is it far?'

The taxi swung into the side and stopped.

'Are we there?' I asked.

He got out and opened the door beside me.

'Are we there?' I asked again.

'What's all this about – money? If you've no bloody money you shouldn't be in the motor.'

'I've got money.'

I named the amount down to the smallest coin and held it out towards him on the palm of my hand.

'Take me that much.' I said. 'Just go on till that's used up. Then if you tell me where it is I'll walk the rest.'

He peered at me. He was in his fifties with a scarf across his chest and vanishing round the back to where the ends would be tied. After a moment he shook his head.

'As far as it'll go . . .'

I could hear him laughing even over the sound of the motor once we'd started again.

'Tell you, son.' I leaned forward to hear. 'It's funny game. Young guys getting off their marks without paying. Bad enough this game without being taken for a mug.'

'Not much chance of me running anywhere.'

'That right?'

He groped under the dash and held up a big spanner.

'I'm getting on a bit,' he said. 'But I've surprised one or two with the speed I can move.'

80

I sat back. My foot throbbed in pace with the engine. I had banged it again going down those hellish stairs in the dark.

'It's a scunner,' the driver said. 'You know what they call this time of night in any other job? Unsocial bloody hours.'

The taxi stopped. Looking out, I saw a wall covered with names and threats. All the paint looked black in the light from the sulphur lamps.

'This it?'

He didn't answer. I opened the door and then sat back deliberately.

'What's up?' he asked turning to look at me.

'I didn't want to worry you.'

'Eh?'

I climbed out and limped forward to pay him.

'You have an honest face, pal,' he said.

Now I wanted him to say the wrong thing. I wanted him to get out of his safe little cabin. I didn't think his spanner would do him much good.

'I have a bloody sore foot,' I said. 'Is that not more like it?'

'Don't be that way, son.'

'Here. Take the money. That's my lot. Call it a tip for your conversation.'

It was awkward for him. I dropped the money a little at a time into his hand.

'You're okay, son,' he said. 'It's just that you're a big fellow and I wasn't sure of that stick. All the best.'

'Thanks and fuck you too,' I said but he had pulled away.

I went into the close that had the right number and climbed the first stairs. With the effort of favouring the bad foot, the muscle of the calf cramped. I crouched kneading it until the knots came out. At every door I hoped to see her name so that I could rest. I got to the top and then I came down again checking all the way. She might be a lodger. She might not have her name on any of the doors. My name was not on the door of the Kennedys' house. I could knock at a door and ask. I thought how pleased someone would be to have me knocking at his door in the middle of the night.

I sat on the bottom step. I had no money and no idea what district this was. At the back of the entry there was a scurrying like the light tapping of fingernails. Even respectable tenements drew rats. There was a door beside me, one of the two on the ground floor. I pressed the bell. In the stillness I heard the dull burring from inside. I leaned on the tiny dull square of light three times; nobody came and I limped past the second door into the street.

The name of the street was on a plate on the tenement wall. It was the right name, but it was a 'Street'. I checked the piece of paper and the name was right, only it was not 'Street' but 'Gardens'. I went round the corner and there was another plate and it had what I wanted. I was back in business.

The Gardens began with one block of tenements. After that there were hedges with neat bungalows tucked behind them. I searched for some clue about the numbering until I was frustrated, exhausted and ready to give up if there had been anywhere else to go. When I got the right house, I found in the middle of the gate the number trickily worked in iron.

It was a house like the others; if you were absent-minded, or hungry enough, you might have rushed by mistake into either of its neighbours and sat down to someone else's dinner. No lights showed, but then it was late. Nothing but the inertia of all the little decisions since I had fished out the fold of paper in the taxi made me open the gate.

There was a bell and it had a little light so that you could find it in the dark. I could not bring myself to ring it. Maybe if I went round the house I would come on Margaret standing at a window. We would get into bed and every time the springs creaked a woman's voice, her mother's, would call out: 'Are you all right dear?'

I tucked the stick under my arm and leaned on the roughcast wall for support as I went round the house. The side window was open. There was no sound from inside and nothing to make out but shapes. I hesitated with my hands on the ledge for what felt like hours then turned back to the front door.

I made a pointless little rapping, too quiet to waken anybody. I rang the bell. I banged with my fist; I rattled the box. At the height of the din, an insomniac stopped at the gate. I turned to look at him. He went away. Under a lamp, he emerged as a fat little man with a white dog at heel. If he was a good neighbour, he had changed his mind.

With a soft rub of wood on wood the window rose. I reached in with the stick and swept it in an arc without touching anything. Please God, I thought, don't make it her parents' room. At least there was no sound of creaking springs. I bent in over the ledge till my hands touched the floor, gathered the good foot under me and hit the floor crouching. Silence.

I had got to my feet and started to edge forward when the door opened. A pencil beam of light crept forward just ahead of the new arrival. If the torch beam had swung about it would have caught me playing statues. The light crept across the surface of the table. There was a vase with white papery discs of honesty standing up out of it and a piece of paper propped against it. The paper was held so it could be read then was taken behind the beam out of sight. The light moved and there was a bump.

'Bloody hell!' a man's voice said. I knew the voice. No name came with it, but I had heard that voice before.

A man's shape spread cruciform against the lighter dark of the window and vanished as the curtains were drawn. The beam wound back across the carpet, a switch clicked and there was a dazzling brightness from overhead.

'Muldoon!' I said. 'I didn't know you knew Margaret.'

His foxy mask gaped in shock, the torch still lit and waving in his hand. His mouth opened and closed a couple of times before he could speak.

'Was that you hammering at the door?' he asked.

'Nobody else, but why didn't you open the door? Is Margaret here?'

But at the first question his tiny eyes scuttled to the drawn curtains and I remembered the window opened behind it. I turned my back on him and went over to pull back the curtains. The glass underneath the catch had been cut out in a half circle. I put my fist up beside it as a measure.

'I don't think you came in by the front door either,' I said. The neat hole was just larger than my fist. 'That's professional. I couldn't have done it. Was that one of the optional extras in the seminary?'

'Never mind me,' Muldoon said. 'Is burglary a new course at the University?'

'I'm a friend of Margaret.' I leered at him like a bad comedian. 'She's expecting me.'

As he didn't answer, my own words put another thought in my head.

'Are you breaking your vows with her?'

He put the torch out at last.

'I don't know what you're on about.'

'You and Margaret. Nothing sinful. Only trying to make little Muldoons together.'

He didn't rise to the bait. There are people who ask to be needled; Muldoon had taken me that way since the day I met him. Sometimes I had the feeling that I did not really care for him. With remarks like that, I could usually drive him into a miniature puritan frenzy.

'You'd better sit down,' he said. 'Before you fall down.'

'You first.'

He shook his head as if he was patronising me – it was very strange – and sat down himself beside the table with the flowers. When he was down, I let myself sit. Every muscle in my body sighed. For the first time I took in the room – a sofa, chairs, a gas fire set into the hearth with a fuss of ornaments on the shelf above it.

'There's nobody else in the house. Is there?'

'Just you and me,' he said.

'Cosy.'

I knew I should be questioning, getting things out of him. My mind was foundering in pillows of weariness. When I tried to get him in sharp focus, bolsters of flesh pressed from below and above to close my eyes.

'The question is,' Muldoon said, 'how you found this house? I was told you'd no idea where the girl lived.'

I tried to think who could have told Muldoon anything like that, but I was too tired. Who had I told? Whose business would it be?

'But you did,' I said, out of simplicity not cunning. 'You knew her house all right.'

'Cut out the dirty talk!' When I meant nothing he decided to have his outburst of temper. 'I've never liked you and that's the truth. That come as a shaker to you? You're one of those fellows think they're great. Everybody has to like them. Not me, friend. Not one little bit – and if you've got it coming, I'll be there to cheer.'

I had been amazed before by someone telling me what I was like – and they never came anywhere near being right.

'If you're ever there when I get something coming, Muldoon, don't cheer. Not unless you want your jaw broken.'

'You're a right bastard!'

He moved as if to go for me, and changed his mind.

'Come and give us a kiss!' I said.

The minutes in the chair or the surge of adrenalin unthawed me.

'Better still,' I said, 'tell me why you're here. Did big Peter Kilpatrick send you?'

Muldoon went quiet in his seat.

'Well Peter's a good friend of mine,' he said. 'It would be possible he sent me. He might be wanting something back.'

'He might be wanting something back,' I mimicked him.

He made an ugly face and leaned forward.

'Peter's sorry he gave the girl the parcel. He wants it back.'

'So?'

'So let me have it and I'll give it back to him.'

'Did you think it was here?' I needed some leverage to make him explain. 'You haven't told me why you came here.'

'That's got nothing to do with anything.'

'I think it does. You tell me why you're here and then we can talk about the parcel.'

He sat back like a man deliberately relaxing.

'If it'll make you happy. I thought Peter would be here.'

'What would he be doing here?'

'What would he not?' Muldoon said. 'Isn't he thick with the girl?'

I thought about that. I had to be stupid to have taken it for granted Margaret would be running errands for someone she knew only casually. He might be a friend of hers; because you did someone a favour it did not mean you went to bed with him.

'I can't imagine Margaret's parents having Kilpatrick here as a house guest,' I said.

Muldoon put his hand in his side pocket and drew out a piece of paper. I remembered the paper he'd lifted from the table.

'Her folks are away on holiday. She's left this note for them – they're due back, but they've been away.'

'Let me see.'

He folded it in his hand. I considered getting up fast but, whatever he saw in my eyes, he eased to the front of his chair. I didn't think I was in condition to catch him before he made it out of the door.

'Why has she left them a note? Has she gone away with Kilpatrick?'

'With Peter?' He looked as if he hadn't thought of that. 'It's possible. He'd want out of here when she—'

'What – when she what?' My brain was too tired; I let the possibilities spill out. 'When she gave me the parcel? Or when she came back and told him she'd given it to me? Why would that upset him? He told her to give it to me – that's what she said. And I was to keep it for Brond.'

'For who?' I had never pictured what they meant when they said a man's jaw dropped – that's what happened, like a box lid on a hinge his jaw fell open. 'For Brond?'

'All I know is I was asked to give him the parcel – and now he's got it.'

Muldoon stood up.

'You've given it to Brond,' he said colourlessly.

I straightened in the chair and took a grip on the stick. It had never occurred to me that there might be something in Muldoon to be afraid of – not till now.

'I gave him a box,' I said slowly, 'and it was wrapped in brown paper tied with string – the hairy kind of string—'

'Are you working for Brond?'

I ignored the question.

'And there was tape, lots of tape. And we took off the tape and the string and the box opened. And there were two things inside.' This was the moment when his face should tell me if he knew what had been in the parcel. He looked worried, tired suddenly – as always, red foxy. I could not tell. 'A cloth and a gun. The cloth had stains on it – maybe ketchup off a fish supper. Somebody had fired the gun.'

Muldoon's face was closed and secret.

'I've been thinking Kilpatrick must have been the one who fired it and that was why he wanted to get rid of it. But now you say he wants it back and I've been wondering why he would change his mind. Has Kilpatrick killed someone?'

Muldoon grinned at me.

'You want to give your head a rest,' he said. 'You're too old for fairy stories.'

I got the stick under both hands and lurched to my feet. Muldoon came back into proportion. He was a little weed of a fellow.

'How would you like me to rest the back of my hand across your mouth?'

'There's no need for that,' he said. 'Listen, Peter'll explain. He's the man that's worrying you – let him do the explaining. I

87

didn't want to tell you he was here until I was sure everything was all right.'

'Here? He is? Is Margaret here too?'

'Of course, in the bedroom. I'll get them.'

And he turned as naturally as that and went out. Even before I heard the outside door close, I knew he had fooled me. Margaret and Kilpatrick were not in this house. I listened to the stillness. The house was empty except for me and I had no right to be here and had to get out. I fell into a chair and tiredness rose over me like a small death. I wondered if Margaret Briody had really gone away . . . If that had been a note Muldoon had folded in his hand . . . If . . .

I woke in a fright. My arm had folded under me in the chair. Out in the hall red light came through the glass door from a street lamp. I took the first likely door and was lucky for there was a bed. My jacket and tie came off easily, then my trousers dragged and tugged with twin bundles of socks tangled in the cuffs.

Under the borrowed blankets, I couldn't stop shivering.

NINE

Kilpatrick's friend? Kilpatrick's friend. Who was Kilpatrick's friend? Muldoon, I remembered, and remembering came awake.

The room was full of light. A white ceiling and net curtains with sunlight behind them. On the other side, a dressing table covered with glass animals. The nearest was an elephant with ears like bright drops of water.

I felt alive and full of energy. I yawned and thought about getting up.

Hunger and a full bladder bobbed me gently to the surface again. Sitting up, I saw a yellow dressing-gown lying on the floor. The pillow beside me showed an edge of yellow and when I tugged on it a nightdress of yellow nylon slipped into my hand. It smelled of Margaret Briody.

There were eggs in the fridge in the kitchen. I put a pan on the hot ring and dropped a knob of butter in it, but by the time I had broken three eggs into a dish the butter was giving off black smoke. It was a fine morning and a strange house. Breakfast should be done properly. I found a dishcloth and wiped the pan clean; put their Cona on with coffee; added black pepper and stirred my three eggs with a fork; put a plate under the grill to warm; threw in butter again and as it spat and sizzled across the pan poured in the eggs. The mix spread and I shook the pan, folded, turned out the golden half moon on a plate. Perfect.

Naturally, I had forgotten to make toast.

Eat or make toast while the omelette deflates: it was like a question from the old professor in Moral Philosophy. I ate the omelette. Later out of hunger, I searched and found half a shop loaf in its wrapper and chewed down slices of it. The butter was good even with that – salt butter from the Orkneys.

It was a well-doing family. In the parents' room, I found a drawer crammed tidily with documents and bills. I lay on the bed and read through them. On one demand note, her father had put a date and quoted as a reminder to himself part of his reply: 'never welshed on a bill in my life'. He had underlined 'never' with three heavy slashes of a pen. From the kinds of stuff he bought, I thought he must be a builder, a slater perhaps, and imagined him as being on his own and wondered how much he made: enough anyway to let Margaret be at university and holiday abroad and have that shiny gloss on her skin. Even in the photograph on the wall, she glowed. I wondered if the proud father noticed how highlights and shadows conspired around those incredible breasts. The photograph beside it was of a little girl dressed for first communion. She looked bridal but familiar. I guessed Margaret must be an only child. Her mother would say to her in a few years: 'We sacrificed but never grudged it – to give you a chance.' I thought she might grudge it ahead of schedule if they found who she was with at the moment. I took it for granted now that Kilpatrick was hiding for some reason and that she was with him. I remembered what I had said to Muldoon. People did kill – it happened all the time. A friend of mine in the first term had been stabbed to death one Friday night outside a pub. A fifteen-year-old had stabbed him with a sharpened screwdriver and it had forced a way between two ribs into his lung so that he drowned in blood.

Margaret in the photograph on the wall glowed and smiled. I thought if I was her father I would keep her locked up. I would buy a machine gun – no problem for a man who settled his bills – and mow down all the men who lusted after her.

In their hearts, I thought, and scratched myself.

A bang echoed round the house and quivering into the middle of the floor I translated it as a front door closing. From the hall came the sound of a woman's voice and the deeper mutter of a man in reply. In a silent frenzy I straightened the spread on the sheets and gathered up bills and letters to lay them back in the drawer. Two fat envelopes spilled on to the floor. I scuffed them under the bed. It had gone quiet. I considered escaping out of the window; and had a vivid picture of being arrested half over the sill.

The door eased open under my hand more slowly than I would ever have imagined. Through the crack I studied the empty hall, suspecting shadows. There was no reason why they should go into Margaret's bedroom. They would be in the kitchen. Hungry after travelling.

In the bedroom I wasted no time. I found my socks in different places and crammed on my shoes barefoot. Stick in one hand, socks in the other, my jacket over my arm – the tie had vanished, a casualty of the night – I recrossed the hall. I was going to be lucky. With one finger I hooked the handle and the front door opened – it wasn't properly shut.

A squat bullet-headed man, old enough to be my father, was reaching up to push the door. He had a case in his other hand and a holdall tucked under the same arm. He blinked at me and then put the hand that had been reaching for the door on to my chest and propelled me back into the hall.

'Now don't let's be hasty, Mr Briody,' I said. He wasn't big, six inches less than me, but he was broad and with my shoelaces undone and holding one jacket and two socks I wasn't feeling at my best.

'Don't tell me,' he said. 'I can guess. Where's Margaret?'

I shook my head.

'Through there.' He pointed to the room Muldoon and I had been in the previous night. I found myself sitting in the same chair.

'Stay there!' he said and went back into the hall.

I put my socks on and got my shoelaces tied. I buttoned my jacket and then unbuttoned it, thinking Mr Briody might get over-excited. My tie remained among absent friends.

He came back and shut the door quietly. The other chair was

too far away apparently, for he pulled it up close to me and when he sat down leaned forward.

'She's not in the house,' he said. 'But I can see her bed's been slept in. Is this yours?'

My tie had turned up again.

I put my hand up to my neck, not claiming the tie but as if to indicate the benefits of an open collar in summer, while, under the circumstances, avoiding any suggestions that the practice might be associated with virility.

'Where's she got to? I want a word before,' he jerked his chin in the direction of the kitchen, 'the wife realises what's been going on.'

A set of responses clattered through my head like lemons in a fruit machine.

'Look now,' he said. 'Let's be straight. I know these things happen. There aren't many young saints around. But I don't want needless hurt. You tell me where Margaret's got to – and then we'll get you out of here before the wife has a chance to see you.'

He was so reasonable I wondered what Margaret got up to usually. I had been too timorous perhaps about delving into that cornucopia.

'Ah,' I said wittily, 'she's not here.'

'I told you that,' he said.

The accent was not just Irish but southern Irish. He was a man from Eire, and one who signalled to a lad born at the sharny end of a country lane that he was a bloody peasant like my father, uncles and so forth.

'You did,' I said. 'You did surely,' I heard myself say with just the fatal hint of an inadvertent brogue.

'So?'

'Yes. Well, I was . . . at a party. At a party here. Very nice – well behaved. No nonsense. A party – with records and . . . soft drinks. Yes, well. My foot – I injured it—'

'At the party.'

'No–no, to be honest with you, shifting a wardrobe. A while

ago. But someone stood on it last night. And Margaret said, you're in no state to go home. My parents are away. You sleep in their bed – my bed. You sleep in my bed, she said, and I'll sleep in their bed,' I finished hopefully.

'She's not in their bed,' he said.

'No, she wouldn't be. She's at work.'

'Where? Work?'

'A summer job. She got it yesterday. That's what she held the party for – to celebrate getting the job.'

'And she'll have made up the bed before she left.' He nodded seriously. 'She was always a tidy girl.'

He stood up and I took a grip on the stick.

'You won't mind going before the wife comes.'

Nodding enthusiastically, I levered myself up.

Softly, at the front door, still with that serious look, he said, 'It's best that you're away before the wife comes through. You wouldn't want to go through all that stuff again about the job and the party – not to speak of the wardrobe on your foot. That's a cruel thing – a wardrobe.' I edged away from him down the steps. 'It must,' he said solemnly, 'have leaped like lightening.'

As a father, he struck me as being on the eerie side.

In daylight, being lost and without money presented no problems. After a sleep I could walk from now till tomorrow even if I had to hop the last hours one-legged. If I kept going I might spot a taxi and he could wait at the Kennedys' while I fetched the fare. Three notes were tucked in the toe of a shoe under my bed so I wasn't flat yet. There was a bye-law too, someone had told me, to the effect that you could ride a bus as long as you gave your name and address so the fare could be collected later. Or was that only children? Anyway the chances were that nobody would ever have told the hard-faced bus conductress.

'Who's boss!'

I glanced up and there was an old lady before a gate smiling complacently at a woman lugging a howling child up the steps.

What I'd heard was the splash of the old lady shoving her oar in: Show him who's boss: don't let him dominate you. Him looked about three years old. As they struck a tableau on the top step, you could see her underskirt was grubby, and her legs just legs with the usual taut strings behind the knees, but still it never failed to be interesting how far up they went. Bent over, she let her irritation get the better of her and smacked the boy's face. The howl shrilled up from assertion to outrage. And at that second he writhed round and saw my grinning face. It was the kind of straw that might help set a character for life. How could I explain to him that I wasn't joining in the female conspiracy against him but only looking up his mother's skirt?

'Hey! you there!' A remembered brogue turned me in my tracks.

A car had pulled up beside me. Mr Briody was leaning across the passenger seat. The door clicked open and he beckoned to me. 'Get in!'

I had a conviction this was the pay off. Like most Irish, he would have been in America. He had been a slater in Chicago and learned from some Sicilian how to avenge the family honour by taking you for a ride.

Since my foot hurt, I got in.

'Where to?' he asked.

'I'm going back to my digs, but anywhere—'

'Would they be near the University?'

'Two or three streets away.'

'Right then. I can find my way to the University. I've given Margaret a run there. You can guide me from that. Right?'

'Great. Thanks a lot.'

He put the car in gear and pulled away.

'It occurred to me you might really have a bad foot and since I'm on holiday with nothing to hurry for I came after you.'

'That was decent of you.'

After a time, I recognised a corner, then some shops. My neck was stiff with not looking in Briody's direction.

'Nearly there,' he said, and added casually, 'I wouldn't have been surprised to see you running up the road like a two-year-old.'

'Mr Briody,' I said with a world of sincerity, 'believe me – I mean Margaret and I haven't – I'm trying to say that I've nothing but respect for your daughter.'

'Margaret? Daughter?' He twisted round to look at me while the car took care of itself. 'You must think I'm a boy from the bogs or the greatest Christian since Matt Talbot gave up the drink. If it had been my daughter, I'd have degutted you.'

'You're not Margaret's father.'

No slouch, I had worked it out.

'Not an unwashed glass or a crumpled crisp bag the length and breadth of the house. But there, I suppose as well as making her bed she tidied up this morning before she went to work. It must have been a hell of a party.' He made a creaking noise and I realised he was laughing. 'Hand it to you for a quick tongue and the devil's cheek. It beats Flaherty running bare-arsed up the lane from the widow's.'

The moment for explaining how shamefully innocent I was seemed to have gone.

'I'm Danny Briody's cousin. Liam. He and Mary are over staying at the farm and we'll be at their house a day or two. Then on to London and home again.' He grinned. 'And it's nice to meet you too since you're a friend of the family, as you might say . . . Don't misunderstand me, mind. Danny's a good skin. It's not the first time Danny's helped with the farm rent in a bad year. And there's never a Christmas but I send over the plump birds that make a holiday a feast . . . It's just that Mary and him go on about that girl of theirs until you'd have thought she was another Alfred Einstein.'

I didn't correct him, reckoning that I'd drawn heavily enough for one day on my good luck account. Anyway for all I knew he might be thinking of another Einstein: Alfred the shyster lawyer or one-armed sheep-gelding champion of County Clare. Something like that.

'Mind you,' he went on, 'I'm fond of Margaret. It's just that I've wondered if she was as quick on the uptake as they say . . . You'll be at the University yourself?'

'Yes.'

'And you'll be in the same class as Margaret?'

'In the same year. We share a couple of subjects.'

'Do you tell me that?' He paused, cleared his throat and then asked in a rush, 'Now, would you say she was doing well? I mean that she was doing *well*? Was she able for it, would you say?'

'We're only in first year,' I said. 'I'm not sure how she got on in the degree exams.'

He nodded satisfied as if, without quite realising how, I had answered his questions. Then we were at the University and for the next five minutes we were busy as I called the turns.

'Left at the next corner. This is me. You could let me out here.'

The car stopped as if he had hit a brick wall. Thrown forward, I caught the padded edge of the dashboard before my head battered the windscreen. Sputtering to the surface again, I saw him gaping through the windscreen at Kennedy. My landlord had one hand on his gate and in his turn was staring at us. The car must have squealed to a stop.

Kennedy looked at me through the glass. I saw his gaze shift to my companion. He took his hand from the gate and walked towards the car.

'Mother of God,' the man beside me whispered. 'What's he wanting with us?'

'It's Mr Kennedy – he owns the house I stay in.'

Kennedy was almost on us.

'Don't tell him who I am or where—'

The door opened and Kennedy bent in to me.

'It's yourself. We wondered where you got to last night.'

He was studying Briody across me as he spoke, but un-expectedly a hard fist in my side shoved me out, forcing Kennedy back as I sprawled from the car. The slam of the door made one noise with the roar of the engine as the car leaped from us.

'Your friend's in a hurry,' Kennedy said. He watched the car squeal round the corner as if chased.

'I don't know him.' Without knowing why, I had decided to do as Liam Briody had asked. 'He gave me a lift.'

'Where'd you come by him then?'

We were moving towards the house.

'I thumbed a lift.'

'Oh, yes.'

We turned in at the gate and he took out his key to open the door.

'I finished up at a party last night. Got a bit too merry and stayed the night.'

'At your age you want to watch the drink,' he said, but not as if his mind was really on it.

'I started walking home this morning and discovered I'd no money. Lucky I got a lift.'

'Lucky,' he said. He still hadn't turned the key. His hand rested on it. 'Especially with him being in such a hurry.'

In the hall, he asked, 'Where was the party then?'

I started up the stairs.

'It was a fellow I met,' I said without looking back. 'I got a lift to it.'

'You've done well with the lifts,' he said, but I kept going.

I lay on my bed like a fox gone to earth. There were no bones around to chew but I had found a tin of biscuits in my shirt drawer and lay nibbling custard creams. My best strategy might be to lie there into the foreseeable future.

Jackie came in without knocking.

'Sorry,' she said. 'I didn't realise you were here.'

She did not look surprised.

'Do you wander about my room when I'm out?'

'There's linen to change.'

'Is that linen you're carrying?'

She was not holding anything.

'You're in a funny mood,' she said.

'Not me.' I took the corner off a biscuit. 'I had this crazy notion you might be a foot fetishist. Sneaking in for a quick sniff at my socks.'

She shut the door behind her.

'You want to watch what you say. You don't want to let him hear you talking like that.'

'He's the one that's in a funny mood. He was desperate to know where I was last night.'

I had never talked to her like that before. After the last couple of days I felt older – not any wiser, just older.

'Why should he care?' she asked.

For no good reason, I took that as an insult.

'You're supposed to be shocked at being called a fetishist,' I said sourly. 'Assuming you had the foggiest notion what I was talking about.'

'Aren't you the arrogant little bugger?' she said. 'Six months ago you walk in here not sure which spoon to eat your soup with and now you're a walking dictionary and man about bloody town.'

I was getting used to people surprising me. It didn't mean I had to like it.

'Do you want a biscuit?'

To my surprise, she came over and sat beside me. I passed her the tin. There were only two biscuits left.

She ate neatly, picking at the edges with her small white teeth.

'You have some dirty habits. The bed'll be full of crumbs.'

'If you're changing the linen . . .'

'Where were you last night anyway?'

'Oh, for God's sake!' I rolled out of the bed explosively. 'Do you know my mother and father couldn't be worse about checking up? I'm only a lodger, you know.'

'Your mother,' she said, looking at me unperturbed, 'did she ever sniff your socks?'

'That's—'

I really almost said it: That's dirty!

'I think you won that one,' I said. I thought about it for a minute then went on, 'I was at Margaret's house last night.'

'The girl who brought the parcel here?'

'Margaret Briody. Somebody gave me her address.'

My jacket was lying on the bed and I pulled out the card Brond had given me. She reached out and took it from me. I was anxious that she should believe me.

'Before that I'd no idea where she lived. I met her in the Reading Room at the University.'

'And she took you home.'

'No!' I said. 'We went for a coffee and finished up going for a meal and when we came out . . . It's a long story. I got the address from Brond – the man who—'

'That was the fellow was supposed to get the parcel.' She was quiet, attentive and seemed changed into someone I hadn't noticed before was there. 'Did she, this girl Margaret, take you to his place?'

'No – nothing like that. When we came out of the restaurant a man was waiting for us. He took me there.'

'But not the girl?'

'I think she might have wanted to come but—'

'How did the man know where you were? Did the girl phone Brond to tell him where to find you?'

I was shocked.

'No!' Even as I protested, I discovered that the idea's shade had been drifting across the back country of my mind. 'No. She wouldn't do that.'

'So anyway Brond got his parcel. What was in it after all the fuss?'

'I didn't find out.'

'He took it and said thank you.'

'Something like that.'

'Was part of his thank you the girl's address? Was it her kept you out all night?'

'God!' I said, 'you and your old man are a pair.'

My voice lingered on 'old man'. Sometimes I thought he was just past forty; other times with his long face and solemn ways he could have been ninety. She sat quiet. I tried to think of something to say but my mind was a blank. She stared at the floor, perhaps so she wouldn't have to look at me.

'It's easy to get the wrong idea about him,' she said. I had to strain to catch her words. 'I forget too till something makes me remember my last year at school. I was supposed to go to college afterwards. My da was very proud that way. But all my da's plans came to nothing that summer. From a child I'd always loved the summer for the town would be full of people and have a bit of life in it. My mother hated it, though – she would never take a lodger, but the shop did well enough so she didn't have to. It was the winter she liked when we had the place to ourselves. In January the foam from the waves would drift down like cotton across our garden. Summer was for the young ones. I fell in love with him that summer.'

Imagining that last schoolgirl summer, it seemed unnatural to think of Kennedy.

'It was one day I went to the beach. There was a rock stood above the sea at one end and a crowd of young fellows, all visitors, daring one another but none of them would dive from it for the height and the white water round it. He was lying among the crowd sunbathing and when he sat up we looked at one another and he gave me a wink and got up. I thought the world had stopped talking when he dived so clean and neat from the very topmost part into that white water.'

'That was—?'

I didn't finish but nodded towards the door. I had the stupid idea she might be talking of some lover she had known before Kennedy came into her life.

'Oh, it's strange to think of it now,' she said. 'We had a wild time. I couldn't tell you half the things he did. In spite of all my father could do, we were married by the summer's end. And then we came here – for he'd bought this house, and was only back to Ireland a short visit on business.' She shook her head as if in disbelief. 'A short visit and him there all summer long . . . until he had me married.'

'It doesn't sound like the same man,' I said, still stupid.

'He changed,' and she shivered as if wakening and looked at me sitting beside her on the bed.

'But,' she said and stopped as if the word could explain itself. She got up and put half the room between us by going to the window.

'He's down there,' she said, 'in the garden. He likes to be by himself working among the flowers – especially if he's worried about anything. I don't know if you've noticed that. He's fond of the garden.'

There was no excuse for what came next. I had been through a bad couple of days but that was no excuse. Jackie was a fine-looking woman – somehow better-looking for being serious than before – who had been talking about her husband and was watching him now as if I didn't exist; but that was something less than an excuse.

'Ah,' I said, 'he's a gardener and a worrier, and a high diver since you say so, and a good bookie's clerk, I'll believe that, and a nice boring little man altogether.'

I thought she hadn't heard me, and then I thought she was ignoring me; and then I hoped she hadn't heard, but she did answer, quietly, looking down into the garden.

'It's easy to make a mistake about him. He's given me enough cause to forget. Only there are things . . . The year after we were married – when – when my baby had died. We were not happy – he had become so different. I cried a lot. I would start to cry for no reason and then I wouldn't be able to stop. One night we went into a cafe and there were these four young fellows who had been drinking. They had the style, you know, of gang boys. A weak mindless look about two of them, and a lad that might have been simple, and another that had a face of pure badness. You wouldn't know which of them would turn nastiest without cause given. They talked at me, not nice talk, until you couldn't ignore it. He got up and went over to them and something happened. You don't need to believe me. I don't even know if he spoke to them or just looked at them. He came and sat down with his back to them and started talking to me again, almost as if he hoped I wouldn't notice what he'd done. And the four of them got up and went out like dogs a man had turned timid with his stick.'

When she tried to smile at me, her lips trembled. I was desolated by something I had not looked for or wanted – an aching flood of tenderness towards her.

'I remembered then,' she said, 'that I had started off being afraid of him.'

The dull blurred Kennedy of every day got in the way so that I could not believe in the reality of those vivid and dangerous memories to which she laid claim. Perhaps that had happened to her too over a long time. If it had, she must have been lonely: married and lonely. She had stopped believing in her memories and then Kilpatrick had come to lodge; 'Peter' with his hard good looks and sudden temper. That bastard wouldn't have hesitated about taking her to bed, and if she had gone I couldn't feel prim any more or disapproving.

What would the husband of her memories have done, though, if he had found out?

TEN

Muffled against my mid-afternoon pillow, the radio leaked music and then for a while, turn about with the advertisements, an account of the arrival of my father's Great Man at the city's top hotel. I had worked as a relief porter at Christmas at Riggs Lodge and it amused me to think how impressed my father would be if I was there still to encounter at close quarters the lofty skeletal figure of the old politician, or get from his own hand a gratuity – some appropriately small coin, of course, since they always get that sort of thing right, those hereditary aristocrats. I thought about that and it stopped being funny and then I fell asleep.

Someone was ringing the front door bell. Late sunlight had slipped from antlers to hooves in the picture above my bed I had christened 'Son of Stag at Bay.' The bell went on ringing after any reasonable person would have given up. When I had that thought, an instinct got me out of bed to answer the door.

'I thought you'd help me,' Margaret Briody said.

She was in jeans with some kind of tatty shirt hanging over them, and she was the most desirable thing I had ever been close enough to touch.

'What kind of help?' I asked.

I sometimes had these bad attacks of caution.

'Please,' she said.

My father had advised me about the dangers of being helpful in an undiscriminating sort of way to girls in the big city.

'Wait here,' I told her.

'If you won't,' she called after me, 'I don't know what I'll do.'

I went upstairs at the fast limp and collected the stick and my jacket. After a hesitation, I took all three notes out of their hiding place in the shoe under the bed. It was only money. If Paris was worth a mass, my father's advice was a fair swap for Margaret Briody even in a mess.

She made a forlorn figure standing at the door. A gentleman would have asked her in; but then no one had ever mistaken me for one of those.

'I don't think my landlady's too keen on you,' I said. 'We can get a seat in the park. It's not far.'

Before we got there she had told her story. We sat on a bench near the statue of Carlyle; the massive head emerged out of a column of uncut stone like a tethered lion. Behind us, the river made quiet noises whenever there was a break in the traffic.

'Let me get this straight,' I said. 'Kilpatrick's hurt. And you want me to help him?'

'To help me.' She was crying again. 'I took him to Daddy's yard. It was the only place I could think of. It's empty because of the holiday.'

'Why, in God's name, didn't you get an ambulance? If he's hurt, he should be in hospital.'

'But he wasn't really bad – not until I moved him. But now he's lying there and I can't waken him. I'm frightened.'

'That's what I'm telling you – he should be in hospital. What else can I tell you? There isn't anything I can do.'

'Help me.' She touched my arm. 'If you come with me – and we could get him into the car – and we could take him to the hospital. You're right – that's where he should be. Only if we took him up to the door, we wouldn't have to go in ourselves. You could help me with him. He might not want to go, you see.'

I saw; suddenly, I saw. 'We take him to hospital,' I worked it out, 'and if he doesn't want to go, I persuade him. But we don't go in with him, because then we'd have to give our names. We just leave him and drive away. That makes everything lovely. Nobody needs to know that he got himself hurt while he was in your house – for some reason, in your house. Not even Daddy and Mummy since they're away on holiday. Are you serious?'

Visibly, she decided to ignore any hint of indelicacy in what might have brought Kilpatrick to her house, Daddy being on holiday. Instead, she clung to the point at issue. 'I'm sure Peter wouldn't mention our names,' she said.

I couldn't think of anything to say to that.

'I've told you what happened.' When she sobbed, her breasts took big silhouettes out of the evening park. 'I don't know why you should want to be nasty to me. I'd gone out to do some shopping. I was going to make him – make him a lovely dinner. And when I came back, he was sitting on the floor in the hall and there was blood— blood—' Her voice edged towards a hysteria that was only half intended.

'He'd been shot,' I said.

She made a movement of protest.

'What do you mean?' she asked.

'Shot. With a gun. You said he was hurt. Now you're talking as if he might be dying. He didn't get into that state falling downstairs. And don't tell me you live in a bungalow.' I felt she was capable of anything.

'He wouldn't let me phone a doctor. I did want to! But he said it wasn't serious and he would phone his boss and find out what to do. He made me help him into the living room and then I'd to go outside while he phoned. And then I'd to get him the stuff to make up a parcel and—'

'You brought it to me,' I said, 'just like he asked. What harm had I ever done you?'

The sun was going down the sky and a little wind stirred in our faces.

'That's not fair to Peter,' she said. 'He didn't tell me to take the parcel to you. I was to take it to an address he gave me. But I was frightened. He'd used the towel I'd given him for the blood and I'd seen the gun although I said nothing – I didn't want to make him angry with me.'

'He was lucky. It didn't matter how I felt, so I get the gun.'

'Do you have to talk like that?' she asked. 'I didn't know for

105

sure what he'd put in the parcel. He asked me to take it to this address he gave me and—'

'What address?'

She could fix those wide violet eyes on you for a long time without blinking. 'I don't remember,' she said. There was no way of telling if she was lying.

'Anyway,' she sighed, 'I couldn't find it. He'd given me directions, but I got them muddled. I didn't think it could be the right address, the streets were so awful. And then this man started following me. I couldn't take the parcel back to Peter. You don't know what a temper he has. And then I remembered you were in the same lodgings as Peter. You always look as if you know what to do – You were the only person I could think of when I was so frightened.'

The brightest woman in the world couldn't have found a better method of persuading me.

'Stop crying,' I said in my rough, competent way. 'We'll work it out.' Something struck me. 'When you gave me the parcel, you said that Brond was going to come for it. Why did you say that?'

'It was just a name,' she said. 'I had to tell you something.'

I shook my head. 'No. That's no good. There has to be a reason. Was it his address Kilpatrick gave you? Were you supposed to take the parcel to Brond? It was him Kilpatrick phoned, wasn't it?'

For instructions. Because things had gone astray. Because something disastrous had happened. A knock on the door, you open it, smiling probably since it's this young pretty girl (damn it, *beautiful*, damn it, damn it) who's come back with stuff for dinner and herself for afters (no wonder the bastard was smiling), only it wasn't her but someone else, someone un-expected. The gun must have looked like a cannon. It was the kind of trick they pulled off all the time now in Northern Ireland. Bang! Bang! you're dead. Only whoever it was must have hesitated since Kennedy had got the gun from him. It hadn't stopped him getting shot though. Smiling, he had

106

probably gone to the door with an erection. It must have felt strange when he realised it was death that had knocked.

'He phoned Brond, didn't he?' I said.

'When I went back, he wouldn't believe that I'd taken it where he told me.' She gulped and bit her lip in a child-like movement. 'I had to tell him I'd given the parcel to you. He made me. And then he was angry.' She made the same child-like and vulnerable movement of her mouth. 'It was worse than that, he was frightened. He said I'd have to find somewhere else for him to hide.'

'Because you'd given it to me?' I didn't understand.

'Yes – till the man he'd phoned could help him. And I thought of Daddy's yard. It's got a room behind the shop with a bed in it. My father used to sleep there often in the early days – so he could be on top of things.'

She said the last bit like a phrase rehearsed in the house so often it had turned into rote.

'How long can Kilpatrick stay there?'

'Till Monday. The men don't come back from holiday till Monday.'

'What men, for God's sake?'

'My Daddy's men. He has more than twenty men work for him.' She glinted lunatic irrelevant pride. 'He has the demolition contract with the District for that side of the city – after fires and things.'

So much for Daddy. He must be rich beyond the dreams of Annandale – or at least of its farm labourers' sons.

It seemed the time for irrelevancy.

'Why don't we get married?' I asked her.

She widened those extraordinary eyes at me. For a panic-stricken moment, I thought she was going to accept.

'I don't think he'll be able to stay there all night,' she said. 'He's getting worse. He can't be there when the men come in on Monday.'

She hadn't even heard me, it seemed. A number of good things about being married to her came into my head.

'Come back with me!' she said. In her concern for emphasis, she leaned close. It reassured me to find that sex put danger out of your head in the real world. 'He'll listen to you.'

I had given up trying to explain that Kilpatrick was no friend of mine.

'Why was he so sure you'd help him?' I heard myself ask. 'Why did you?'

She blushed. It was unmistakable. Not, despite the year, merely an allergic reaction or the reflection of a holocaust on the far side of the hill. It started out of sight, under the shirt in the soft dark, and spread up until it warmed her neck and the high bones of her cheeks.

'You must be pretty close,' I prompted.

'We're good friends.'

There was no answer to that.

'Come on!' I got to my feet and she looked up at me without stirring. 'If we're going, let's get started.'

The flush ebbed from her skin and it was white under her mane of black hair.

'You won't come?' she whispered.

It wasn't what I meant, but her misunderstanding gave me one bonus chance, the last; to be sensible. It was a pity my idea of myself didn't square with walking off and leaving her to her troubles. The girl being beautiful and frightened and helpless were poor reasons for putting my head on the block.

'That's not what I said. Apart from anything else, if we don't move they'll lock us in the park.' I started to walk and she came into step with me. Close to me, even her sweat smelt of tears and honey. She moved with a loose graceful stride that almost matched mine. I wanted to stroke her hair and touch her. It didn't make any sense, but I felt marvellous. The vast stone head of Thomas Carlyle peered at me across the twilight, and I wanted to yell at the old fraud, You're dead, but I'm alive! I laughed out loud, and when she stared said to cover it, 'We'll have to spend the night in here.'

Innuendo would be my speciality; common sense could be someone else's.

'Oh, no,' she said. 'We could climb the gate. I'm good at climbing.'

I wondered if she could be mentally retarded. Kilpatrick might have won her heart by poking nothing more sinister than Crunchie Bars into her.

I put an arm round her waist. She shied like a skittish horse, then relaxed against me, but when we came into the street she took my hand and lifted it away, not unpleasantly but as if it was the proper thing to do.

We walked until we came to a subway station for she had decided against bringing the car from her father's yard. Going down the steps, I remembered trips on the subway as a child when we had visited the city.

'It used to smell differently,' I said. 'It used to smell of ozone.'

She looked at me uncomprehendingly as we went down side by side.

'Stuff that you get at the seaside,' I explained. 'You take deep breaths. Makes you feel better.'

Waiting on the platform, I began to laugh. It was as if I had been drinking and had taken too much. She looked at me as if I was mad and I remembered a silly story as an explanation.

'My Uncle James lived in Largs when he was a boy. Do you know Largs?'

She nodded.

'I've never been there. But he used to tell me how with the other boys he'd walk out to the Pencil – it's a monument thing outside the town.'

'It commemorates the Battle of Largs,' she said seriously. 'The Scots defeated the King of Norway.'

'We were the people,' I said. 'Anyway, I laughed because I remembered him telling me how the tourists would stand on the sea wall out there and take deep breaths – aa-ah! aa-ah! And in those days the boys knew they were standing right above the pipes where the town's sewage emptied. So much for ozone.'

The train poked its snout out of the tunnel. We travelled in silence. The walls of the tunnel slid past; then a station, two or three people, an Indian with a whistle who waved the train out again; more walls.

'This is ours,' Margaret said.

When we came out of the station, it was night. Between the pools of light from the streetlamps, it was dark. I wondered about putting my arm round her again, but before I could she said, 'Please God, let him be all right.'

I thought she wanted to draw me into that feeling, but maybe she just wanted to share it. She must have known I would not turn back at this stage. We came into a main road with sulphur lamps set on long swan necks. In that street, her eyes turned some shade from outer space for which the name had yet to be invented. Out of it, we defiled into a wadi of darkened tenements. It was a place for ambushes. I felt endangered.

'Margaret, he must have told you who hurt him and why?'

'No.' She turned her head away from me.

'That's hard to believe. Did you ask him?'

'No.'

She stopped walking and we were outside a shop. I had been looking for a wall or a fence round what she called her father's yard. There was a lane though at the side big enough for a lorry to go through. Her father's name was over the door of the shop front.

'Well,' I said. 'Have you a key?'

Her breath hurried in little gasps.

'I didn't ask him,' she said. 'I don't ask him any questions.'

'Have you got a key? Give it me and I'll go in first.'

She shook her head.

'I don't know what he'd do.' Her voice was so quiet I could hardly hear it. 'It's better if he knows I'm here – so it's all right.'

She had opened the door before I thought of the obvious. I caught her by the arm.

'Has he another gun? One of his own, I mean.'

I felt her trembling.

'I don't know.'

But she pulled away from me and I followed her inside. There wasn't enough light from the street to see anything. We stopped and she called, 'Peter! Peter? It's only me. Peter?'

In the silence I could hear the sighing beat of my blood, the sound of her breathing, a faint thrum of traffic from the main road we had left.

'Oh, God!' she said. 'He's unconscious.'

When I tried to follow her, I blundered into the edge of a counter. It caught me on the left side under the ribs with the force of a punch. I couldn't find another door. I had a touch of panic I'd felt as a child sleeping in a cupboard bed. I would waken and feel around in the dark until I was sure there was no opening but only walls on all four sides.

A light came on in the back shop.

'He's not here.'

Her voice was drained of life.

I pushed past her into the room: a desk, filing cabinet, a battered table supporting a typewriter and a pile of clip folders.

'Shut the door of the shop,' I told her. 'Or we'll have somebody wandering in off the street.'

She went through obediently. I heard the door bump shut and then her locking it. Beyond the back shop there was a smaller room with an electric cooker and sink. There was a bed against the wall. I lifted back the soiled grey blanket that covered it. On the sheet there were rusty smears like the marks on the cloth that had wrapped the gun.

I was sitting on the bed when she came back.

'What will we do?' she asked.

'Are you sure he's gone?'

'I'd left him in the bed. He was too ill to move.'

I didn't like the idea but I knew I would have to check the rest of the place. He might be lying somewhere too weak to move or call. Or crouching delirious, waiting for a head to appear round a corner so that he could blow it off.

'We'll have to make sure,' I said.

A practical streak I hadn't expected led her back out to the desk from which she produced a heavy-duty torch cased in rubber.

'The only other place,' she said, 'would be the yard.'

A side door took us out into a paved court. It felt cold like a place the sun never reached. In reaction I looked up and felt a silly relief at seeing a patch of stars above the tenement walls. The torch beam ran about the court into corners, across dark stains of oil and a litter of wind-blown trash. She settled it on an unpainted door that was heavily padlocked.

'He couldn't have got in there,' I said.

'There's nowhere else.'

To show her how silly that was, I walked over and shook the door. The heavy shiny padlock fell open and hung gaping from the catch.

'It's not locked,' she said.

'I think it's more than that.'

I heard myself whispering as if someone just outside the reach of our light might be listening. I lifted the padlock off and there were marks scored into the top.

'It's been broken,' I said and added as she put her hand out to the door, 'but whoever did it hung it back on the door. He can't be in there now.'

She gave a push and the door swung open.

'I can't find the switch for the light,' she whispered. 'I don't know where it is.'

We stood in the doorway and let the torch play over dim bulks of sacks and ladders lengthy on the wall. I took the torch from her and put the light round again myself. Neither of us moved.

'He wouldn't be here.'

'No,' she said.

We came out and I hung the impressive padlock in place again.

Back in the room, she crouched on the edge of the bed. She looked pale and defeated and beautiful.

'I don't understand,' she said. 'He was too ill to move.'

'Maybe it's not your problem any more,' I said. 'Will I take you home?'

'Yes,' and she added in a lost way, 'nobody'll be there.'

'Not Kilpatrick anyway. Not if he was as anxious to get away as you say.'

As I spoke, I opened the cupboard over the sink and rummaged inside.

'There's coffee and sugar. No milk . . . And here's a tin. It's chocolate biscuits. Looks like supper.'

She sat watching me while I filled a pan with water and sat it on to boil. I found two cups, surprisingly of china, each with a matching saucer. I even found a jar with milk powder. 'Just like home.'

She took the cup and I sat beside her on the bed.

'Sweet drink and a biscuit. Take a biscuit. My prescription for shock,' I said.

She wouldn't take one but as she sipped the coffee the colour came back into her cheeks. I had put three rings of the cooker to high and left them on. As we sat, the little room grew warm. I remembered eating breakfast in Margaret's house.

'You'll have to knock when you get back or your visitors will think they're being burgled.'

'Visitors?'

It occurred to me that I hadn't told her about spending the night in her bed.

'Your father's cousin and his wife.' My mind went blank. I couldn't remember his name. 'From Ireland. Your parents are over there just now.'

'Uncle Liam?'

She stared in disbelief.

'That's right. His wife and him. They're going on to London – but they're at your house tonight.'

'But what time is it?'

I looked at my watch. It was nearly one in the morning.

'Holy Mother of God!' she said. 'How can I go home now? What would Aunt Rose tell my mother? She never liked me.'

'Oh, I don't think so,' I said. 'It's just that they find you being perfect a bit hard to take.'

'What are you talking about?' At least she didn't look defeated any more. She had come alive. 'Are you telling the truth?'

'How else would I know about your Uncle Liam? I went to your house this morning—'

'And they saw you? Oh, what did you have to do that for? She'll tell my father for sure – she'll make a real story of it. My life won't be worth living.'

'Your Aunt didn't see me.'

'It doesn't matter. He tells her everything.'

'Oh.'

He had more to tell her than Margaret realised.

'I can't go home at this time of night,' she said. 'Not with her there.'

I took another biscuit. They were good although they must have been there since before the holiday fortnight. The sellotape round the rim must have kept them fresh.

'Sleep here,' I said casually.

A spray of crumbs spoiled the effect. She brushed them mistrustfully out of her lap.

'There's the bed,' I said defensively.

'What about you?'

'No problem. I can walk till I get to an all-night bus stop – or until I get home.'

'And leave me here on my own?'

It would be an eerie place to be alone. The old building settling in the dark; the bulky shadows in the store across the yard.

'I don't mind staying.'

'You're not sleeping in this bed.'

'I'll sleep in the chair.'

That idea seemed to ring a bell for her. She must have seen somebody doing it in a movie. In the films, though, the chair wasn't an upright, wooden-seat cane-back tucked under a desk.

'You'll sleep through there,' she said.

'It's cold through there.'

Before she could argue, I went through and cleared the typewriter and folders off the table. I lifted it into the small room and went back for the chair. I set them both by the wall as far from the bed as they would go. She didn't really have a great deal of choice. There was no way she was going home or that she would spend a night alone here without protection.

'Will you give me a chance to get ready for bed,' she asked in a little voice.

'Sure. I'll wait in the shop.'

I didn't want to risk putting the light on and attracting attention from that dark side street and so I took the torch. It didn't take long to exhaust the sights. Standing in the dark, I got childish: I spun the light in circles, threw it up and caught it; stopped when I decided this was one night I particularly didn't want to spend in a police cell. I stood quiet and let the light make discreet passes. As if it had a life of its own, it kept sliding back to a cash register on the counter. There was an illegal feel to the dark. I wondered how much Margaret was taking off to go to bed. There seemed no harm in looking at the register. It was an old model. When I tapped one of the keys, nothing happened. I tugged at the drawer but it wouldn't open. There was a faint shout from Margaret. She must have got into bed. I got the trick of it – the drawer opened when you leaned on No Sale and pulled. They kept the petty cash in it; no notes but a lot of coins. I picked out the big ones and dropped them in my pocket. Softly I pushed the drawer shut. My heart was pounding till I thought it could be heard outside. Apart from cakes out of the bakers as a schoolboy, that was my first theft.

All that she had left outside the blanket was her face and a spread of black hair across the pillow. Trying not to be obvious, I looked around for her clothes. I thought she might have climbed into bed fully dressed until I saw her stuff folded at the foot of the bed. She had spread her shirt on top so it was impossible to tell what was under it.

'Put the light out,' she said.

'Where's the switch?'

'There by the door. No, the other side.'

I put the light out and then put it on again.

'I'll need a minute to work out where things are or I'll break my neck.'

Conscious of her eyes dark and wide over the blanket like a fugitive from a harem, I padded around adjusting the chair so that I could tip it back against the wall and pulling the table forward to where I could lift my feet on to it. I'd never seen an unlikelier sleeping arrangement.

'That's it then. It's about as good as it's going to be.'

I went back to the door and charted the route.

'I'll put the light out.'

The blackness was total. I stood still trying to get my eyes back. Suddenly, a breathless whisper asked, 'Where are you?'

'Here. By the door. It's too dark to see.'

'Oh.'

'I'm giving my eyes a chance to catch up.'

Gradually I decided I could make out shapes. The hatch window to the left of the sink didn't so much give light as qualify the darkness. Slowly I edged forward. The side of my left hand knocked wood and I knew I was by the table. I bumped the chair and it rattled away. When that happened, I heard her gasp. I lowered myself into the chair and tipped it back gingerly until it rested against the wall. I put my feet up one at a time on the table. The silence was perfect.

'Good night.'

'Good night,' I said. The chair cut into the back of my neck.

'It was good of you to come with me.' Her voice was low and husky. 'I couldn't have come by myself.'

Surprisingly, I slept. Perhaps it had something to do with the warm glow of righteous self-approval I was generating.

Even righteous sleeps end.

It was still dark.

'Margaret?'

No answer.

I cleared my throat and tried a little louder.

'Margaret? You asleep?'

Carefully I lowered the legs of the chair to the ground. It was a miracle I hadn't tipped over and broken my neck. When I got up, my knees buckled. Blood must have stopped reaching them some time earlier.

In the dark I started undressing. As I pulled off my trousers, change spilled jingling from the pocket. My breathing stopped until I heard the deep rhythm of hers. Mother naked I set out for the bed.

This time I could see a little better but the bed was only a shape full of shadows. I thought she might be awake listening to the sounds I had made, pretending to be asleep or pretending it was a dream. I was ashamed enough to go back to my upright chair until I imagined trying to find that scatter of clothes. A small cold breeze licked my buttocks and I explored the cleft of pillows and sheet, peeled back the clothes and slid in.

She rolled over and put her arm round me. One problem solved: she wore bra and pants to bed. I lay still for a year or two and then softly ran my hand down her back. She had skin like warm velvet. I eased under her pants and on the last little bone I came to, rubbed gently. She sighed and snuggled comfortably closer. I stroked my fingers down one side of her soft parting and back up the other and pressed in between her cheeks.

'Peter,' she murmured and opened her legs so that mine slipped between them. Then I felt her hand come down and hold me.

Conscience apart it should have been all downhill sledging from there, but when I brought up my hand and touched her on the breast she trembled, let go as if I'd turned hot and threshed like a swimmer going down.

'It's all right. It's all right.'

I thought she was having a fit. She quietened.

'What are you— Is that— Get out!'

'Look,' I whispered reasonably. 'I've slept in that hellish chair. It must be your turn.'

There was a pause. She was still spread half under me. The size of my interest puttered against her thigh like an over-crowded motor boat.

'That was a terrible thing to do,' she said very quietly.

'You haven't sat in that chair for hours.'

'But you've taken all your clothes off.'

'I didn't want to get my vest crumpled.'

If she would only laugh, things might go right even yet. It was like lying beside a furnace. The heat of her body beat round me. I licked her shoulder. It tasted salty and smelled like warm milk and apples.

'You'll have to get out,' she said calmly.

'No.'

'Please, now, you wouldn't do it if I didn't want you to.'

Somewhere about the middle of the next day, I would brood on what might have happened if I had yelled Yes and got on top of her.

'Good God, no,' I muttered soothingly into her neck. 'I wouldn't force myself on a girl. I'm not like that. I've never needed to force myself on a girl. We'll do whatever you want.'

'Get out of the bed, please.'

'Apart from that. It's bloody cold out there. I won't stop you if you want to sleep in the chair.'

'Don't be stupid,' she said. There was an intensely practical strain in her.

Another pause. After a bit, I moved my leg closer imper-ceptibly; only she perceived it and said, 'Will you lie still . . . And we'll go to sleep. That would be fair.'

She freed herself and turned away. The dim bulk of her back was presented to me. I put my hand on her backside hoping for some repetition of the earlier effect. She reached behind her and picked it off.

'Go to sleep,' she said. 'That's fair.'

'Fair!' I heard my voice squeak and deepened it for the next bit. 'How can you talk that way?'

'You're a decent fellow,' she said. Her voice began to trail away. Either she was the best actress since Sarah Bernhardt screwed on a wooden leg or she was falling asleep. 'You've been good to me. I trust you.'

Sometime before morning, I fell asleep without abusing myself or murdering her – which must prove something about the resilience of human nature.

ELEVEN

There was a smell of frying bacon and since it was an illusion I kept my eyes shut, not wanting to be disappointed. Thoughts of the middle of the night ebbed into the forebrain. By cautious fractions, I stretched in the bed.

I was alone.

'You're awake then,' a measured cheerful voice asserted. 'You're a good sleeper when you start.'

Reluctantly I peeped out of one eye. Margaret was bending over the cooker turning something in a frying pan. She had found a kettle, too, and a wisp of steam plumed merrily into the air. It was a scene of pleasing domesticity. I rechecked my memories of the night and clenched the eye shut again.

'It's a beautiful morning,' she said. 'The sun's splitting the stones.'

I could hear the spatter of fat. Despite myself, my mouth began to water.

'That can't be bacon. Where would you have got it?'

Her laugh, like every sound and move she made, was music.

'I found a little corner shop. There's ham and eggs and coffee. And he had rolls. Do you like rolls?'

'What could be nicer?' I said, keeping my eyes shut.

'There's butter with them,' she said coaxingly.

I put my forearm over my eyes.

'Come on!' she said. 'It'll spoil if it has to wait.'

If only, I fretted, she had thought about that during the night.

'Chuck me over my clothes,' I said.

'In a minute. Do you like your eggs turned?'

Flesh and blood could stand no more. Resolutely I put back the blankets and stood up.

'Sweet God!' she said. 'I hope you're not one of those exhibitionists.'

With more awkwardness than grace, I progressed to where she had piled my clothes neatly on the edge of the table. Among her other virtues she seemed to be house-proud. I got into my underpants with difficulty. She could not resist another glance over.

'No need to peek,' I said. 'It hasn't recovered from the mauling you gave it last night.'

'Oh, now,' she said seriously, 'don't talk like that or I won't think well of you.'

'Turn them!'

'What?' she asked in fright.

'The eggs – I like them done both sides.'

Fat hissed as she tipped them over.

'I fried them in butter.'

'You'll give me a coronary one way or the other.'

Dressed, I came over and had a look.

'You should fry bacon on a dry pan,' I said.

'Don't be silly.'

'It's true. A dry pan – heat the bacon and slant the pan. Press the fat out as it fries. Makes the crispest bacon you could eat.'

'I suppose you'll manage this though.'

She sounded offended. I began to feel better. To tell the truth, I began to feel unreasonably cheerful. We had two eggs each as well as the bacon. She was a good eater. There wasn't much talking until we had finished.

'I'm going to be coarse again,' I said.

She looked relieved when I scrubbed the plate with the buttery end of the last roll.

'Run out and get the same again, would you?' I licked pale flaky crumbs from the wet tip of my finger.

'Are you still hungry? Would you like something else?'

There certainly seemed to be a hint there that she was ready to forage out again with her little shopping list. That was very compliant of her. She seemed to split her personality between the night and the daylight hours.

'Don't tempt me.' A thought cracked my jaw in mid yawn: 'Kilpatrick will be missed at his work. He told me he worked in an office somewhere.'

'Oh, no. When he left the Army, he joined—'

She stopped abruptly, and though I waited she didn't say any more.

'Well, anyway,' I said, 'wherever he is, he's not here.'

I wondered if the look in her eyes could be relief. If it was, guilt made her more emphatic.

'I'm worried *sick* about him,' she said.

'I know, you lay awake all night worrying.'

She looked more seriously offended this time. I watched uncomfortably as she cleared away and ran water over the dishes.

'That won't clear the grease off them if the water's cold,' I said.

As a way of ingratiating myself, it didn't work. She slammed off the tap.

'What are you doing?' I asked.

'It's obvious, isn't it?'

She was cramming back into her shoulder sack all the odds and ends that had got themselves unpacked.

'Going?'

'And you,' she said. 'I'm going to lock up.'

'No, Miss Briody,' a voice said behind me. 'I can't let you do that.'

Without turning round, I knew who it was. Margaret stared over my shoulder wide-eyed with shock at the interruption. As Brond spoke, he moved into the room until I could see him.

'If you would wait here, Miss Briody,' he said, 'it would only take us a minute to make sure.'

'Sure of what?' she asked.

He tilted his head and almost smiled: the whole effect seeming to say, If you want to pretend, that's your business, of course.

'Who are you?' Her voice trembled.

But it was his name she had used when she brought me the parcel. She had met him at Professor Gracemount's party – but, of course, that was weeks ago. Perhaps I was the only one who could not forget what Brond looked like.

At a movement of his hand, I followed him through the door into the passage that took us out into the yard. We left Margaret standing by the table, her ridiculously crammed shoulder bag swinging from her hand.

'There's no one in there,' I told Brond as he crossed to the unpainted padlocked door.

'You've looked?'

'Both of us looked.'

'Last night? I see. Miss Briody has a key then.'

'You don't need one – the padlock's broken.'

I pushed it open with my finger and lifted it clear. He took it from me and examined it, then looked about as if searching for a place to lay it. There was a box round a standpipe and he stood the lock on top of it at a careful angle.

'Didn't you find it strange?' he asked.

Without waiting for an answer, he opened the door.

'Didn't you find it strange that a businessman should go off on holiday and leave his property so badly protected?'

'I didn't give it a thought,' I lied stubbornly.

'Extraordinary,' Brond said, looking at me with interest.

The store seemed smaller than during the night. Builders' material was stacked everywhere. What I had taken for ladders were lengths of timber propped against the far wall. There were ladders as well, hung on hooks from a beam. Light drifted down from dirty skylights. Slowly Brond paced the length of the place.

He stopped in front of a pile of empty sacks in the corner farthest from the door.

'Well?' he asked.

I could see no reason for the question. It seemed to me he was playing another of his obscure games with me.

'Well?' he asked again and swung his forefinger like a pointer. I could see nothing.

'Are you joking?'

'What an odd impression you must have of me.' The note of his voice was as solemn as a Sunday bell. 'Doesn't it seem strange that the floor here is so clean?'

There was a path through the dust.

'Shift them away.'

The sacks were dirty. I lifted one and a shower of grime settled on my shoes. I held up my hands. Each was oiled with a sooty smear.

'This is stupid.'

'Don't stop. It would look bad if you refused.'

The bewilderment he imposed on me and the fear I would never admit made me turn again to the task. I tugged at the next sack trying to slide it off to keep down the mess. It would not move. I pulled again but something was holding it. I was doing Brond's bidding. What kind of man was I? In blind anger I took a double grip on the sack and, too excited to be careful, gave a great heave. It came with a sudden release and I staggered back in an uprising cloud of dirt as the body of Kilpatrick turned stiffly out from among the sacks and sprawled at my feet.

Fastidiously, Brond waited until the dust settled. He bent over the body and turned back the shirt to look underneath.

'Shot,' he said. 'It's a nice question who killed him. The person who fired the gun or the one who brought him out here. If the two acts are traceable to the one culprit, the problem resolves itself.'

I did not understand. A broad smear of black grease striped the dead face from one eye to the side of the mouth. I felt in my pocket for a handkerchief although I never carry one.

'Why did he come out here?' I hardly knew what I was saying.

Brond stood up impatiently.

'Come out? Without help? And burrow under the sacks? First being agile enough to bind himself.'

With the shoe that had the thick raised sole, he touched the body's legs at a place where they were tied with a piece of cord.

'His thumbs are lashed together also.'

The same shoe lifted the body over without effort. It was true. But what horrified me was to see how poorly the body was dressed – trousers, a cotton shirt, the feet were bare.

'This would be a cold place at night,' Brond said as if reading my thoughts. 'He'd lost so much blood, of course, otherwise he would have struggled from under there at least. He must have been half dead already.'

It was too horrible to accept.

'He must have been dead.'

'No.' Brond's shoe scuffed at the sack. The body's clenched fist lay on a corner of it as if to claim possession. 'He bled on this while he was lying here. Not much – but then by that time he didn't have a great deal left. Given his all for Queen and country. Or whatever he did give it for.'

I had never seen anything colder than Brond's smile.

The door we had come out by lay open and so did the next two, until in the front shop I stared blankly at the last door which lay open to the street. Margaret was gone. Outside stood the sleek hulk of the car that had taken me to see Brond a lifetime ago. Primo sat behind the wheel.

'Why didn't he stop her?'

'Would you have wanted that?'

'Yes. Why would she—'

'Well?'

Well? Well?

I shook my head. Was it conceivable that Margaret could have known while we lay in bed together that Kilpatrick was dying out there in the cold under a bundle of greasy sacks?

Nothing could make me believe that.

TWELVE

The man in the grey shirt and old flannels asked, 'How long is that now?'

He had been asking at five minute intervals.

'More than an hour,' I told him.

'It's incomprehensible to me,' he said.

'Something's happening.'

We listened to the sound of running feet and a voice shouting with an edge of panic.

'I never imagined it would be like this,' the man said.

There is something wrong about uncontrolled noise in a police station. You associate police stations with discipline. If anyone does anything violent, you expect it to be done quietly and off-stage. My mind shied off images of violent policemen. Thoughts like that are weakening when you sit waiting in an interview room.

'To the police, of course,' Brond had said.

I had been astonished.

'Where now?' I had asked, desperately casual, watching the vast shoulders of Primo as he steered the car through the morning traffic.

'To the police, of course.'

He had turned on me a look of mild reproach.

'I hope,' he said, 'you realise the seriousness of what we found.'

'We found Kilpatrick,' I said.

'We discovered a murder,' Brond chided. He was enormously the good citizen, expensively dressed, with Primo as chauffeur, leaning forward with a folded handkerchief to wipe a trace of greasy dust from his shoes. 'In the event, that leaves us no choice. It would be unthinkable to do anything else.'

Until the exact moment we entered the station – even while we were climbing the steps – I did not believe him. My first reaction was an enormous relief. Someone was going to sort out the pieces and let me have my life back.

The whole station heaved with confusion. An unanswered telephone was left ringing. Three constables passed at the trot. Brond spoke to the sergeant at the desk. I could not hear what was being said. I saw his face change, then it was as though the same virus affected him. He hobbled away at an incredible pace down a corridor to my left. That was the last I had seen of him.

A plain-clothes man had taken me by the arm. Five minutes, ten, had passed while I waited for Brond to come back. A sense of some vast catastrophe built up round me. It was strange to be at the centre of so much activity and be so excluded.

'In here,' I'd been told.

'What's going on?' I'd asked.

'Wait here. Someone'll be along to talk to you in a moment.'

He might have been deaf. As I asked again, he gave me the look policemen use to put you on a different planet. Then he shut the door.

The only other person in the room was a brown-faced, elderly man in shirt and flannels. Despite the stains on the flannels, he had that air which mysteriously but unmistakably signals prosperous respectability. Like me, he had been waiting. We had passed the time listening, trying to make out from the confusion of sounds what was causing the panic. Once the door was thrown open and we jumped up, but it was a flustered sergeant who stared at us as if we had no right to be there.

'I've been—,' my companion began.

'Sorry, sorry. Later. Really sorry.'

The sergeant disappeared. I had never heard a policeman offer so many apologies. It was like a measure of disorientation.

We sat down slowly.

'This is impossible,' flannel trousers said.

'Something serious is going on.'

'Yes.' He nodded. 'But still . . .'

We sat in silence. It was a miserable place. High on one tiled wall there was a narrow strip of window. I pulled the table over and stood on it. Pushing up on the toes of my good foot, I could just see out. It was some kind of air-shaft. Within feet of me, there was a featureless brick wall.

'I don't see any need for that,' my companion said.

I climbed down.

'Did you see anything?' he asked inconsistently.

I offered him a sneer.

'All I meant was that if there's some emergency we'd best let them deal with it. All we can do to help is be patient.'

'Splendid attitude,' I said. 'Admirable. You're not a criminal yourself then.'

He flushed with annoyance.

'Good heavens, of course not. Do I look like—'

He broke off, looking at the unsightly flannels.

'I was gardening. That's why I'm here. I'd bought onion sets. The roses at the back haven't been doing well. Too sheltered perhaps. Anyway I'd decided to have them up and I'd bought onion sets. So I took out the bushes and raked and I had the sets in a pail. They'd been in water, you see. I pushed the dibble in – to make a hole, you see, for the set – but when I pulled it out the dry soil ran into the hole and ran and ran. And I stood up and stepped back and there was a roar and a gasp as if the earth itself had taken a breath. And half the garden was gone and I was standing right on the edge of a black hole I couldn't see any bottom to. I mean it just went down, and I could hear little stones and clods still falling.'

He looked at me wide-eyed, reliving it.

'You're the first person I've told,' he said.

I wondered if he was a lunatic.

'Earthquake?' I asked. 'Surely not in Glasgow?'

'Earthquake?' He looked at me as if I was the one who was mad. 'Who's talking about earthquakes? Subsidence! My garden had slipped into an old pit shaft they'd all forgotten about.'

'Jesus!' I said.

'Oh, yes. Lanarkshire, you see, rests on old coal mines.'

Not long after that someone came and took him away. Very politely, so it was possible his story was true. I waited. I had never been in this situation so it was hard for me to tell if the noises off were settling back to normal. Twice more I stood on the table. Brick walls don't change much. Two and a half hours went by. The door was not locked. I tried it once. There was no physical barrier to stop me from going out and asking what was happening. I sat down and waited.

The short fat one took notes. The other one did the talking. Neither of them explained who they were; no names or ranks. My name. My age. My occupation.

'How well did you know Peter Kilpatrick?'

'Not well at all.'

'How many of you lodge there?'

My mind scrabbled.

'Three – no, four.'

'Uh-huh. All of you students, isn't that right?'

'No – two of us. Willie Clarke and me. Muldoon isn't. Neither is . . .'

'Uh-huh?'

'Kilpatrick. Peter . . .'

They knew that.

'So you're a student. At the Uni.'

He mouthed the word in the way Davie had just before he tried to butt me in the face – yoo-ni.

'That's right.'

'Uh-huh. Why didn't you like him?'

'I didn't say I didn't like him.'

'Ladies' man, are you?'

'Me. No.'

'Big fellow like you. Not bad looking. All those stories about students.'

129

The fat man snorted appreciatively.

'I asked you a question.'

'I answered it.'

'Uh-huh. Incline the other way?'

I didn't know what he was talking about. When I looked at him uncomprehendingly, he made a limp movement with one hand.

'That way, are you? Fancy the boys?'

'Not much.'

He hesitated and I thought I'd not been emphatic enough for him, but it was only a needle. He came back to what he was really after.

'Ladies' man, are you?'

'I don't run round bloody mad, if that's what you mean.'

He turned to the fat man, who kept writing.

'That what I mean?'

The fat man glanced up at him then at me. He sniffed.

'No. Didn't think so. Have a steady?'

'A what?'

'A steady – girl you go about with.'

'No.'

'Big healthy fellow like you. How long you been here?'

'Since the session started – last October.'

'All winter. And no girls. Funny.'

'I didn't say no girls. I've been out a few times. Took a girl home from a dance a few times . . .'

Walked the streets a few times. Howled at the moon a few times.

'Names.'

'Eh?'

'Names. Give us their names.'

He waited. I thought of them being questioned by the police.

'I'll give you a name,' he said. 'Margaret Briody.'

'She's not a girl friend of mine.'

'Where'd you sleep last night?'

Some time later he said that she'd been interviewed. Not long after that another man came in and stood listening.

'Jealous of Peter, were you?'

'Why should I be jealous of him?'

'You're telling us that you didn't know he was sleeping with her?'

'With who?'

'Don't play the funny man, son. Just answer the questions. You're in a lot of trouble. You can do it the hard way or the easy way.'

The light in the narrow window had faded. Since the morning I had been sitting in that room.

'I'm hungry,' I said.

'Sorry,' he said. 'Get him a sandwich – no, I'll go.'

He got up and stretched. The man who had been standing silent sat down. The one who had been questioning went out.

The new one sat with a pencil turning it on the table. The door opened and another two newcomers appeared. One sat down and took over from the fat man. The fat man yawned and left.

'I want to piss, too,' I said.

'In a minute. Tell me first about Margaret.'

'You must have heard – I've said all there is to say about her.'

'Tell me again. When did you find out about her and Peter?'

It must have been an hour later when I remembered about the sandwiches. Nobody had brought me any. But the room gradually filled up. More men kept coming in. Some were in uniform. Two or three would ask me questions taking it in turn. The men in uniform were not constables – I didn't know what ranks but they looked important.

It was just after I felt the strangeness of this roomful of men that the last one arrived. I was being asked a question and it stopped abruptly. The new arrival closed the door and waited as if he wanted to gather every eye. I watched him as if I too had been waiting for news.

He nodded – Yes. Yes.

There was a release of breath, a mingled sigh and snarl, like the purr of a hunting cat. Then every eye turned back to me.

The man who had just come in bent over and whispered to one of my interrogators and another one got up and he took his place.

Everything changed then. Although I had been frightened before, I could make sense of what was happening. Now the questions made no sense to me.

Had I ever been a member of a political party?

Where had I met Kilpatrick?

How did I feel about the Royal Family?

Had it been in a club I met Kilpatrick?

Some kind of society or organisation?

What group did I belong to?

And then over and over again:

Where had I gone during the night – while Margaret Briody slept – before I climbed into her bed – God, they knew about that – where had I gone? What time had I slipped out? Where did I go? Did I know – this house, that street, this hotel?

Had I been inside that hotel?

Riggs Lodge – but, of course, I had. It was the hotel I had worked in as a relief porter at Christmas.

When I said that, there came another of those strange sighing chuckles, fat and satisfied and at the same time hungry.

My watch had stopped. It felt like the middle of the night. I had at the back of my mind the thought – this is wrong; and I thought that I would say nothing more; I would insist on something to eat. Dully, I realised that I wasn't hungry any more. I was tired. The questions kept coming and I answered them while behind their distraction I conducted with myself this other argument – that it was wrong; but until I settled it what else was there to do but keep answering?

Earlier when it was still daylight they had taken my finger-prints.

'No,' I had said.

Two big men looked at me incuriously.

'You don't want to be printed?'

'No', I said in a small voice.

'Up to you,' one stone face said. 'Case last year in Edinburgh. Fellow felt the way you do about it. They broke one arm on the Tuesday and the other one on the Wednesday. Thursday the Court said that was reasonable force. Thursday afternoon he got his fingerprints taken. Right?'

Right.

'You know what this is?'

A large sheet of stiff paper crackled out between us. A meaty hand spread it flat. There was a bruising across the knuckles that reminded me of Primo's hand on the apartment door, the fat swollen pressure of blood and offended tissue. He put a finger down on the paper.

'Here,' he said. 'You know what this is?'

It was a plan of some kind. A blueprint: the sheet was covered with detail. I understood enough to see that it was a building and that it must be very large.

The finger tapped, tapped.

'Here. Stop bluffing. You know what this is.'

I didn't; I knew nothing about reading plans. When I bent closer, it dissolved into a jumble of lines.

'Through that door, right? And then up the outside.'

Somebody leaned over his shoulder and said, 'They're sure.'

The one who was asking the questions looked up at him irritably and that let me understand it had not been a statement aimed at me, but a question, 'They're sure?'

Now he stared down at me.

'Possible,' he said. 'He's a big fellow. But, Christ!'

That started them off on a new line.

What sports did I play?

Climbing? Had I done any climbing? In the University Mountaineering Club, wasn't I?

'I'm afraid of heights.' The admission of something I had always been ashamed of angered me. Even watching those old movies where the comedian teetered on a ledge above toy cars and people scurrying like ants, I would tense up and have to look away.

In or out of uniform, they were all bulky men, beef to the heels, with a lot of beer bellies hanging out in front. The room wasn't all that big and the temperature had climbed. Spreading patches of sweat darkened the shirts of those who had taken off their jackets.

A red misshapen face lowered over the table at me when I admitted my fear of heights. 'You've been told,' he shouted. 'You've been warned about the funny stuff. You've had it easy. Don't think this is the only way. Do it easy or do it hard. Open your mouth and get it over with. If you get turned over to the heavy squad, you'll think we're angels.'

He went on too long. Not that I didn't believe in his heavy squad, just that he went on too long. I had been questioned and shouted at for hours.

'Why don't you,' I said quietly, 'go and play with yourself?'

After that I did not answer any more questions. To everything I shook my head. No more words. After a while, they stopped. People discussed in whispers; there was a general movement out.

Soon there were only two of them left. It was like when we had started so many hours ago.

'. . . of that of that none of that none of.'

I sprawled and gasped, came up like a bad dive in the pool, ears sore, pain in my chest. Someone shook me by the shoulder.

'None of that. This isn't a fucking doss-house.'

I wrenched myself out of his grip.

'Just keep awake.' He had an unpleasant grin. 'A guy like you shouldn't sleep. I couldn't sleep if I'd done what you did.'

'I've done nothing.'

'Hey!' he said. 'He's found his tongue again.' He leaned over me. 'Why don't you tell me all about it? Nobody here but us. All the big brass away. Tell me about it and we'll get a statement. Then you can have a sleep.'

He had lowered his voice in an elephantine gesture towards

friendly persuasion. I shook my head for the millionth time. Routine.

Except that he lost his temper – or was a natural actor. A hand like a bunch of rocks bunched the front of my shirt. What must have been his thumb pushed into the hollow of my throat until I choked. I writhed back but the chair swayed and I was held off-balance.

'Nobody here but us,' his voice said in the distance. It echoed in the dark that washed over me. I got both hands on his and tried to pull it away but could not move it. I had not eaten. Even if he was a strong bastard, it was also true that I had been weakened by lack of food.

The hand came away. Slowly the room settled. By the door, another man was standing. The one who had been massaging my throat swung round and then came to a kind of attention. His trousers wrinkled across his fat rump. The man by the door looked vaguely familiar as if he might have been one of the onlookers in the room earlier. He was in plain-clothes but wore them like a uniform; grey hair, a big beaky nose, about fifty; you could tell he was an officer and a gentleman.

'Did I see correctly there?'

His voice was unexpectedly high and thin.

'Sir! I was—'

'Never mind all that! Was he trying to pull your hand away?'

My tormentor had lost the thread. He mumbled and stopped, finally offered, 'I suppose so.'

'I mean *trying*. Putting an effort in.'

More confidently the answer came fast, 'Yes, sir. He was trying.'

'No luck though?'

Complacently, 'No, sir.'

The man paced closer.

And you're not Tarzan, are you, sergeant?'

The fat sergeant was lost again.

'So it would follow chummy here wouldn't be the world's

strongest, eh? Big fellow,' his eyes measured me, 'plenty of muscle. But you've handled worse?'

'Yes, sir. Plenty worse, sir.'

'Well, then, sergeant,' the voice squealed with frustration, 'would that suggest anything to you? You did hear the technical boys' opinion about what had happened? Does that sound like chummy? Or was he bluffing about fighting you off?'

The sergeant seemed to understand all of this. He looked at me thoughtfully. I hadn't expected him to think as well; it seemed vaguely unfair.

'He wasn't bluffing, sir. I'm sure of that . . . Doesn't mean he couldn't be an accessory. If he knew the hotel, he could have given the inside plan.'

'But we'd still be looking for the man we really want to find.'

They studied me together.

'If this one knows . . .' The sergeant let his voice die away.

'You'd like me to take a walk. Come back in half an hour or so?'

'If he knows, I'll get it out of him.'

Above the beak nose was a pair of pale blue eyes: they looked not at me but at a sum of problems filling the space I occupied.

There was a gentle tap at the door. I had never imagined I would be glad to see Brond.

He smiled peaceably at the picture we made.

'There you are, sergeant. I wondered where you had got to,' he said, ignoring the other man. 'I hope you haven't been living down to your reputation.'

'I don't know what you're hinting at, Brond,' the officer's thin voice sounded strangely subdued, 'but what happens next if we don't run this maniac down?'

From behind his back Brond produced a stick which I recognised as the one he had given me.

'You left it in the car,' he said, and passed it across the table to me.

'What kind of tomfoolery is this?'

'Our friend here had a broken foot,' Brond said reasonably. 'The stick supports him.'

Both the sergeant and his officer gaped at me. I was beyond surprise at anything anyone said or did.

'Foot? Foot!' the officer squealed. 'Get up! Up!'

I got to my feet and almost keeled over. I had been kept in that seat since the questioning started.

'Good God!'

'Quite,' Brond said. He sounded complacent.

'But this is—' He mastered his temper with an effort. 'Not the world's strongest man. And just to round it off he's a bloody cripple. Why did no one say he was crippled?'

'I'm not a cripple,' I said. My tongue felt as if it had rusted. 'I hurt my toes moving furniture.'

The officer jerked his clenched fist. He looked as though he wanted to strike me, the sergeant, somebody – anybody perhaps but Brond.

'A monkey on a bloody stick!'

'With respect, sir,' the sergeant said, 'doesn't mean he isn't an accessory.'

'Charge him!'

'Surely not,' Brond said. 'I'd leave the hotel side of things – for the moment.'

'I take it that's not meant to be anything more than advice,' the officer said. I think despite himself, it came out sounding like a question.

'I leave the details to you,' Brond said sweetly. He began to laugh, 'Take care of the ponce and the pounds will take care of themselves, eh, sergeant?'

They didn't think that was funny. The officer said so. 'Not funny. You know what happened at the hotel is all anybody is going to care about. But we don't forget that the boy Kilpatrick's father and his uncles – damn it, the whole family were policemen. The father John Kilpatrick was a well-respected man on this force. We don't like it happening to one of our own.'

'I disapprove of murder,' Brond said, 'as a general principle. That overrides its particular applications. If you feel so strongly

137

about Kilpatrick, bring a charge. I still doubt if the other matter is ripe . . . Stick to Kilpatrick. It's not certain anyway that the other business will have much to do with you by morning . . . You stick to Kilpatrick – if the two are connected it might give you a toehold in the big one. Keep the London boys from pushing you completely out of it.'

The sergeant looked from me to Brond. Clearly this was not his idea of a conversation in front of a suspect . . . from the way his eyes flickered down to avoid his superior officer, I guessed he did not feel hearing this would do him much good. Muddled and frightened, I had the wild idea Brond was trying to give me some clue as to what was going on, but all I could think of was Kilpatrick: that he had been a policeman and that he was dead.

Not long afterwards they took me out of the room where I had been questioned. Brond went away somewhere and left me. While the men spoke around me, I could only see that there was a wash of grey light across each pebble of frosted glass in a window. The night was over.

They charged me with the murder of Peter Kilpatrick, and then they put me in a cell where there was a bed and allowed me at last to sleep.

THIRTEEN

I had only been a prisoner for a day and some part of this day, and yet as they hustled me out to the car my heart hurt me with the relief of being under the sky again; and as we were driven through the streets I could not have enough of looking at the women on the pavements. How could I come to harm when the city was full of mothers buying food and bargaining?

We were held up at the lights outside a jeweller's. Above the door I saw the words Mappin and Webb and we edged forward and there were three clocks arranged in a window. As I watched, their hands shaped eleven o'clock in unison and in my silence I imagined their chimes.

I was wide awake; everything was sharp-edged and clear; I was beyond exhaustion. They had shaken and lifted me out of sleep. It was like the times after parties this winter when I had wakened in the morning still drunk. I thought my mind was clear. At intervals I considered that I had been charged with murder. It was a true event which referred to someone else. Under all that pretence, a silent mouth inside me screamed.

The dark man's stomach rumbled.

'So much for sandwiches on the plane,' he said pleasantly, as much it seemed to me as anyone.

The fair-headed one on my other side grunted agreement. On the next corner, he eased himself up and farted.

'Sandwiches,' the dark one said and they laughed.

They were both Cockneys. The Noel Coward song kept jingling in my head, 'Maybe it's because I'm a Londoner . . . Maybe it's because I'm a Londoner . . .'

'What a bloody dump!' the dark one said.

'The arsehole of Europe,' the fair one said.

They both laughed again. They were like a cross-talk act. The dark one nudged me.

'That bother you, Jock?'

'I don't come from Glasgow,' I said. He seemed to think I was a member of the Tourist Board.

'Funny that,' the fair one took it up. 'You not getting angry. I'd have thought that would have made you angry. Believing what you believe.'

'Eh?'

'Easier to shoot your mouth off in a pub?' the dark one said. 'With your mates. In pubs like. Not so easy here. Tell me! I'm listening.'

I kept my mouth shut.

'Fucking berk!' the fair one said.

I wondered what the driver thought of the conversation. Yes, sir, I'd heard him say when we came out. He had a Glasgow voice.

Fortunately the journey ended quickly. We got out and I felt sick at the sight of the hotel I had been questioned about the previous night. They put a hand each on my arms, just above the elbow. They didn't grip hard but it was extraordinarily unpleasant.

Inside, I saw the manager who had spared a quick word to me and the other temporaries at Christmas. The doorman too I recognised, and one of the porters. It felt as if everyone was staring at me, but I doubt if any of the guests realised what was going on.

One of the hotel staff led us along a corridor.

'We'll manage from here,' the dark one said to him.

'Do you know how to find your way upstairs? There's a back way.'

'Don't worry about it. We'll come back to the desk. You can take us.'

'I could wait. The hotel would prefer as much discretion as possible.'

They looked at him silently.

'Well,' he said uncomfortably, 'I'll be at the desk.'

When he'd gone, one said, 'Discretion – make you bloody sick,' and the other agreed, 'Much they care.'

'Show us the door.'

'What door?'

'Games. They said you were a comedian.'

The hand on each bicep urged me forward. Before the end of the corridor, we stopped beside a door. It had the look of painted metal like a fire door.

'Push it.'

'Give it a push,' the other one repeated.

I shoved and it swung open. There was a narrow area ten feet or so square. The windows facing us had ventilators set in at the top. You could not see through them but one had been pulled down and there was a clatter of kitchen noises and a man's voice mauling a pop song. I had washed dishes somewhere behind those windows.

'Lock's been broken.'

The dark one was doing all the talking now. He pulled me round by the arm.

'Take a look.'

There was a metal bar that must have been intended to slot into the wall.

'It's been forced,' I said.

'That's right.' He sounded like a master whose dimmest pupil had just managed an answer. 'You know anybody who could do that?'

'I don't understand.'

'People come along here all the time,' he said. 'Somebody would notice if you messed up the wall. Whoever did this did it so there was no mess. And he must have done it fast. Fast as a bleeding gorilla. You know anybody like that?'

'Jock here could do it,' the fair one said, finding his voice again. 'Feel your muscle?'

And he put his hand back on my arm and rubbed the bicep.

'Ooh, ooh,' he did a parody of camp appreciation.

'Cut it out!' I said pulling away.

'Watch it! We'll turn you over for attempted escape.'

'Might hit us with his stick.'

'What's he bleeding got it for anyway? Ridiculous. Desperate character and they leave him with a weapon.'

He took the stick out of my hand and weighed it reflectively.

'It ain't heavy, but it don't mean you couldn't manage a bit of GBH. He could poke you in the balls with it, Wally.'

'I need it to walk. That's why they left it. I've hurt my foot.'

'No!' he said in sympathetic disbelief.

He moved too quickly and anyway his grinning face gave me no warning. Before I could react, he stepped on the injured foot. The pain was so bad and unexpected that I blacked out.

It could only have been for a second. I was leaning against the wall – the fair one had stopped grinning. He held out the stick. I took it.

'Sorry,' he said. 'I wasn't looking where I was going.'

And he grinned.

'Outside,' the dark one said and moved me out into the area. When I looked up, the sky was blue and far away at the top of the funnel.

'We're interested in the window four floors up. Don't need to tell you, though, do we?'

'Why not? I don't—'

I broke off. What was the use?

'You don't . . .? Nobody ever teach you it's manners to finish a sentence?'

'I think I should have a lawyer.'

The laugh they gave sounded genuinely amused.

'Bit late for that, my old son,' one said. And the other, 'You've been watching those late-night movies. But this isn't fucking America, it's England.'

'Like fuck it is,' I said.

They looked at me as if I had given them a present.

'England starts a hundred miles south of here,' I said lamely.

'You're a bit of a fanatic, aren't you?' the dark one said.

'Because I don't think this is England? That's not fanaticism, it's geography.'

'He's full of chat, isn't he?' the fair one said.

'Full of piss.'

The singer in the kitchen beyond the lowered window had his repertory of pop songs interrupted. Something had gone wrong and an immediate uproar of angry voices flared until it subsided under the dominance of a single spate of heavily accented cursing.

'Another piss artist,' the fair one said. 'Bleeding wogs.'

I wanted to smash them down. That night in the Union when I had bumped the elbow of the guy who turned out to be a medical student. Sorry, I'd said. Some of the beer splashed on his trousers. Just spots. It was nothing. Beer from his glass poured down the front of my jacket. I remembered that and his fat fee-paying-school face mouthing at me, but I didn't remember hitting him. Although his jaw had been broken, they had smoothed things over. No penalty: mostly because I had been ill that night. Nobody knew how much it frightened me that I couldn't remember.

The Homicidal Pacifist, Donald Baxter had named me after that.

'You're wasting time with me,' I said. 'Can't you get that through your head? I'm not stupid – I don't know anything about – this.' I jerked my arm free and pointed to the windows above us. 'Somebody broke in from the corridor – somebody climbed up there. I don't know why anybody would want to do that. But I couldn't. Do you understand that? I hate heights. I don't know what happened up there. I don't know why— why you should blame me.'

They looked at me seriously. For a moment, I thought I had got through to them.

'Like a handkerchief, flower?' the fair one said.

'You didn't know who, did you? Not at Christmas,' the dark one said. 'Not when you were planning it. But somebody, sooner or later. Place like this, stood to reason, sooner or later there'd be somebody your lot wanted. Only as usual with amateurs you got caught.'

'We can fit you up for this one. You're in the shit.' The fair one mouthed the word like a soft fruit. 'We're the only friends you've got left.'

'He's right, you know,' the dark one said in a kindly way. 'He's a bit rough, but he's not wrong. Take the rest of your lot. Suppose they stay in the clear. Who's left? It's all down to you. They'll put you inside and post the key to Robert the fucking Bruce. Since he's dead – it'll get lost. Your old mum'll be dead before you get out.'

'Your kid bloody sister'll be dead.'

'How did you—'

I shut up again. It was stupid to show I was upset by anything they said. It was just that I hadn't expected them to mention Jess, who was only eight years old.

'We know everything worth knowing about you,' the dark one said. 'You'd be surprised how much we know about anybody – if he gets important enough.'

'Important!' the fair one spat between my feet. 'Bloody amateur! His lips are sealed. He's in a dream world. Honour among thieves.'

'Not thieves,' the dark one said. 'Idealists. That's the word, isn't it, son? Idealists . . . Patriots.'

I was like a ball they passed back and foward. We looked at one another. Their game was one I didn't know. The rules changed. I lost.

'Patriots.'

Going up in the lift, the dark one said, not maliciously, but in a quiet way, like advice, 'You don't want to mind your head about geography, son. We'll decide the geography. That's our job.'

'We're geography teachers,' the fair one said.

In the suite on the fourth floor, there were two men I recognised. They had been two of the quiet faces, elderly watchful men who had not intervened in the questioning but had gathered glances during the hours of the night. I had known they were the ones who mattered.

My Cockney cross-talk act gave them scant respect. The 'sirs' were perfunctory.

'The bedroom? Through here would it be, sir?'

I had no choice but to join the procession. It was a bedroom, but with a television and all the required bits and pieces to remind you the riffraff were kept outside. The food was good too – I had scraped enough of it off cold plates to remember that. The bed hadn't been made.

In luxury hotels beds don't get left unmade – unless something has happened.

Even then I didn't realise. I thought of a robbery – or someone caught in bed with the King of Spain. The Cockneys carried that shade with them – of diplomats blackmailed, refugee scientists; people like them had been around since the Medes invented laws and a state to justify them.

'His own detective heard nothing?'

'No. He became suspicious, though, and it was he who found—'

'Yes.' The dark one interrupted him. 'But since no one's told chummy here anything about that he doesn't know what was found. That's right, isn't it, son?'

I hated him more than anyone I had ever met – except his fair partner.

'You're satisfied things were tight at your end?'

'Of course,' one of the older men said frowning. 'We're not unused to this kind of thing. Car park had been checked out – no access in case of any bomb nonsense. Surveillance – discreetly – in the corridors and the rooms gone over with a toothcomb before . . .'

'Maybe you were too discreet,' the dark one said.

The man who had described the security arrangements went a strange purple colour. Before he could say anything, the other senior officer crossed to the window.

'Who could have anticipated this?' He twitched aside the

curtain. 'A quite exceptional affair. I still find it difficult to—'
His voice faded as he leaned out. He re-emerged looking
persuasively startled. 'And that door downstairs – incredible.'

'Incredible like in fake?' the dark man asked.

'Fake? What fake?' For a distinguished senior officer, he
sounded inappropriately tentative.

'You said "incredible." I wondered if that's what you meant
. . . sir. Unbelievable – that's what I wondered. If you don't
believe all that – the door downstairs, the window.' He too
went over and peered out. 'It's a hell of a climb, and then doing
a window like this from outside . . . I can see anybody might
wonder if it was a put up job.'

The senior officer gave him a look that seemed to me full of
dislike. I have unusually sharp hearing, not always a comfortable gift. I can eavesdrop on a conversation three tables away in
a restaurant. People don't realise. Now I could hear them as
they murmured at the window.

'Don't like your attitude. The detectives immediately involved – as usual – weren't our people. If you want to suggest
an inside job, you'd better start looking nearer home.'

'Don't misunderstand me, sir. I wasn't suggesting—'

'That's all right then, isn't it?'

'Certainly. But you understand we're here to get results—'

'Well, what about this fellow? Do you prefer to have them
standing around while you discuss possibilities? Is that how you
people handle suspects? Or am I missing something – new
technique, is it?'

'Not a technique, no. We don't need technique for this
fellow. Seems to me he's a dead duck.'

I missed the rest of the conversation. I was thinking so hard
about what he meant that I lost my sense of the place and sat
down on the bed.

'Get up out of that!' the second of the local men screamed in
rage.

I fell off the bed – shot up like a cat that has had its tail
pulled.

'He's a cool one,' the dark man said. He and the older man came forward from the window. The four of them made a half circle hemming me in against the bed.

'Cool? Cold-blooded. That really is cold-blooded.'

'And bloody insolence,' the other senior officer said.

The Cockneys ignored this local repartee. They waited quietly, two solid men like matched bookends or a pair of duelling pistols. Even standing relaxed, they had their weight balanced. I didn't fancy my chances of making a break for the door. Even if I had, there would have been no point. If they were secret police, I had no border I could cross to get away from them. There was nowhere for me to go.

'You don't mind sitting on a bed where someone's died?' the dark man said.

I should have known that it was death that had brought us here. Accusing me of one murder without reason or sense, they could extend the list until I had more victims than Jack the Ripper.

'Somebody's died in most beds,' I said.

'Not recently.'

'Not this recently,' his partner offered.

'Last night recently.'

'You know where I was last night. God, I have the best alibi in Glasgow. I was with these two for a start—'

The two senior officers looked confused.

The fair man frowned: 'Not *last* bleeding night. Night before last. Same night you did the other one.'

'Not me,' I said.

'We have two bodies,' the dark man said reasonably. 'One's in a shed – under sacks?' The older of the local men nodded. 'And the other one's, well, he's under these soft sheets.' He rubbed a sheet between thumb and fingers like a patter merchant on a stall at the Barrows. 'He's dead too.'

'There must be plenty of people die in the city – every night of the year.'

I didn't know why I kept talking. Even in my own ears, I

sounded like a criminal defending himself. A cold-blooded customer – and bloody insolent.

'Well, now, that's a point of view.' The dark man was enjoying himself. 'All those slums. No Mean City and that. Razor slashers chopping each other's sporrans off. Dozens of murders every night, I expect.'

The two older men still looked like officers; they even looked distinguished; it was just that they didn't look powerful any more.

'Only thing is you don't get dozens of them tied up first.'

Tied up? I had an image of Peter Kilpatrick with his legs and wrists bound. And the smear on his face I had wanted to wipe away.

'Want to say something?'

I shook my head – no. What was there to say?

'Plenty of time to change your mind,' the dark man said comfortably. 'We were talking about coincidences. Two killed – that happens. Both tied up – could be. Tied up with the same cord – second one tied up with cord cut off the piece used on the first one. That's no fucking coincidence, not any more.'

'Who was killed?' I looked at the bed. And then by an involuntary reaction tried to move away from it – but the fair-headed man was in the way. He crowded me against it.

'He doesn't know,' he said.

'I don't.'

'He only works here. He only works it all out. He only plans it. Didn't you care who got killed?'

The dark man took over from him. He had such a gentle and reasonable manner, I had begun to prefer his partner.

'Of course, he cared,' he said. 'Not much point in killing just anyone. That would be murder. That's right, isn't it? You wouldn't call this murder. Of course not. Idealist. Don't think I don't understand. We make a study of it. Plenty of idealists about nowadays. Planting bombs. Blowing up schoolkids. Shooting down old ladies at airports. And this kind of thing,' he nodded at the turbulent bed, 'not murder. Assassination.

Oh, you've got what you wanted. Every paper in the world this morning has what you've done in a fat headline. In London and Berlin and Rome – even in Rio de Janeiro, I expect. Wouldn't surprise me if even the Chinks had it on their telly – how you murdered him. Pardon – telling how you assassinated him. They admire that kind of thing.' He had talked himself into a controlled fury. 'We don't. You're going to be surprised how much we don't – especially where he was concerned. Put it this way – if some people, even some of your people up here, could get their hands on you they'd tear you apart piece by piece for what you did to him.'

He stopped, breathing hard, the muscles in his thick neck swelling. 'Lucky, isn't it,' he asked putting his face into mine, 'that we're in a bleeding civilised country?'

'Like the cavalry,' Brond said to me in the car. 'I came over the hill for the second time.'

And he had. At that moment, the cavalry image seemed exact to me – pennants and a brave show of horsemen to the rescue. My Cockney Indians had frightened me more than any of the tough cops who had surrounded me during the night. I said that to Brond.

'Their technique would have been different.' His plump cheeks crinkled in a smile.

'The tall man with grey hair, he asked them if it was a new technique to have me standing there while they argued. Is that what you mean – some psychological technique?'

Brond laughed. I thought it was the only genuinely amused sound I had heard him make.

'They'd have beaten it out of you. Either here or at the house in Chelmsford. What was going on last night would have seemed a waste of time to them.'

I felt sick. There was no question of not believing him. Everything he said carried authority.

'But why did they let me go? Was there new evidence? Has someone confessed?'

Brond looked at me carefully.

' "Let go." I don't think we could say that, not exactly "let go".' I watched Primo's hands turn the wheel. The sun had gone behind a cloud.

'Are you going to take me back to them?'

'I hope not. Think of yourself as being in my custody. Not let go, I'm afraid.'

'Are you a policeman?'

'We seem to have arrived,' Brond said.

I hadn't recognised the streets, although I should have. We were at Margaret Briody's house.

Primo got out of the car and came with us which surprised me. I couldn't think of him as being any kind of policeman. He hadn't been with Brond at police headquarters or even later at the hotel, although when we came out he had been sitting in the car waiting for us. Maybe it was because the first time I had seen him he had been a workman. I remembered the removal man Davie with his snot-yellow grin and the thud of Primo's blows beating into his flesh. Perhaps no one was what he seemed. (Except Andy surely – how else would he have got the knack?) Now Primo stood a step or two behind us in a grey suit which was an imitation of Brond's, only since it was less expensive the cheaper cut made the brute width of his shoulders seem disproportionate, like a parody.

'Can I help you?' the woman who opened the door asked.

As soon as I heard the Irish lilt, I knew she must be Margaret's aunt who had to be kept in ignorance of the facts of life. If it had not been for her, we would not have spent the night at the yard or been there in the morning when Brond came to search the place. I might have been lying now on my bed thinking idle thoughts of Jackie as the sun idled lasciviously down the stag's horns in the picture on the wall.

'Margaret's not here,' she said when Brond asked. 'But she'll be back soon, God willing. Is it something to do with the University?'

'That's it,' Brond said soothingly.

He exerted on her the charm of authority.

'Would you want to wait?'

We sat in the living room where Muldoon had bluffed me such a long time ago. When she called, the uncle came through drying his hands on a towel.

'Well, now,' he said. 'I'm Liam Briody. And you're from the University?'

But, even as he was speaking, those quick eyes had run over us. Considering us, he wiped the towel over his knuckles slowly.

'Would you leave us for a bit,' he asked his wife, 'while I have a word?'

She looked flustered but got up. At the door, she asked, 'Would you be wanting some tea?'

Before we could answer, Briody told her, 'No. We'll have our chat first.'

He waited until the door had closed and then, in a different tone, wondered aloud, 'The University? Is that what you told my wife?'

It seemed to me Brond deliberately waited to let him take the next step.

'I know the young fellow there. According to him, he's a friend of Margaret's. He's here and then yesterday Margaret appears looking as if the world had stopped. Now three of you. What's it about?' He made a calculation then, like a light switching on as the notion took him. 'Police! Is it police, you are?'

Brond waited appreciatively.

'Not ordinary police,' Liam Briody said. It wasn't a question.

'We're interested in Margaret,' Brond said at last.

'She's done nothing wrong.'

I admired that. The tone was very different from what I had taken to be his casual mocking attitude towards her.

'I'm very willing to believe that,' Brond said. 'Although, of course, it's not something that's settled – not at this stage – not yet.'

'She's a good girl,' Briody said sturdily, but he was no kind of match for Brond, who pressed people into the shape he wished.

'This wouldn't have anything to do with Michael Dart?' Briody asked. Suddenly he looked like the old dealer in horses who came over from Cork to the market my father took me to as a boy; he would spit on his hand and shake with the man he was getting the better of to show the deal was made. He was a great one, that old man, for trading to and fro – giving to get, what you wanted for what he needed.

That was how I heard the story of Kennedy, who Briody told us was in reality a Southern Irishman called Michael Dart.

'His father had been a hard core man who'd taken the gun with De Valera against the Free State. But that was a long time earlier – and this was before the new troubles and the new deaths. Then, in the North they went quietly collecting their welfare benefits and unemployment money; while in the Republic most of us were too busy trying to live to worry about the Border. But Francis Dart, Michael's father, would still be arguing and living the old battles. Michael took in the talk of dead heroes with his mother's milk. I think he must often have been with the Hound of Culann sitting at the knees of Sencha and Cathbad instead of labouring in the mud of a poor farm. When he was fifteen it came to be known that he was one of four that had boobytrapped an RUC post on the far side of the border. They blinded a fellow of twenty or so – a man with a young family. Both the hands on him were blown off by the same bomb. Michael was marked from that time on, and it's true that some of the foolish young men thought he was a hero . . . It must be hard to be a hero when you're only fifteen.'

'How long did it take him and who did he kill?' Brond asked.

Briody blinked at him.

'You've worked it out. The last day I saw him I met him in the street. I wasn't sure if I should speak with him for he and my brother had had hard words. I asked after his father – poor man, he was dead within the month, and I wouldn't say

Michael's trouble wasn't the larger part of it. Two days later the news was all over Ireland. Michael Dart and two others had raided a bank in Dublin. Something went wrong. The chief of them – an old fellow the boy looked up to – got into a panic. He made a hash of it somehow and they couldn't get to the car and then he took a bullet in the leg. The third fellow threw down his weapon and ran for it. Michael stood over the old fellow and fought it out. He got to the car – God knows how for he had to carry the old one. Before night they'd recovered the car – with the old one sitting up dead in it for he must have taken another wound while the boy was carrying him. Michael Dart was away and one Garda dead and another fit for nothing after that with a bullet in his lung. I've heard tell the third fellow, the one who ran for it, was found dead later and that might have been Michael's work too.

'It must all have been planned the day I spoke to him, yet you would never have known for he was so merry and talkative. He was a reckless boy who could call birds down from the trees with the charm of him.'

He looked at us puzzled.

'I knew him at once. Though he looked forty years older if the truth were known.'

'Twenty years on the run will have rubbed off his charm,' Brond said.

'I've no doubt that's true.'

After Briody we sat not talking. Brond seemed content to wait. Primo stood behind him – every so often he half turned to look out of the window. I was watching him when he leaned forward to check outside and then back so as not to be seen. I knew that someone must be at the back door. A minute later I thought I could hear voices and then that I was imagining them.

'Was that what you wanted?' Briody asked. His voice trembled, which upset me for he was a fine solid man, who had done nothing to have Brond set against him.

The noise of voices came loud, one dominant, a woman's

voice sharp and angry yet with that timbre so right it could be no one but Margaret. Next moment she was in the open door and looking at me as if I was alone in the room. Her face was full of hate.

'Why aren't you in prison? Oh, it's not fair that you should be here.'

'What's he done?' Briody asked, alarmed. What's he done to you? was what he meant. And I almost shouted out, We only slept in the same bed. Nothing happened.

'You killed him,' she said, never taking her eyes from me. I had never seen such loathing. 'Oh, I can't understand or imagine it.'

But I was innocent of the death of the old politician. They had not needed to tell me it was his bony skull and noble skeleton that had been murdered in the hotel bed. Who else would cause such excitement? Even my father when he heard of it, though he would not be capable for any reason of tearing a human being to pieces, might manage a moment of hatred.

'How could anybody do that?' Margaret wondered. 'To leave him out in the cold place to die.'

Then I knew she was talking about poor Kilpatrick and had been told that I had killed him.

FOURTEEN

When we came to Jackie's house, Brond dealt brutally with her.

'He has no right,' I said, without believing it since Brond seemed to have the power to do whatever he wanted, 'he has no right at all to go tramping round your house.'

Jackie huddled in a chair that seemed too large for her, and Primo gave less sign of having heard me than a rock in the Trow burn at home. He was not watching us but was simply there, while overhead Brond's limping step passed from room to room.

She had been puzzled to see us on her doorstep. She started to ask me some question but Brond laid his hand on the door and with a steady pressure took it back out of her hand. Without haste he crowded her back and, Primo behind me, I had no choice but to follow him. It must have seemed to her like an assault of men. We filled the hall. Brond walked through into the front room and she followed him as if mesmerised.

'Is your husband in the house?'

She shook her head.

'He's in serious trouble. Did you know that?'

'Trouble?'

'You know he's done something. What's the point of lying about it? Are you a political activist as well?'

'Politics?' She said it like a word in a foreign language and then stupidly, touchingly, said, 'But he works for a book-maker.'

'Well, he's miscalculated the odds this time,' Brond said with the heavy humour of the dullest, most brutal of policemen, and Primo smiled.

Now, returned from searching upstairs, he began again, 'Where is he? Out planting a bomb somewhere?'

She was astonished but behind that something else as well; as if, perhaps because she was Irish, only the mention of that word in this nightmare began a nightmarish possibility of sense.

'Bomb,' Brond repeated, making a thick pat with his lips, 'poof! Pop! Like that,' and he splayed his fingers, and then picked at the grey cloth tight over his thighs as if lifting off tiny seeds he had shaken from his finger tips: 'and then a body here, a leg, a finger perhaps . . . what would this be?' He lifted nothing between a careful thumb and forefinger. 'Too pulped to tell.'

And he opened his fingers making us look down as if some horrible fragment would lie on the carpet she swept so clean each morning.

'My husband?' The absurdity of the idea released her. 'My husband! He's not fond of . . . I mean, he's a Loyalist all right. But never to go further than a grumble over the papers. Oh, I mean if you knew him. If you only knew him.'

She looked at me for confirmation. That dull stick Kennedy – Oh, I should confirm it. But I had listened to Briody's story.

I remembered as her smile faded, that strange thing she had told me: how he had got up from among the young men on a beach and done contemptuously what they had been afraid to do, being daring only in talk.

'Not Loyalist,' Brond said. 'The other lot.'

Any doubts I had felt about her vanished. She showed no smallest sign of understanding; it was beyond anything she could have contemplated.

'Your husband's a terrorist,' Brond said impatiently, 'with a list of Protestant dead notched on his shillelagh.' He looked at her sharply. 'And you, what do you want to be taken for? A good Ulster girl of Loyalist stock . . . Yes. Well, if that's so, some of those dead may be yours. Think about that.'

I had known her for a winter without seeing that she was admirable. When she spoke, it was with a firmness there would be no shaking.

'I don't understand any of this,' she said, 'but there's only one person I want to explain it to me.'

'You want him, I want him. Our interests seem to be identical. Where is he?'

'I don't know.' She made a gesture to stop him from saying anything. 'Not exactly. I really don't know. He got a few days' holiday and went away fishing. He went up north, but I don't know where.'

'Alone?'

'Yes. He likes to be on his own.'

'Well, he would,' Brond said and gave her a sweet smile. 'It must be a strain to live a lie every waking hour. Even with the one closest to you.'

She bent at that but would not break.

Outside the house, I was put into the car by Primo's hand. Even in the interrogation room, I had not felt so entirely at someone else's disposal. Brond said something to him and then got into the driver's seat.

We drove off leaving him on the pavement.

'What is he going to do?' I asked. The sound of my own voice surprised me. I found in myself a feeling for Jackie which I did not want. There was no future for that feeling; not any real future of the kind my mother would understand. 'Why have you left him behind? He won't hurt her?'

We climbed the circling ramp that led to the bridge over the Clyde. Across pouring ranks of cars I saw dock cranes and a glitter of light from the big river.

'If you went into that water,' Brond said, 'jumped, pushed or driven off the edge in a car, first requirement when they fished you out – if they fished you out – would be a stomach pump. Look there!' I caught a glimpse of a racing boat, young men pulling back on the oars. 'Jolly boating weather! When they lift it out the hull will be plastered with swabs of used toilet paper.'

We curled down and back on earth were held at traffic lights.

'Primo won't hurt her?' I repeated stubbornly.

' "Primo". That's rather splendid.'

I had never thought of him as anything else, but it was only a joke, a malicious joke by the removal driver Andy.

'Primo.' He rolled the name between his lips like a cigar. 'It's not a bit like his real name, which is redolent of glens, swinging kilts and dawn trumpets at Kandahar. Hurt her? You're a poor judge of human nature. Primo is a chivalrous man, another of the world's idealists.'

'I had the impression,' I said with a sense of danger, 'that he would do anything you told him to do.'

'Did you?' Brond stole a glance at me and then turned his attention to the traffic. We left the main road and went along beside tenements of black scabbed stone. 'Was that the impression you had?'

He sounded childishly pleased.

The front shop had Licensed Bookmaker and the usual kind of name beside it. I thought it must be the place where Kennedy worked. Brond got out and left me. There was nothing to prevent me from opening the door and walking away. He had left the key in the ignition and I could drive. I could drive up any road until the petrol ran out. When Brond came limping back I was still there.

'He had a phone call,' he said, putting the car into gear, 'from his wife.' I thought for a moment that Jackie had managed to deceive him. Afraid for her, I searched his face for a sign of anger. He did not look angry; but then he did not look surprised either. I did not believe in the possibility that Jackie could trick Brond.

When I recognised the route, though, and realised we were going back to Kennedy's house, I grew afraid again for her sake.

Primo was standing where we had left him, talking to someone. When I saw it was Muldoon, I wondered if everyone in the world belonged to Brond; but, as the car stopped, he turned away abruptly as if to go into the house then changed his mind. I understood why as a change of angle showed me Primo's hand covering Muldoon's arm like a rockslide.

'Open the door,' Brond suggested and I stretched back and put down the handle.

Muldoon came into the car half lifted on Primo's grip.

'What's the game?'

He was close to blubbering; the narrow face fragmented by fright and ratty anger. That was what I would have expected of him, so why did I feel he was acting? Acting as he asked what was going on, what kind of mistake had been made, who they were.

'My name is Brond.'

Perhaps very special actors have bodily control that will let them drain colour out of flesh and leave a face grey and sick. I didn't believe Muldoon was that kind of actor.

I wondered what the name Brond meant to him.

In Glasgow you can drive out of a slum street into one beside it that looks like an Adam terrace in Edinburgh. It is a city of contrasts. The house Brond stopped the car at was handsome. It was like the house some friends lived in; five students in a ground floor flat; they ate in a room that had a carved wood mantelpiece thirteen feet high. It was the kind of house the merchants and the shipping barons built for themselves when the city was rich. Now in my friends' flat holes like woodworm in the mantelpiece showed where the lads played darts after they had been drinking. This house, however, was Brond's. He said so when Muldoon, trembling, asked where he was.

'My place,' Brond said. 'Come on.'

There were patches of green grass cut close on either side of the path. I noted every detail as if we were moving very slowly, even the dry yellow circles where cat piss had burned the lawn. When we went up the stone steps to the front door, I thought Brond would ring and that one of those smooth young men, like the ones who had whispered to him in the corridors at police headquarters and later in the hotel, would open the door to us.

Instead he took out keys and turned one, then another, and a third lock. The hall was dirty and shabby. The air smelled stale.

The only furnishing was a low table with a telephone, but as we passed I saw there was no cord to connect the instrument to the wall. Our feet beat on the uncarpeted staircase. On the landing, we were faced by an open door. I glimpsed a sofa and a table with papers but we walked on down a crooked strip of matting until Brond stopped at the last door in the corridor.

'My parlour,' he said to Muldoon. 'Walk into my parlour. You'll know the verse.'

It was black until he reached inside and touched a switch. One unshaded bulb stirring in the draught threw a hard light on peeling walls, bare boards, heavy wood shutters sealing the windows.

The room was empty except for a kitchen chair under the light.

I understood the function of the room. There was a quality Sunday paper that condemned examples of torment with dates and details until the sufferings flowed together, even the ages and jobs of the victims seemed identical, and only the names of the continents changed. Stories of torture were the pornography of the middle classes on this island.

Muldoon sat down where he was told. That was strange too, since he knew what the function of the room was.

'I want you to tell me about a young man – a boy really – called Peter Kilpatrick,' Brond said. 'I want you to tell me when you saw him last. I want you to tell me about Michael Dart.'

'Michael who? I don't know that name,' Muldoon said.

There might have been a signal or maybe it was time, but Primo leaned down and hurt him. I waited and did not throw myself to his defence.

'I'll speak more clearly this time,' Brond said.

'I won't stay here,' and I turned for the door sure that they would try to stop me and then I would have to act.

Brond glanced round.

'Wait along there,' he said. 'Don't be foolish about going off.'

I sat behind the table of papers in the room at the head of the stair. From the sofa that once had been expensive, tears leaked dirty brown wadding. I remembered a night when I had been ill with bad wine and fever, how I had lain on the steps trying to grab Muldoon by the crotch. I had never liked him. And then I sat forward and put my hands over my ears and pretended I could hear only the shell sighs of my blood. Staring at the desk, I had a stupid idea. I imagined that everywhere over the whole world where people were being abused – political victims, children, frightened women – at this very moment the thumb of God would appear out of the air to crush each tormentor out of existence. I imagined that over and over again until a light touch fell on my shoulder.

It was Primo.

The touch of his hand was a horror to me but, as I flinched from it, he pulled it away as if my shoulder burned.

'I never thought I'd sympathise with the IRA,' I said. 'You've done that for me.'

His face was shiny with sweat and he looked unwell.

'Not ordinary policemen, Briody said that to you. By Christ, he was right!'

I took courage from the sound of my own voice and his silence.

'I don't think Brond's a policeman. I don't think anybody knows what he really is. Has he been pretending to the IRA that he's one of them?'

'Damn the IRA,' Primo said in a slurred voice like drink, so that I could hardly make out the words. 'What country do you think you're in?'

Then I saw among the papers scattered across the table an old newspaper clipping. There had been rumours of Scottish republican movements, secret societies, but no one took them seriously. There had been a trial though. I remembered the headline. The government had set it up as a propaganda exercise and the papers were ready to play along; but it had crumbled under their fingers in court into a farce of blundering amateurs and comic opera robbery. Only the sentences had been serious. I held up the scrap of newsprint towards Primo.

'Something new,' he said. 'Not like anything before.'

'And Brond is part of it – a government spy.'

Primo lifted his clenched fist quivering above my face.

'Because of him,' he said, 'this time things will be different.'

Beyond his arm, I saw Brond appear in the doorway. At the same instant, Primo felt his presence. His arm fell to his side.

'Our friend next door is sleeping,' Brond said. 'Would you make sure that he is comfortable?'

When Primo went out, Brond closed the door.

'Like the cavalry again,' he said.

Appearing over the hill to rescue me; and like before I was glad that he had come.

'You shouldn't upset him,' he said looking towards the closed door. 'He's like a soldier. A good soldier.'

'I know. Kilts and trumpets at dawn. You told me before.'

'It's quite true,' Brond said, sounding serious, even indignant, until he spoiled it by beginning to laugh. 'He went off to fight in Malaya – a mere schoolboy furious with the Communists for trying to subvert the British Empire. The first time he tried to volunteer his father chased after him and fetched him home because he was under-age. He got there though, and did *splendidly* well.'

Some confused perception of the finality of his contempt – for Primo, for me, for everyone; maybe even for himself? – gave me the courage of anger.

'If I get out of here—' Why had I said that? I would get out of there. They weren't going to kill me. 'When I get out of here, I'll talk. Even if you take me back to the police, I'll tell them.'

Somebody would listen.

'Tell them what?' Brond asked. He watched me expectantly, and that puzzling anticipation chilled my anger.

'About Muldoon,' I said hesitantly. 'You can't do – what you did to him – not in this country.'

'Nothing else?' Brond wondered. 'Isn't there something else

you want to tell them?' I shook my head in denial. 'Muldoon's not really very interesting,' he went on. 'We knew about him, of course. His whole family is up to its unwashed neck in Irish Republicanism of one stripe or another. His father was interned during the war and has spent most of the last fifteen years enjoying Her Majesty's same brand of hospitality. We suspected there might be a bigger fish, but never got near to thinking it was Kennedy. Michael Dart!' He tasted the name appreciatively. 'Oh, he was good. He knew that hiding wasn't a matter of putting on a false moustache. You have to put on a false life. He lied to the world. If he was a sleeper, he was one of the best. There's a price, though, for living in ambush behind your eyes. That little wife didn't know who he was. But who *is* he? He's her husband Kennedy night and day, and Michael Dart for an hour a month – perhaps not so much. Or he's not Kennedy at all except as an actor – not even when he's holding her in his arms. Michael Dart all the time and always pretending. I think that would be hard to do. In the end, who was he? . . . I find that interesting.'

Suddenly, as he finished, he came round the desk towards me. Despite his limp, he moved very rapidly and I shrank away from him in my seat. Bending above me, however, he slid open the file drawer and began to rummage inside. 'That, yes, interesting,' he said, as if to himself, groping at the back of the drawer. 'Muldoon, no. Muldoon now is a dead letter. You'll have to do better if you want to tell a tale. Isn't there something else you want to tell?'

I saw a bridge in bright sunlight and a boy scrabbling to draw himself up to the parapet.

'Eh?' Brond said, touching me on the shoulder. 'Something else?'

'No!' I cried too emphatically. 'Just Muldoon. There wasn't anything else.'

He had taken a box from the drawer and now, turning away from me with a look of disappointment, plucked out a fat white chocolate which he popped into his mouth. Muscles in his plump jowls writhed as he smacked upon it. 'I almost forgot I'd left these on my last visit. Fresh cream, but it's cold here and so they keep.'

If he had offered me one, I would have refused it. He didn't offer. Instead, reaching with the hand that held the chocolate box, he caught up one of the papers scattered on the desk. As it dangled, held between his third and little finger, I saw that it was the newspaper clipping about the trial of the Republicans or radicals or revolutionaries – whatever they were, Scottish certainly.

'What do you make of this then?' he asked, flicking it at me. 'You read it while you were waiting?' I nodded warily. 'Trust a student, of course. And?'

What country do you think you're in? Primo had asked me.

'Is he— is Primo one of them?' I gestured at the clipping.

'Primo,' he savoured the name, amused again by it. 'Yes . . . I don't think he'd refuse that as a description. Modify it perhaps here and there. They always fall into factions, these people.'

How much contempt he had in him; and I remembered that Professor Gracemount had been a spy and that Brond was his friend; and I wondered if a spy always despised his victims. It was an insight I did not want, but the thoughts ran through my mind too fast for me to control. Because I was afraid he would read them in my face, I blurted out the first thing that came into my head: 'But you said he was a soldier. You said he ran away to be a soldier.'

'All the way to Malaya,' Brond said seriously, 'and did splendidly. Most white men couldn't stay in the jungle for more than a few weeks, but he had a platoon of blacks – come from Africa to fight the Chinese. I expect they were keen on the Empire too, you see. With his platoon, he would stay in until he couldn't get to sleep because his bones were sticking into the ground. Then they would include rum in the parachute drops – and he drank that until he could sleep. He really was a hero.'

'He's a funny kind of hero now,' I said, glancing towards the door and thinking of what he had done to Muldoon.

'A good soldier is an instrument,' Brond said solemnly. 'I imagine then he tortured some little yellow men in pyjamas – it's the kind of thing good soldiers have to do. He is a good man, and he took no pleasure in what he had to do through there. I suppose it's difficult for your generation to appreciate a sense of duty.' He paused and I suddenly reheard his last sentence as if it had been some kind of impersonation. Something must have shown in my face for his voice changed. The words were still serious but his voice was different. 'He is a dedicated man. To lose your only son and in a stupid, pointless accident. That's cruel.'

He widened his eyes compassionately, but the voice kept that altered, inappropriate note.

'Tragic,' he said. 'And so unnecessary – that's what is hard. The child was playing on a bridge. And he fell.'

FIFTEEN

'Yorkshire cock. 9 inches plus.'

I sat on the toilet seat reading the legend on the tiles. I could never remember what the sizes should be – and, of course, the average worrier about such things typically over-looked the phenomenon of foreshortening. Anyway, now we were in Europe was it not time our graffiti went metric?

Below the legend there was a drawing of something that looked like a length of limp hosepipe. Tucked under it were two pendulous moons that to me resembled women's breasts. I congratulated myself on another proof of my heterosexuality – of such things as much evidence as possible is comforting.

On the hosepipe was printed, 'Anybody want it?' And there again – nine inches after all – while the answer might be yes, the practical problems would have to be faced: supposing I did manage to cut it off him, how would I manage to attach it to myself?

The ambience of the occasion engendered reflection in those areas – philosophy, linguistics, symbolic logic, that kind of thing. Why I was there was a different matter and a speculation I had suppressed along with so much else. From the moment Brond had come over the latest hill like the cavalry, I had surrendered myself into his hands. Now – despite flashes of terror like lights thrown into a darkened room – I floated with events as if he were my protector, my best wishes safe at his heart. It was inexplicable, but I rested in my darkened room rather than searching for doors to escape by or a window to see from – the survival instinct had ebbed low, or perhaps that was the way it served me.

We were at a party given to celebrate the last night of an

Open University Summer School. The School was being held in a university near the city. After the mansion house and Muldoon's ordeal, we had got back into the car and driven away. Behind us in the house we must have left Muldoon – conscious I hoped. I told myself it was stupid to be afraid that he might not be alive.

I was in favour because of the company I was keeping.

'Professor Gracemount has been a good friend to the University,' said a bald little man who had been introduced as a Professor of something. 'He pulled strings for us in the early days when we were establishing ourselves, worrying about buildings – we have to be guests in so many places – and how our courses would be judged by the conventional institutions. It was our good fortune to have friends then. Now our units are purchased in colleges and universities in the United States,' he gave what one of those units might have described as a self-deprecatory laugh, 'Canada, Australia, New Zealand, several of the new African states as well as here at home in England . . . I suppose I should say,' another laugh, ' "here in Britain." '

'North Britain,' Brond said, with a wink at me as if to share the joke.

'People don't,' Professor Gracemount said, sniffing impatiently – was there a hint of evil-smelling cheese in the air? – 'sensible people don't fuss about that any more. If they ever did! I imagine sensible people must always have been concerned with substance rather than shadow. Problems of war and peace, economic problems, problems of social organisation. Good God! when Carlyle defined the Condition of England Question, he wasn't interrupted by some fools piping up, "Britain please, Condition of Britain, if you please!" If he had been, I can imagine the short shrift they would have been given. Carlyle surpassed the parochial. I don't think he would have tolerated his countrymen confining him as a Question to the Condition of Ecclefechan. And how much less that narrowness of vision is tolerable now, when we're in the midst of the last of the wars of religion – Communism and Capitalism in conflict – and any smaller thought's impossible.'

I was surprised by the energy he put into this, sounding at the end even poetic. I had thought he went in for languor rather than excitement, but then, apart from that one evening at his house, I had only encountered him before as a lecturer.

'You divide the world so neatly,' Brond said, 'it sounds dull. Boredom may become the main motive for committing treason.'

'Betrayal,' the bald little Professor said in a North of England twang, 'won't wash for the old reasons that moved Quisling or Pétain or even von Stauffenberg. The only music we'll pay attention to is that played by the "Rote Kapelle" – a tune that made us dance when it was Germans betraying Hitler – but that set our teeth on edge when Nunn May, Maclean, Burgess, Philby and the rest, came under the baton of the Great Heresiarch . . . Karl Marx, you see,' he added in an aside for my benefit, who visibly hadn't seen. 'It's possible to reject their actions without denying them idealism.'

'We know where your sympathies lie,' Brond said with a pale smile in the tone of someone indulging a child.

'I am a Man of the Left,' the little pedantic Professor said, turning his head towards a bray of horse-laughter from a group of students by the bar. 'The Irish contigent,' he explained, 'they're with us this week.'

'The land of Sir Roger Casement,' Brond said, 'speaking of traitors.'

'He sinned against the British Empire,' the little Professor said, mouthing the phrase with distaste, 'another religion, mighty and immoveable – but it passed like a dream between one night and the next morning's awakening.'

'Not entirely passed,' Brond said cheerfully. 'I had a friend who tortured little yellow men in Malaya for the Empire. And another who killed a child that had stumbled on some dangerous information – sense of duty, you see.'

'That's not duty as they understood it in the heyday of the

British Empire,' the little Professor said. 'It's trumpets and brass blaring over a secret longing for defeat. It's wallowing in post-imperial vomit.'

I think he was trying to be rude, but he could not manage the effortless offensiveness better bred Britons brewed at pre-paratory school as a distillation of seven-year-old homesickness.

Distilled essences of Celtic sorrow, blended or malt, were equally hard to come by that evening – two litre bottles of Italian wine, beer, martini and unobtrusive sherries making up the booze scene. There seemed, however, to be a general resolution to shift as much of it as was humanly possible.

'Ever heard,' I asked, 'about the old Italian peasant who was dying? "Gather round my sons." So they gather round. "All-a my life, I make the wine. I teach you to make the wine. Now I am dying. We make a big-a fortune from the wine. Now I tell you my last-a secret. How to make-a the wine from grapes." And all the boys fell back in astonishment from the bed, and then the oldest son says, "Poppa. You mean you can make it from *that* as well?" '

'I love the way you Scots talk,' she said. 'Say something else.'

We were sitting on the floor. She was a big girl with a strong face that had something in it to draw me across the room to her.

'Don't laugh at my funny accent,' I said, 'and I won't laugh at yours. Where are you from?'

'London. What do you mean "accent"?'

' "Maybe it's because you're a Londoner . . ." ' I crooned to her.

'But I don't talk like a Cockney,' she said. 'I talk like ordinary people who sound as if they don't come from any-where. My mother has an accent, though – that's why I wondered.'

'Your mother?'

'We came from Hungary. My mother and brother and me. I was only a baby. My brother was shot in the hand. He's a lot older than me, and until then all he had wanted out of life was to be a violinist. After he was shot, he couldn't bend his hand.'

'That was the Russians?'

'Yes. It was the second time my mother had left Hungary. She left before to get away from the Germans. This time it was the Russians. I don't remember any of it. But my older brother can't play the violin. If you could believe my mother, he was a child prodigy.'

'That's the thing about great disasters. Each one is a mosaic of personal tragedies.'

I was very solemn. I really liked her and her long strong face, her brown Jewish eyes and her long legs curled under the wide skirt that suddenly looked Hungarian. I could have wept for her brother. I had a desire to stroke her face and talk to her in some private place; something sparked between us and the feeling was not only mine. I really liked her.

A squat red-faced man half stood on me. Instead of apologising, he glared down, a tumbler in each hand.

'You want to keep your legs in!' he snarled in a thick brogue.

'Talking of accents, a boy from the bogs,' I said.

'He's a nasty bit of work,' she said looking after him. 'Rosemary – you know Rosemary – said that he walked her back after a lecture she'd given. He was carrying her books and he tried to touch her up. When she stopped him, he threw her books down. She told him to pick them up and he walked away. But next morning he came and apologised and said he hoped it wouldn't prejudice her against his work. He'd been so smarmy to her before that I'd thought it was sickening – like a kid at school sucking up to the teacher.'

' "Servile when you must, insolent when you may." '

'Who is?'

'That's what Liam O'Flaherty's Liverpool landlady wrote to him – "You are like all your race, servile when you must, insolent when you may." '

'Seems rather harsh.'

'Understandable. He had preferred fleeing as a fugitive from the British army to staying in hiding with her and having to marry her daughter.'

'They're a funny crowd the Irish.'

'Like the Hungarians. You've been too long among the English.'

'Here! – I am English. So's my husband.'

'So was O'Flaherty's landlady. It's a small world.'

By that time, it didn't matter too much what we were saying. I was sensitive to everything about her, her eyes and the way one arm took her weight as she leaned towards me. Discreetly, we fed off a shared excitement.

'Why don't we go somewhere private?' I suggested. 'Have a drink away from all this racket.'

The Irishman who had offended Rosemary was at the centre of a group just in front of us. The group was laughing at or with him.

'I'd like that. Shall I bring this?' She held up her glass of red wine.

'No problem.' I reached under the chair and eased out the bottle I'd hidden there earlier. 'Best wine on the table. I liberated it just after I arrived.'

'What would happen if everyone did that?'

'I expect some of them have. Old Scots custom. Necessary foresight of a small nation kept poor by a maniac imperialist next door.'

'Sad,' she said mockingly.

'Don't cry over my history and I won't cry over yours.'

We climbed to our feet and stood swaying gently and smiling at one another.

'Let's go,' she said. 'Is your room in the main building?'

'I don't have one. I'm a visitor.'

'Be my guest.'

At the door Primo materialised.

'You have to stay here.'

She looked at me as if I had grown horns.

'Who's he?'

'Nobody.' I half turned from her and muttered desperately, 'Look. We're going outside . . . you know. We'll be back. No funny ideas. Brond said it – where would I go?'

He looked at me impassively.

'Back inside.'

'What is this?' She touched my arm. 'Are you coming or not?'

I shrugged.

'No – it doesn't look as though I am.'

'My God!' she said. 'I mean I've been stood up but . . . Oh, God!'

To my embarrassment, she looked hurt more than angry. As I shuffled, she gave a shiver and turned back inside. She stood looking at the bright room and then swung round and pushed past us. She vanished into the lengths of the corridor.

'She thinks you're my boy friend,' I said to Primo.

He didn't react. The idea was too silly to touch him.

'No, not you,' I said. 'Not the Scottish soldier. Jesus! Has nobody told you? There's no Empire any more and all the Chinks are colonising the restaurants.'

'I don't go for that Empire stuff. I've seen through all of that,' he said. 'But you don't listen, do you?'

'Here!' I shoved the bottle of wine at him. Reflexively, his big hand closed round it. 'A present. Stick it up your kilt!'

The Irishman was still being the life and soul of the party. Brond was on the edge of the group listening with a little smile.

'Did you have to spoil my chances?'

'Chances?' Tasting the word, Brond found it, like the wine, cheap.

There was so much distraction we exchanged words in a cocoon of privacy.

'Not for anything you'd understand,' I complained, sounding petulant.

'Oh, chances. The girl. Did you try to slip away with her?'

'Make love not war. Why did you bring me here?'

'To pass some time. It was too early for where we have to go. Anyway I had been invited and I thought you would enjoy the cultured atmosphere.'

'Wonderful,' the girl in front of us said. Like most of the people at the party, she was English by the sound of her. The man who answered was as well.

'Mm. He tells marvellously funny stories.'

'Tell us a story,' the girl called, 'about your Uncle Danny!'

General laughter.

'The one about the pig!'

The Irishman grinned vastly. His nose was beaded with sweat.

'He was known for it in the village,' he cried. 'Did I sing you the song about him?'

A rearrangement of the circle left me in front of him. I composed my face into my ethnic interest look – the one that went with visits to folk clubs. As a fellow Celt, I wished him . . . He looked at me and shook his head.

'I can't do it,' he said. 'Not with you looking so Scotch and dismal at me.' The entire crowd smiled and rippled. 'Like an ould Protestant minister at a funeral.'

In a leprechaun suit and a green hat, he would have made a splendid undoubting Uncle Thomais.

'Did you ever hear,' I asked, 'about the Irishman who blew up the bus? . . . Got his lips all burnt.'

A determined outbreak of small arms talk peppered me away. I refilled a tumbler and found a chair by the wall.

'A present.'

Brond sat down and put a bottle of wine between us. I recognised it as the one I had thrust on Primo.

'The condemned man drank a hearty dinner.' I topped up my glass.

To my surprise I found that some of the consonants had gone rubbery.

'Don't overdo it,' Brond said. 'We'll be leaving soon.'

Across the room, I spotted the Hungarian Cockney talking to a man who looked as if he had passed all his exams a long time ago. She had come back then.

'Suppose I didn't leave. Suppose I just sat here and finished this bottle and held on to the seat and screamed if you tried to get me to leave.'

'You know better than that.'

'No, I don't.'

I filled my glass which seemed to be emptying by itself. Soon I would have to find another bottle.

'Suppose— suppose I shouted out loud – right now – that I saw you throwing that boy from the bridge? I mean, right now!'

The words fell out of my mouth sobering me with terror so that I was unable to look at him.

'I think it was Primo's boy you killed. I saw you.'

But of course, he knew that. He must have known that from the beginning.

'Why did you do it?' I asked, and then the second question which, though it shouldn't have done, mattered more to me: 'Why didn't you care that I was there?' Thinking about that, I rushed on my own destruction. 'Did the boy overhear something that you couldn't risk him telling to his father? He was only a child. It must have been something simple enough for him to pass on, but you couldn't let him tell his father. Simple enough to pass on, even if he didn't understand it. Or maybe it was a letter you had left lying about? But why would you do that? You're not careless. Nothing happens unless you want it to happen.'

'You confuse me with God,' Brond said, purring. 'I must say I have a weakness for you. And for Belgian chocolate, of course. And boredom – which is another weakness. I get bored easily.'

'Do you despise us so much?'

'I don't despise a bereaved man enough to torment him with fantasies,' Brond said sharply. 'Primo – as you call him – lost his son in a silly stunt on a railway bridge. The boy had been challenged by two friends to cross it on the outside by scrambling across the girders. The two boys saw him fall. A group of spectators, including a police constable, saw him fall. One of the neighbours ran to fetch the father – Primo – and he arrived just as his son fell.'

'But I saw you,' I said.

I tried to hold on to that; it had been taken from me once; I tried not to let it happen again.

Brond kept silent until I looked back at him. He was smiling.

'You saw something or imagine you did in some unnamed place at some time which is indeterminate. And now you're not sure. How can you be since you did nothing at the time? That must make you wonder about yourself. Suppose now you report this extraordinary event, claim that it happened, and there is no death nor any record of one – But that's what you're afraid of, isn't it? You must feel like someone in the process of a mental breakdown.'

He shuffled my certainty from me like a conjuror mixing a card into the pack.

'Stand up!' he ordered and waited until I did. 'Let's settle this nonsense. Take a deep breath. Now, shout out what you imagine you saw!'

The party washed over me as if he had opened a sluice gate. I drowned in that laughter. He was Brond the good friend of Professor Gracemount who had the power to pull strings. I bent and picked up the bottle. My hand held it at the level of his face. It was heavy glass at the level of a face, which was only bone, after all, and flesh. He hung me from the strings of rage and fear, and the little bald Professor came between us ignoring me and took his seat beside him.

By this time the Irishman was coming on like Brendan Behan. He would probably get two extra credits for this from Social Studies – assignment on living down to expectations.

'How about,' I asked in the first pause, 'the number of Irishmen it takes to screw in a nail? Anyone? Eh? Ready? Five! One to hold the nail and four to spin the wall round.'

I thought that was genuinely funny and laughed for a bit.

When I finished, the place had got quieter.

'How about you and me going outside?' Uncle Thomais asked. He had done one of those lightning changes from extrovert good nature to black rage.

'How about . . . How about the way to make an Irishman burn his ear? Do you know how to make an Irishman burn his ear?' He watched me dangerously. 'Anybody? Anybody know how to make an Irishman burn his ear?'

Nobody wanted to play that game.

'I'll tell you how to make an Irishman burn his ear . . . Phone him while he's ironing!'

Somebody laughed. It was good to be a success. I joined him and went on for a while after he'd stopped.

'Time to go.'

Primo had come for me. When I looked back from the door, the group had dispersed. The Irishman was by himself over at the cabinet of drinks. It looked as if I had altered the mood of his celebration.

In the car, the engine throbbed softly. Lights on the dash threw a dim glow up on Primo's face. Double rows of headlights flowed at us as we came on to a motorway. The needle climbed and successive silhouettes peeled behind us into the darkness.

'The Irish joke,' Brond said conversationally. 'It's a shoddy response to the troubles across the water. The flood of jokes about Irish stupidity isn't really a sign of the fabled British sense of humour.'

In the silence, I thought with the clarity of exhaustion about how often I had heard the word British that day.

'It's useful politically to persuade your own public,' he said, 'that any people you have to treat firmly are sub-human.'

'The great British public. Primo and me both,' I said. 'Scottish soldiers.'

As we followed the path of our lights into darkness, Brond took my stick from where it lay across my knees.

'Are you afraid,' I asked remembering the bottle that I had held by his face, 'I might try to use it as a weapon? It's too light for that.'

'So much for curiosity,' he said.

His hands moved and the stick lengthened between them.

'It's a piece of craftsmanship,' he said. 'You don't appreciate my gifts. It was cored out on a hollow mandrel lathe using a spoon drill and a hand rest – they bore in about twenty inches from each end to meet – then plug here and hold it with a pinned ferrule; there a double silver fitting on the drawing end; lastly it's packed with two pieces of split cane to hold . . .' his hands moved apart, 'twenty-seven inches of tempered German steel.'

It was melodramatic and foolish, a kind of joke, except that nothing Brond did was foolish and if he joked it was in a foreign language about events on another planet. He handed me the stick and I took it, not mine now but his, not a dead thing any longer but like a sleeping servant – or a bad master.

He said, 'It's their unexpectedness I treasure.'

I wondered if unexpectedness was his euphemism for treachery.

'Where are you taking me?'

'To the capital.'

I had a blurred terrifying image of a house in a quiet town near London – a giant nest of rooms every one empty except for a single chair. In mindless reaction I tried to stretch the stick between my hands. Brond laughed.

'The Prevention of Crime Act 1953 – it's against the law to carry a weapon in public without lawful reason or excuse. Did you know that? Anyway, a sword stick really is not a practical weapon in a car.'

I forced my hands to lie still.

'You gave me the stick in the interrogation room,' I said, 'in front of those detectives.'

'Fortunately,' Brond said, 'like yourself, they weren't sufficiently curious.'

The car slowed as under our lights orange strips on the road rippled. On the roundabout, we passed a sign for the Forth Bridge and took the next exit.

I knew the city now but not why we should be going there.

'Glasgow has street walkers,' Brond said as we passed along that long straight entry into the mother of Alba, 'and an unpalatable collection they are. It has to do, I suppose, with the lack of a substantial middle class. Edinburgh has those, of course, but offers a more genteel service in addition. The advantage, one must suppose, of having the Faculty of Advocates and a plethora of civil servants about the place.'

We came to the Haymarket and went up the hill to the right instead of going forward into Princes Street. After a maze of dark winding streets, we came out on to a broad road and a little later, as I ducked my head searching for some sign I could identify, the car stopped. Primo switched off the engine and I followed Brond out on to the pavement.

Away to our left curved a terrace of substantial houses. In front of us there were stone pillars marking the entrance to a driveway. We seemed to be on a street set above the main road for through the railings behind us the orange lamps shone level with where we stood. Their light followed us into the drive which was longer than it looked from the street, with plenty of space for cars to park discreetly. There was only one at the moment, but I recognised it as a Porsche 911 because the estate owner's son at home had one; Trailtrow's son, just turned eighteen, roaring past with a girl beside him, a French girl, an actress, and the calves blockily in flight kicking up their heels.

'If it is a brothel,' I said loudly, 'neighbours in a district like this should object. They should send for the police.'

Primo who was behind me grasped my arm in warning, but Brond looked back seemingly unperturbed.

'Even discreet brothels,' he said loudly in a kind of humorous parody of my tone, 'make a noise from time to time. I expect their neighbours have learned to ignore it.'

A carpet of pebbles gleamed under our feet. Traffic murmured with an effect of distance. We might have been lost deep in the country, coming to knock and ask our way.

The woman who opened the door looked young at first glance, but at a second I thought she was in her fifties at least; and then again there was something not easily defined – she was well dressed, expensively perhaps, nothing immodest – that made me understand Brond had used the exact unvarnished word to describe this place we were about to enter. Maybe that should have made me feel safer, but it didn't. I didn't feel happier or safer; just puzzled when she did not admit us at once.

'Last time was a mistake,' Brond said, and he leaned forward and spoke to her too softly for me to hear.

'. . . last time,' the woman said. '. . . last time . . .'

It was eerie to see Brond refused. The illusion of his omnipotence had been imposed upon me. What she was doing filled me with anxiety. I wanted her to stop before something terrible happened. At that moment, however, a car swung into the drive, jerked to a halt in a scatter of pebbles behind the Porsche and ejected a plump bouncy little man whose hair gleamed silver in the light from the open door as he approached.

'Evening, Maisie.'

He had the air of a familiar guest. As he went to pass us, he glanced at Brond and stopped abruptly.

'Good God, Maisie!' he said. 'Don't tell me you're keeping this man on the doorstep. I'll vouch for—'

'Mr Smith,' Brond interrupted him, very easily and as if making a joke. 'And friends.'

On the ebullience of the little man, all four of us were carried inside. We followed the woman through the hall into what you would have thought of as the front room of a family house. When I looked round for the little man as a protector, he had vanished. There was a table with glasses and bottles and when she asked us what we would drink I noticed for the first time that she had a trace of an Irish accent. The glass she put into my hand was an expensive whisky tumbler, solid and comforting.

When the door opened, I looked round expecting to see the little man who had vouched for us. Instead it was a young girl who might have been seventeen. She was wearing a tweed skirt and a soft wool sweater – the kind of outfit worn by daughters of what my father would call 'the gentry' – very genteel.

'Yours, I think,' Brond said.

On her cue, she smiled at me.

'Angela,' she said. 'Nice to have you here. Would you like something else to drink?'

I said, no. Mine?

'I think you're wanted somewhere else,' the Irish woman called Maisie said sharply as if she had authority, but the girl ignored her.

'Perhaps you'd like to see upstairs?'

I looked at her. In my head, I knew she had given me an invitation and what it meant; but in my stomach I did not believe it. Not because of Brond and all the dangers and strangenesses that had brought me here – that would have been too rational. I believed in the place as a brothel. What I did not believe was that any girl who spoke and dressed like the expensive daughters of the gentry would ever get into bed with me.

But she did.

Undressed she still looked expensive. She had little breasts and her stomach was flat. Her skin shone. She looked very healthy.

'Let's fuck,' she said, and it didn't sound like a whore, but like one of the expensive permissive girls I had dreamed about meeting at a party and seducing with my charm.

I got on top of her and as I slid inside could not help a little cry of triumph.

When we had finished, she half sat up on the pillow and yawned. The sheet was caught round her middle. She held one of her breasts, rubbing her hand on it back and forward.

'That was your first time,' she said.

I felt too good to care. In a little while, being one of those who took pleasures sadly, I would start to worry about herpes, crabs and the rest of the sad litany of public lavatories.

'I'm a late developer. A country boy.'

She had a nice accent. I wondered if it could be genuine. Maybe she was a rich man's daughter doing this for excitement – and going back later to some rich girls' boarding school, in Surrey, say, or St Andrews.

'Should we get up now?'

'No hurry,' she said.

From what I had read about prostitution, it seemed to me this must show we were in a very high class establishment indeed. Maybe I would save her from herself; we would marry and I would be taken into daddy's business.

'Let's see what's going on,' she said and rolled like a cat out of bed.

I lay and looked at her. She was brown all over except for a narrow band of paler colour round her hips. Even her breasts were lightly tanned.

'Come on,' she said and held out her hand.

She was standing in front of what I had taken to be a mirror.

'Put out the light.'

'Why?'

'Go on! Do it!'

I did not know what all this cost but it began to seem like unusual value. The lamp by the bed was lit and I switched it off. At first it was dark but then I could see the shape of her glimmer by the wall. My sex stirred and rose as I moved towards her.

She must have touched the mirror in some way for I found myself looking into a room. It was brightly lit: lamps by the bed and door, an overhead cluster of bulbs, all were on.

Brond was kneeling in front of a woman. He was naked but he still had on his shoes and black socks. I think the idea must have been that this would be humiliating. He was holding up to her a long tube or series of tubes, tapered at one end and with a thick handle at the other.

'It's an electric prod,' the girl's voice said beside me. 'They use it on cattle.'

He was showing the woman something on the handle. It might have been a ratchet he turned. I saw his mouth moving but no sound came to us. The woman took the tube from him and laid the end of it between his legs. Suddenly his body convulsed and jerked away. The woman beckoned him back into place. He shuffled forward and she laid the tube again in the same place and nothing happened and then his body jerked away for the second time. The woman stood unmoving and made the same beckoning gesture, but he hesitated. She stood with the tube in her hands and said something and she looked at the handle and made some kind of adjustment.

I felt a hand on my back and the girl ran it down and rubbed against me. Her warm breath tickled my ear.

'You can put it to different settings,' she said. 'She's giving it more power.'

This time when the prod touched him his body was thrown back, but when she gestured him forward he came at once. When he had reached his former place, she stepped back and he had to approach her again, but again she went back two or three paces. As he crept nearer, she made the same movements as before on the handle.

'My God,' the girl said, 'she's going to give him more.'

It should have been marvellous to feel unafraid of Brond for the first time. It should have been marvellous to catch her smell mingled with my own like the sharp tang of citrus fruit; it should have been marvellous to think how healthy we were and how natural as we stood there watching.

At last she laid the prod against him and his body did jerk and shudder but his instinctive movement was so immediate that it must hardly have touched him. That seemed to anger her and she tugged him by the hair to his feet and set him with his face against the wall.

'He won't be able to get away from it there,' the girl beside me said. 'Christ, she's giving it more. If she gives it full power, she'll destroy him.'

Brond stood with his arms at his sides so that his forehead and the palms of his hands were against the wall. He opened his legs and the tip of the prod went into his body in the passage between his buttocks. His hands flew up in clenched fists and his spine arched impossibly and then he crashed to the floor; his heavy body writhed like a cut worm and with a final shuddering of the legs lay still. Too still. The woman backed away with both hands over her mouth. There was no way for us to know what kind of noises she might be making.

'Oh, God,' the girl whispered. 'Look.'

The head of the corpse was slowly raised from the floor. Then Brond stood up. He was naked and in those ridiculous shoes with the black stockings wrinkled round his ankles; and he looked as terrible and as frightening as on the first day I had seen him. He gathered up his clothes and began to put them on and he must have said something to the woman for, as he was dressing, she stripped. She was not a young woman and her flesh sagged and hung on her like strips of soiled dough. Her face was half crazed. When he picked up the prod from where she had dropped it, she stood with her face against the wall but he must have told her to turn round. The hair between her legs was grey and he put the prod there and she bent with the pain of its entry. Although the woman's body winced in expectation, nothing happened. As the prod slid free and nudged the nipple of each breast in turn, her head hung watching in helpless confusion.

'It's a fake,' the girl said. 'There's no charge in it at all.'

He slapped the woman as if angered and her head flew back and struck the wall, and at that he seemed to lose all control. As he caught her by the throat, she might have been screaming. Before his shoulder hid her, I saw her tongue stretched forward and the spittle fly out of her open mouth. The girl's hand rubbed at the base of my spine.

'He'll kill her,' I sobbed. 'He's killing her.'

I saw her die. With his hands about her throat he laid her down on the floor and then put out the lights one by one. At the door, he looked back at her lying by the wall and then he had put up the last switch and it was dark.

'Kiss me!'

The voice whispered at me.

'Where's the light? The light. We need the light.'

I tried to push her away. She pressed against me and then I felt her tongue lick my face.

'Get away!'

I lurched from her and fell against the bed. When I found the lamp and lit it, she was gone.

In the empty corridor I stood listening. It was a very quiet house. The carpet was thick under my feet although it was dirty and unswept. On the wall between two doors there was a brass gong, figured with elephants and a procession of Indians dancing. I put out a finger and touched the tiny ecstatic figures as if to make sure that something in this world was real.

'Birds in their little nests agree,' Brond chanted almost in my ear, he had approached so silently.

My heart thundered in fright.

'I saw you.'

He sketched surprise.

'I've seen you kill twice now.'

'Yes?'

'On the bridge.' I was full of hatred for him. What a fool he must think I was! 'And the woman just now.'

'Mrs Kennedy? She seemed well enough when I had a look at her.'

'Jackie? What's Jackie to do— Don't despise me. I despise you. I saw you—' it was surprisingly hard to put into words to a man like him, 'begging and being— and being— I don't know how you could do that.'

He made a little humming noise; incredibly he seemed pleased.

'It really did seem extraordinary to you? Not the impression I make at all . . .'

'I think you must be mad.'

He clicked his tongue disapprovingly.

'Oh, come now. It's not so bad as that. I imagine the country's full of clergymen and retired lieutenant-colonels and bus conductors all doing or daydreaming along roughly similar lines.'

'You killed her.'

I became conscious that he was speaking normally while I was furiously whispering as if the fear of discovery were mine alone.

'We've a busy night ahead of us,' he said, 'but let's spare a moment. Come along!'

He crooked his finger and I followed him like a schoolboy. The big front room had people in it now, two or three groups of them, and a piano was being played softly and some of the girls were handing out drinks. It might have been the party at the University earlier. The only differences at a first glance were that the girls were younger, the men rather older and looking conspicuously more successful.

'Recognise anyone?' Brond asked.

Before I could answer, we were approached by the bouncy silver-haired little man who had come with us into the house; smaller than Brond, he did not come up to my shoulder.

'She let you stay then,' he said jocularly.

'Thanks to your good influence,' Brond said.

'Ah, influence.' He seemed to be at the stage of drink where one mood passed easily into its opposite for now he became solemn. 'I suppose we're both exerting as much of that as we can – not that anything seems able to help much. Dear old William Roughhead's world of Pritchard and Slater and Jessie McLachlan is very small beer now. Endless vandalism. Crimes against the person . . . There's a rot in the body social. What? Oh, it's you.'

One of the girls had brushed her fingers, decorously, along the back of his neck and he followed, head bobbing like a lecherous sparrow.

'I doubt if a reporter,' Brond said watching him go, 'or a blackmailer would last long if he interfered with these nice people.'

And he smiled benevolently on the room like a widdershins archbishop.

'Why did you say that Jackie— that Mrs Kennedy was here?'

'Did I?'

'Is she here?'

He turned his head from the crowd and looked at me; his lips still smiled.

'Perhaps. That murderous animal her husband certainly is.'

'He's not the only murderer – and his murders were long ago.'

'You have an odd sense of humour,' Brond said contemptuously. 'Who do you imagine killed Peter Kilpatrick?'

But before I could answer, the silver-haired man rejoined us. He was shadowed by a gaunt anxious man whose shoulders were spotted with scruffs of white dandruff.

'Alex here tells me,' the silver-haired man gestured towards his companion, 'that E.M. Forster used to worry because his bum was full of hair.'

'I didn't know that,' Brond said. 'It's one of those evenings where everybody learns something new.'

'It certainly gives "only connect" a new connotation,' the silver-haired man reflected.

'You already made that joke.' The anxious man was not amused.

'I know – that's why I came over here to get a chance to repeat it.'

'It's a joke in bad taste,' his friend said. 'I believe in the virtues of liberalism. I'm even willing to believe that Forster was a thoroughly nice man.'

'Nice people.' The voice was high and uncontrolled. It didn't sound like me at all. 'Dachau must have been surrounded by nice people.'

The two men stared, lingering on the edge of being offended with me until Brond took up the idea smoothly: 'Nice farmers, nice schoolteachers, nice lawyers too, taking the children on nice family picnics – chorusing with Brunnhilde, "*O Heil der Mutter, die dich gebar!*" – and never one to notice there was a stench of burning flesh on the air. But then a defective sense of smell is a medical condition not a moral one.'

'You're young,' the anxious man said to me. 'You have a lot to learn. You'll learn.'

The silver-haired man affected a transition to the combative. 'That's not an argument, Alex. The matter has still to be taken to avizandum. Just you suppose some wretched dictator builds and fills a camp at Swanston – and you wake up one morning with a smell greasing the air – "*Wer ist der Held, der mich erweckt?*" eh, Brond? – What on earth could you do, Alex?'

The anxious man hesitated. 'We-ell . . . I shouldn't stay there. I should certainly move. I'd even be willing to take a loss on the house.'

And suddenly not looking at all anxious, he began to giggle and they moved off together, well pleased with one another.

'No question of it,' Brond went on as if there had been no interruption, 'Kilpatrick had been sleeping with that charming married woman you call Jackie. That was something no one had foreseen. You see how I resist the temptation to impress you with my omniscience? I didn't foresee it. I might claim to have improvised rather well once it did happen.'

'Improvisation,' I said, '– the mark of the artist.' The words weren't mine. It was a favourite phrase of Donald Baxter's. Brond blinked at me. It may have been the only thing I ever said which surprised him.

'No matter how wonderful our policemen are,' he said, 'a woman of that sort always offers a temptation. I shouldn't imagine she put up much resistance, and Kilpatrick seems to have had a weakness for women. We all have our weaknesses.'

'You want me to believe that Kennedy killed him for sleeping with his wife?'

'He killed him twice over – and why not for that? Kennedy isn't a citizen of the permissive society. A violent man – jealous of that neat little wife of his. That gun you delivered to me was Kennedy's and it was Kennedy who used it.'

Not Kennedy. Not that sanctimonious keeper of a lodging house. Michael Dart had killed poor loud-mouthed Kilpatrick. And despite anything Brond said or thought about Jackie Kennedy, I didn't believe she had ever betrayed her husband before she met Kilpatrick. Poor Jackie had forgotten to be afraid of the man she married; and he had hidden all there was of him to love.

'Twice over,' I said stupidly. 'How could he kill him twice over?'

'According to the helpful Mr Muldoon, they traced him to where the Briody girl had hidden him. It was inevitable after the stupid girl chose you as her saviour and brought the gun back to Kennedy's own house. That was a joke, but an unfortunate one for the amorous Kilpatrick. While the girl was fetching you, he was tied up and carried outside to that dirty shed to die of exposure. Muldoon helped with that. I'm afraid Kennedy was a touch vicious there; being cuckolded does that to a man. The slowest way to die is the hardest way.'

It was possible that Kennedy-Dart had done that; but Brond had known where to find the body. And the old politician who had been beaten to death in the Riggs Lodge hotel ('of ancient Scottish family' – 'a man of honour' – 'much loved': the

188

newspapers said so; how else would my father know what to believe?) he had died that same night while I shared a narrow bed with Margaret Briody. But before he died he had been tied up with a piece cut from the same cord that had bound Kilpatrick. Whether it was Kennedy or Brond himself who had carried Kilpatrick out and hidden him under the sacks to die, I had no way of knowing. The only evidence from my own five unsure senses was a hotel door wrecked by a strength like Primo's.

The silver-haired man wandered through the idle groups to confront us again.

'Remembered a funny story,' he said. 'Maisie had heard it.'

He was perceptibly less sober.

'Excellent,' Brond said. 'My friend here loves a good story. He's amused me a number of times.'

And he caught my arm and turned me so that I blocked the way for a woman who was moving past us out of the room. I knew her. Some kind of social apologetic foolishness came to my lips. I knew her—

It was the prostitute I had watched Brond strangle to death. The look on my face alarmed her and she stepped back, directing beyond me a conciliatory grimace.

'So simple.' Brond patted my arm. 'It's all so simple. Why did you think people came here if it wasn't to buy illusions?'

He followed her out, but when I started after him the little man took me by the sleeve, a full handful with his weight behind it.

'Don't be a boor. I've to tell you this story.'

'Let go!' I gave a jerk that tore my sleeve free, but he snatched again.

'Listen!' he shouted.

There was silence and then people hurried back into talk. Side glances policed us. The room was too full of portly, prosperous, guilty men. I stood still and fixed a smile on the little man.

'It's about this chap who's on the bench for the first time. It's his first time – local government kind of chap. Knows nothing about the law. First case – drunk and disorderly. Ten a penny sort of thing. Thirty shillings or thirty days' imprisonment – usual sort of nonsense.'

Shillings? He must have retold his joke on years of occasions like this.

'Chap listens to the evidence. Then – worst case in my experience; this kind of thing will not be tolerated; I was born and bred in this town; stamp it out – fourteen years' penal servitude. Consternation in court! All gather round him – psst psst psst. Whisper whisper whisper. Chap clears his throat – hum – heh – hum. On further consideration, I will commute that sentence to thirty shillings or thirty days. Bring in the next criminal.'

Bring in the next criminal.

'It's supposed to be funny.' He released my sleeve. 'No one tonight has any blasted sense of humour.'

In the hall, Primo was near the front door. He had a glass in his hand, but standing there alone it looked like a disguise, something put there to pretend it was only by accident that he could watch anyone coming in or trying to leave. Brond was nowhere in sight, but the woman was in front of a mirror tidying her hair.

'The gentleman says you've to see him in the room up the stair.'

She had a broad Glasgow accent nothing like my golden girl's. She smelled of stale sweat; her cheeks were scarred with acne pits; on a corner of Bath Street she would have been in place any wintry Saturday night.

'What gentleman? The gentleman you were performing with up— the stair?'

She dangled her disgusting udders at me, belching bad air and bewilderment.

'You were seen. I was watching – and I wasn't the only one. We were watching you earn your money.'

I hated her bovine corruption.

'Ah didnae know.' She was not resentful. She wanted to explain 'He wis angry wi me. He had tae keep tellan me what to do. Every damnt thing, he said he'd to tell me. But ah've been hurt masel. One morning ah tried tae get oot o bed and ah was stuck. Ah had weeks o pain after that, doctors an jags an operations. Since then ah don't know why people would want to be hurtit. Ah know ah wis wrong. Ah didnae mean tae make him angry. It just slipped out – ah tellt him – ah've been hurt masel. And that's when he lost the rag. But, ken, it was just that ah've been hurt masel.'

In the upstairs corridor, the Hindu faithful still danced on the rim of the brass gong. I looked in the room where I had stopped being a virgin, but it was empty. I ran from one room into another and found Jackie Kennedy sitting on the bed. She stared at me in horror.

'In the Name of God!' she cried, like an Ulster cleric preaching of Hell, 'where did you come from?'

'Get up! We've got to get out of here. Get up!' I reached out as if to pull her up from the bed. 'Don't you know the kind of place this is?'

'Get away from me!' She pushed at the air between us. 'It's you that shouldn't be here. The young fellow didn't say anything about you.'

'Tell me when we're out of here. I don't—'

'Listen to me!' she cried. 'He came to the house. Just a young fellow, well dressed and nicely spoken. Listen! It was him I came here with. Somebody has to listen! He said terrible things to me.'

She was wearing her best coat, brown cloth with some kind of fur at the collar that I had seen her put on to go visiting on a Sunday. I had a picture of one of Brond's smooth young men talking quietly at her as she sat beside him in a car, very upright in her best coat for visiting. I wondered what smooth words he had found for telling her that in their eyes she was Kilpatrick's whore and that her husband had killed him for it.

'I'm sorry,' I said. 'Please!' and I held out my hand to her again.

'Why didn't he trust me?' she asked, and I didn't know whether she was talking of her lover or her husband.

'Please, come!' Stinging tears of frustration; I pitied her and I was afraid. 'It'll be all right if you come. I won't let them hurt you.'

'You're only a boy,' she said. 'What could you do? I have to wait here. He's going away tonight – out of the country. Oh, God, I'm so frightened.' She swung her head from side to side. I had seen a fox caught in a trap doing that. 'I feel he's watching me.'

If the lie Kennedy had lived for so long was unimaginable to me, how strange a judgement she must feel he had passed on her. Yet this play-actor had killed for her.

'I don't know how he would come to know a place like this,' Jackie said so quietly I had to strain to hear. 'I won't believe that he sleeps with that woman. I don't know why they tell me such terrible things. She put me here and told me to wait.'

I sat beside her on the bed and put my arm around her shoulders.

'Her name's Maisie,' I said. 'An older woman with an Irish accent.' And trying to help, 'Maybe it's just that he knew her a long time ago – in Ireland. She'll be a friend.'

Jackie shook her head.

'No. She was young. Just a girl. And very nicely spoken.'

My golden girl. I had lain with her on the bed in the next room. In an hotel room, I had sat on a bed – and they had yelled at me that a man had died in it – too suddenly for me to evade it, Kilpatrick's poor dirtied corpse lolled out from under the sacks.

'I'm so frightened,' Jackie said. 'I'm supposed to go away with him tonight.'

'You don't have to go anywhere with him. If we can just get out of here, I'll look after you.'

I meant it. Sitting on the whore's bed, I could have been in love with her. I touched her cheek with my lips and she did not move away.

Above her head, I saw the bed and squalid room reflected in the mirror, and her in my arms. I feel he's watching me, she had said. Kennedy was watching us. Gently I put her away from me, and getting up went to the mirror, close against it – so close my own face blurred into eyes. The cold glass touched my skin.

'Don't be upset.' In the mirror, she held out a hand to me. 'There's not anything you can do.'

A dark line drawn behind her on the bed turned into the stick I had been given by Brond. I had not brought it into that room. There was no time to warn her, perhaps there was no need, as the door came open. Like children, we stared at the shining weight of the gun in Kennedy's hand.

'Oh, you impossible bitch,' he said. It was a voice full of love and rage and hopelessness.

'I'll go with you,' she said. 'There's no need to hurt him.'

I went towards her. Even now I believe it was because I misunderstood which of us needed protecting.

'You cowardly bastard!' he shouted and I realised he could not fire because I was too close to her. I think he called me a coward again, but all my fear had left me. I picked up Brond's unlucky stick and a turn shook free the blade.

He was coming towards me, trying, I suppose, to get some safe angle from which he could fire but Jackie kept turning with him. I even had time – I was in such control – to realise what Brond had brought about in giving me the stick; by death or guilt both Kennedy and myself were to be silenced. He knew my fatal temper and he had given me a weapon with which I could kill or get myself killed, but I would laugh in his face. He knew my temper but not the speed of my mind or the athlete's strength in my body. I was young and nothing was impossible to me, and as Kennedy came forward I took him with the sword point on the wrist. He was to be disarmed and no great harm done. That was a thing impossibly exact, but I was mad with confidence and the gun fell out of his hand.

Brilliantly coloured blood came out of him in gusts as he tried to kill me with his hands. The heart, that tough muscle, becomes its own murderer when an artery is cut. Untended or if there were no natural defences, it would empty the body. He came at me and I did not understand what had happened. I even had a moment of terror that the blood was mine. I had nothing to defend myself for as he went for me a shock went up my arm and the stick was snatched out of my grasp. The bed took me behind the knees and I went back with him on top. He might have strangled me but it was my fortune that the nerve in his wrist had been cut so that the four fingers of his right hand would not close. I rolled and carried both of us off the end of the bed. As we landed I came down on him with all my weight and it seemed to stun him. With each heartbeat blood spurted from his outflung wrist. All I wanted was to save him. I knew that a tourniquet above the elbow might stop the blood but that the arm would at once begin to die. I did not lack knowledge. As he lay still, I pulled down the wadded sheet and pressed with all my strength on his wrist. The sheet soaked and I gathered more and pressed. The curtain of blood over my eyes put a drench of scarlet over walls, roof, bed, everywhere. The only bloodless thing in the room was his face, like a white parcel emptied and thrown aside. I thought I had saved him until I heard a whisper under the mingled thunder of our breath. On the white front of his shirt there was a small unremarkable shape like the lips of a child opening on a sigh.

At last I had to look up at Jackie. In the mirror of her eyes – not Jackie but Val, Michael Dart's wife – I saw a man of blood on his knees beside a corpse.

SEVENTEEN

I had nothing to do with Peter Kilpatrick's death and for it I had been arrested and interrogated and put in the shadow of imprisonment. I knew less than nothing about the assassination and I had fallen into the hands of secret police and been threatened in the hotel; the impress on a bed of the man haunted me and with it a dead face from under a pile of sacks. I had killed Kennedy; I had stabbed him and he had spouted blood; I had stabbed him and he drowned in a cupful of it; and that night I was returned to my father's house and woke the next day in the bed I had slept in as a boy.

The window rattled in its frame. In any kind of wind, it had done that ever since I could remember. I had never noticed before how it sounded like hasty footsteps. Everything familar looked strange that morning. This was my bedroom, Jess, my sister, had the tiny room across the landing; downstairs, the kitchen was the only other room in the house and my parents slept there in the bed set into a recess in the wall. The ceiling of my bedroom sloped and bumped to fit under the roof; Jess's room was even worse. Her bed was unmade and clothes and schoolbooks lay in a casual archipelago; at her age I had been forced by my mother to be tidy. With a small shock, I recognised the clock on her bedside table: the alabaster lady. Jess must have persuaded my mother to let her take it from its pride of place downstairs. Green marble and on top of it a woman in white drapery, Grecian, flowing – the alabaster lady I called her to myself: the word was like an incantation – alabaster, alabaster. Her breasts were bare and nothing else like that was ever allowed in the house. For years it puzzled me until I decided that probably they had never noticed. Once when I was about seven I went down in the middle of the night and took her back to bed with me. I held her between my legs and fell asleep, but when I woke she was gone. I was terrorised by shame but neither of them ever mentioned it.

I put out a finger and touched her cheek and two little breasts of stone.

It was always dark in the kitchen. The ceiling was low and the wooden beams seemed to pull it down towards your head. There was a small window at either end, but the back one looked out on a bank of earth and the tree that hung its branches over the house. Even on sunny days I wanted to put on the light. When I did, my mother would put it out: we could not afford it. She had spent her married life in this room.

'Ten o'clock. I slept in this morning.'

I had always to apologise for sleeping late. With the hours my father worked, it seemed indecent to lie in bed.

'This morning,' she said looking up at me from where she knelt. She was wiping round the hearth. 'This morning. Well, you'd an excuse.'

I tried to keep my back to her while I cut and made a sandwich of cheese.

'There's an egg.'

'Fine,' I said. 'This is fine.'

I poured milk into a glass and chewed looking out of the window as if there might be something new and surprising to see. The sandwich tasted like cardboard.

'Who was he?'

I remembered her face last night as she tried to see past me to where Primo bulked in the dark at the end of the path.

'Just a friend. He gave me a lift home.'

'You told us you had a job.'

'I had a job.'

'How could you be here if you have a job?'

Her voice was thin and querulous like an old woman's. I put what was left of the sandwich wastefully back on the plate hoping she would not notice.

'My friend's a kind of doctor. He advised me to stay here for my health.'

'Just a kind of doctor? And what does that mean?'

'Till classes start again. I'd like to stay till it's time for next year's classes.'

'Something's wrong.'

'Everything's fine,' I said without looking round at her. 'I'll walk up and see Dad. He'll be up past the brig?'

Turning from the window, everything in the room was dark.

'I'll not be long.'

But she followed me to the door.

'You've spoiled your chance.'

'What?' My voice cracked like an angry child's. It was as though she were laying a curse on me.

'Tell him your lies. You've spoiled your chance.'

She closed the door in my face.

Beyond the bridge were fields of crops. On our side of the burn, there were cattle and some sheep. I walked slowly in the warm sun. The bridge was three broken planks wide. Even since last summer, it had got worse. It would be made to last, though, till it rotted into the water. On the other side, sparrows balanced on the feathery heads of barley. They rippled into the air as I went by, resettling as the wind stroked the yellow swell back and forward. I heard my father before I saw him.

Crouched over, the canister strapped on his back, he swung the nozzle like the blade of a scythe. The spray hissed and stopped, restarted and hesitated like an asthmatic breathing. I had come round by the far end to find him. He was very methodical, making his way towards me as if the big farmer in the sky oversaw his efforts. In shop windows sometimes in Glasgow I would glimpse myself slow plodding as if mired in the glaur of a farm lane; then I would put back my shoulders and march away from the sight picking up my feet as I went.

'Hold it! You'll have me sprayed as well.'

He straightened, blinking in slow pleasure.

'Aye, son.'

Easing the straps, he set the load down off his back. After a stretch luxurious as a yawn he fished with two fingers into his shirt pocket and fetched out a tattered pack of cigarettes.

'Want one?'

'You know I don't.'

He grinned, pleased with himself. The blue smoke paled from his lips. It was warm in the shelter of the hedge watching the wind move through the barley. After a minute, he eased up one leg and let air go.

'Pardon. I thought you'd have picked up some bad habits by this time.'

'Like farting,' I said.

He gave the unexpected laugh that took him sometimes like a giggle when you surprised him with a joke. He was a small man, not up to my shoulder – broad though, a good worker.

'That wouldnae do, if your professors heard you saying that.'

'All some of them are worth. It's a great thought – yon big lecture hall and right at the climax, just when he makes a point – "Shakespeare's father was fined for his dung heap" – a whole year, hundreds of us, up on one side and giving him a blast.'

'No' easy tae get the timing right,' my father reflected and we laughed and fell into a comfortable silence.

'A bit o an overlap, mind, wouldnae matter,' he said and laughed again. He was fond of jokes like that.

'Decent o that chap giving you a lift home.'

I looked at him thinking he was probing, but that was all he meant. Whoever had given me a lift home had been decent.

'He was passing this way.'

'Still . . . Some car. Cost a bob or two.'

'It was a big car.'

'I'm glad you're making that kind of friend.' He cleared his throat, and gazed intently at the patched blanket of fields thrown across the little hills in front of us. As always, he would never look at you when he was saying something serious. 'It's with you being at the University. In my day . . . See, in our day, you never had a chance. You'd no chance.'

I clapped my hands and flights of little birds bickered up into the air.

'What was that about?'

'Ach, I got tired o them bobbing up and down and stuffing their stupid faces.'

My father laughed.

'Auld Robertson'll never miss what they eat. He can afford it . . . It's good to have you back. You're needing the rest.'

'I'm not staying.' I didn't know till that moment that I had decided. 'I'll really need to get back. I've work to do.'

He cleared his throat.

'I'd think twice about that, son. It's up to yourself, of course. You've been ill, remember. I mean if it's the money . . .'

'Not that kind of work. Nothing heavy. Not real work, just studying. Playing on my backside.'

Still without looking at me, he wondered, 'Could you not do that at home?'

'I wouldn't have the books. They're too dear to buy. I can work in the library – at the Mitchell or the University. It's a good time to get the books, being quiet in the summer.'

He sighed out a breath.

'Aye, well, the studying comes first. I can see you would need tae get back.'

Back. To my good friends with the big cars.

EIGHTEEN

The car rolled to a stop and he said, 'I leave the main road across there, but you'll have no bother getting another lift.' I climbed out and, to prove his truthfulness, he signalled carefully right, turned across the three lanes and slipped out of sight under an arch of branches.

About it being easy to get another lift, he had made a mistake. Cars came fast and showed no inclination to stop. A cluster of three went by like that and then a big Ford trundled along sedately. The driver, an elderly man in glasses, leaned forward to hold my gaze until at the last moment he gave me two fingers and accelerated away.

After that, the entry under the arch of branches on the other side of the road seemed cool and secret. I looked at it while cars snarled past, and then crossed over. Beyond the arch there was a narrow lane sloping sharply down. Under the big intermingled screen of beeches, it would have been easy to miss. In the still air, under the dappled light, it was like going down a tunnel, except that fields showed between the trees on either side, unpleating over little hills. Half way down there was a patch of waste ground and a young couple beside a car making apologetic noises to a tall stooped man with the look of a farmer. As I walked down, they disappeared into the car and began to edge it back and forward trying to turn. I stood aside to give them room and at last they beat a retreat up towards the highway.

'They didnae understand a word.' The farmer shook his head at me.

'They were German,' I said. 'At least that's what the plate on the back said.'

'Ah couldnae make them understand there's a bit ground on

the far side o the brae would've done them fine. They were settan up a tent here – but there's nae water and God's plenty o midges.'

Tumbled stones of a ruined but and ben cottage were almost buried among chickweed and dandelions.

'I'll sleep here,' I said. 'If it's okay with you.'

'Ye'll be eaten alive.'

'I'm immune to midges.'

The farmer laughed and as he walked away a black dog that had been crouched in the grass sprang up and followed him, looking back at me over its shoulder. When he had gone, I walked up the brae until I found a good site. I unrolled the sleeping bag and lay listening to the burn and eating the last of my chocolate; over and over in the trees behind me, a chaffinch did his run-up-and-bowl song; it sounded sweeter than the ones at home, but like people chaffinches have different dialects; I thought about that and then I thought about sleeping and then I told myself it didn't matter as long as I rested. A fox barked. Waves kept running up the shore and I came properly awake and it was traffic on the main road and I was out of that night into another day.

'Ye changed your mind then.'

It was the tall stooped farmer. His face was brown with deeply scored lines in the cheeks.

'That's right. I decided against the midges.'

He walked at my side back across the long field.

'This is the life,' I said, 'We could be a million miles from anywhere. We could be on an island out in the middle of the Atlantic.'

'An island . . .' He spat into the grass. 'Ah canna bear the sea. Ah've bided here all my days. Except the one time. And ah got all the travellan ah'd ever want oot o that. In a khaki uniform tae the other side o the world. The Japs took us the same day the auld "Prince o Wales" was sunk. This place does me fine – ah'll no leave it a second time.'

At the top of the slope, we were ambushed by the main road.

Container lorries in convoy shook the air and left an ache of silence. 'Ah don't regret going. It was a thing that had tae be done. Mind ye,' he finished with a serious nod, 'thae three years ruined me.' I had no answer to that, and he walked back through the washed early morning light with the black dog at heel.

Later in the afternoon, I was going through a village when I heard my name called. 'This is me at home,' Donald Baxter said, picking seeds from the pouch of his lower lip. I had thought he lived in an armchair at the Men's Union, the oldest student in captivity. Despite the plaid shirt open at the neck, his concession to countryside and summer, I suspected the woollen underwear would still be there and all the way down to his ankles. Clutching a bunch of black grapes, he had appeared from a dark little cave of a village store and stood blinking in the sunlight. 'Back to the big city? Why not?' he pondered. 'Any excuse for a party.' He came back in a clapped out Marina, one wing punched in and gaping from a past collision. As he braked to a violent stop, flakes of blue-daubed rust detached themselves from the injured part. 'Auntie's car,' he said, and somehow that explained what 'home' meant and in getting away from there I knew he was doing himself a favour. It was nice not to have to feel grateful. A day-old copy of *The Herald* was lying on the front passenger seat; as I shifted it to make room for myself, I saw a banner headline telling of murder and a picture of the old politician who had died in the Riggs Lodge Hotel. Glancing, Donald Baxter said, 'Full of years and dishonour. A treacherous old bastard from a long line of them going back to Flodden. In any decent country of self-respecting Christians, he would have been assassinated long ago.' Driving one-handed, he groped on the shelf and produced as in a way of celebration a bottle of whisky. We passed the bottle back and forth.

Passed it too often. Drunk on an empty stomach, I ended up in Baxter's room intent upon getting drunker. At some moment during what followed, he made the old silly jibe of calling me the Homicidal Pacifist and, when I objected as before, reminding him that he had been a conscientious objector during the war, he cried, 'Not a bloody pacifist! Not then or now. Like Young, I held to the articles of the Treaty of Union. I would join no army but the army of an independent Scotland.' That seemed so silly to me, I began to laugh, but then when I thought of what I had read about the Nazi horrors and remembered that poor devil of a farmer I had met in the morning, I grew angry and told him that he might not be a bloody pacifist but he was certainly either a bloody coward or a lunatic.

'I understand why people get irritated when Scots go on about independence,' Baxter said in a tone of disinterested kindliness. 'I feel the same about Shetlanders – or about the Orkneys. Little piss-pot islands. Whining, "We're Orcadians. We're not Scotch." Bugger them, I think. Let's send a gunboat. A wee gunboat. A wee wee *particularly* wee gunboat,' and collapsed laughing at his own joke.

Later we were bottle friends and comrades and I heard myself telling him about Brond; about Kilpatrick; about Muldoon being tortured; but not about how Kennedy died. In the still centre of my drunken brain, an ape congratulated itself upon being too cunning to tell him how Kennedy died.

'That's not real,' he said, his great dish face pouring sweat. 'That stuff you're telling me. Don't try to kid a kidder. That stuff doesn't happen in never-never land. I don't believe you. Nobody here would believe you. We know real things happen on television and always somewhere else. Not here. If you want to pretend something that matters is happening here, you'll have to tell it in dreams and parables. Dreams and—'

That was when I punched him. Blood flew out from his mouth and he fell backwards on to the floor, looking up at me but keeping very still. His lips had burst on his teeth.

There wasn't anywhere you could hide from history, even when that was what you had settled for.

In the morning, I wakened with a stiff neck. I had slept with my head on the table. The room was empty, but as I climbed up the steps from the basement to the street I heard a noise and, looking down, saw Donald Baxter swaying with a glass in his hand.

'You've changed,' he said. 'Stories end in corruption. Everybody's does. But you're like me. One of the sad ones. The worm gets to us early.'

He wept a single tear of malice.

It wasn't far to the Kennedy's house. Even walking slowly, it didn't take me long to get there. I let myself in and went through all the downstairs apartments. I opened the door of one room and had such a vivid memory of the night I was ill that I expected Jackie to be there and Kennedy at the end of a shaft of light watching us. On the carpet in the parlour there was an overturned Guinness bottle and a tumbler.

As I came back into the hall, a man rushed downstairs at me in a jiggle of gold glasses, plump waistcoat, a squeal of 'What are you doing here?'

'I live here.'

'Not now, you don't;' a fat man settling, as he worked it out, into a merely professional wariness. 'Were you one of the lodgers? Haven't you heard? Mr Kennedy and his wife are selling up.'

'You've seen him—'

He would say yes and Kennedy would be alive.

'There's no doubt the property is for sale. We have authorisation from their agent. They are going abroad.'

I did not have to ask for a description of that agent. I had seen those smooth young men of Brond's. Perhaps it had been the one who took Jackie to Edinburgh, talking softly to her in the car.

'I'd like to wash,' I said.

'I should really ask for some proof of identity.'

'Just to wash. I'll collect my stuff later.'

He looked at the blood on my outheld arm and stood back from the stairs.

Sometimes you need to wash more than to eat. I stripped to

the waist and took my time, pouring cool water over the dirt and sweat. In my room I put on a clean shirt. Someone had piled my clothes and books in the middle of the floor.

When I came down, the man said, 'I'm not sure that you should still have a key.'

He did not manage to sound like a man who would insist.

In the garden outside there was a 'For Sale' board. Perhaps it had been put up while I was inside.

'I'd like a lift.'

'A lift?'

'I've no money. If you give me a lift, it would save me walking. I have a weak ankle and it's too hot to walk.'

To my surprise, he let me into his car and when I told him where I wanted to go he had to pass it on the way to his next desirable property. Ten minutes brought us outside Margaret Briody's house. As I opened her gate, she was coming out of the front door.

'I didn't kill Peter.'

Till I heard the words leaving my mouth, I had not known that was what I had come to tell her. She didn't shut the door but waited as I came along the path. If she was grieving for Kilpatrick, grief wasn't good for her. She was very pale and pimples at various stages cropped out round her mouth and on her left cheek. As I walked closer, instead of her beauty I saw the yellow sores of squeezed acne.

'The police wouldn't have let me go if I'd killed Peter.' Because of those stupid unexpected pimples, I was quite calm. I coaxed her. 'That stands to reason, doesn't it?'

'Can't you see I've had enough?'

Her tone was dull and tired but in spite of herself the separate notes chimed like water over pebbles. She didn't try to stop me as I went past her into the house. I thought she would follow me into the front room, but her steps crossed the hall. A door closed.

This was the room where I had surprised Muldoon the night he broke into Margaret's house: a pair of burglars. I wondered where Muldoon was now. On the table where Margaret had left the note for her parents, a newspaper lay open in a patch of sunlight. I remembered pale fingers of torchlight probing the darkness. Margaret was speaking to someone. I looked at the picture on the front of the newspaper: crowds lining a street, soldiers on horseback, carriages. More than ever, murmuring in the distance her voice was like music.

'You'd better not be here when Dada gets back,' she said behind me.

'Who were you talking to then? Somebody's here. Your Uncle Liam?'

'No – I mean yes. My uncle's here – you'd better go.'

She was a bad liar. I realised there was no one except us in the house.

'Of course, I'd forgotten the phone. You were using the phone in the bedroom.'

'Please go away. There's nothing for you here. I can only ask you.'

'Do you know what I'd like? I'd like to wait here until your father comes back, and if he has anything to say to me that would be all right, too. You know what happened. He can ask me anything. And when he's finished I'll tell him I want to marry you. I'm a university student, I'll say, and I want to marry your daughter.'

'You frighten me.'

'Is that a reason for not getting married?'

'You're trying to frighten me,' she said.

I had not meant it as a threat or a joke. While I spoke I had seen two respectable young people walking up the aisle to get married.

'I *am* a university student.' I held out the idea like a talisman.

'Have some pity. Don't you know how I felt about Peter?'

'*I'm* not a policeman.' Kilpatrick had been a policeman, which after all was also one of the professions and respectable. 'I'm just – My father works on a farm.' Why did I never tell the whole truth about him? 'He's just a labourer. He's a farm labourer. But you might like him. He's a kind man. He'd be very impressed by you.'

But not as impressed as he would have been if I could have brought home my expensive whore in her Pringle sweater and soft wool skirt to patronise him in the voice of the gentry. From the beaches of the south and sunlight off ski slopes, the whore's skin (and what did it matter if it had been a sunlamp in a stinking sauna and massage parlour?) had burnished brown and pure.

'What's wrong? If you're ill, won't you go?'

'Everything's spoiled,' I said.

We faced one another across the little table. I could have reached out and touched her. In the shop we had slept together and I had touched her then; but afterwards I had held my whore's little naked breast between my hands, fucked her, watched with her as Brond knelt under the rain of the fat woman's sweat.

The doorbell rang. After a pause, it started again and did not stop.

'It doesn't sound like your father,' I said. I knew who it was.

'I asked you to go. I said please go.'

Pretty please.

'Did he give you a number to ring, just in case I came? He likes to play games, you know. It's because he gets bored.'

'Leave me in peace,' she said.

As I waited for her to let him in, I looked at the high black headline above the newspaper picture. He had been an old man, and whatever he had done probably he had thought it was right. He had been born to it, as my father would say; but, then, hadn't we all? He hadn't deserved to be beaten to death in an hotel room, because no one deserved that death. They had given him a fine funeral, though, and he would have appreciated that since it was the kind of thing he valued.

'Don't you understand I just want to be left in peace now?' Margaret Briody said.

Somebody else who wanted to opt out of history.

NINETEEN

Of the rooms Brond had filled with his presence, this was the shabbiest. Wearing a black overcoat that seemed too big for him, he sat in a tangle of blankets on a narrow bed. The room looked worse because of the neat respectability of the rest of the apartment. Primo had led me through past a woman and a young girl busy folding clothes into two open suitcases. As the woman looked up – pale round face, too tired to be any longer pretty – Primo said, 'It'll be all right Beth,' and I knew she was his wife and the girl must be his daughter.

Once, hitchhiking, I had slept overnight in a doss house, which should have been an adventure but had left me feeling desolate. This room was like that, despite being neat enough and clean; it was a bleakness of the spirit. The only decoration was a photograph in a cheap wood frame hung over Brond's head on the wall behind the bed. The photograph seemed to have been torn from a magazine and was deeply creased as if at one time it might have been carried folded in a wallet. Putting stuff like that on the wall was the kind of thing children did or what my parents would have called 'the lowest of the low', meaning those who were poorer than we were and feckless in their poverty.

'Notice how human they are,' Brond said, following my gaze to the photograph. 'The little scrubbed sac naked between their legs like innocent testicles. Very human, helpless and detestable.'

'Like Kilpatrick,' I said, 'or him.' The newspaper on the bed lay open to display stately carriages in procession.

Primo made a sudden gesture at the corner of my vision and my mouth dried with fear. It had been he who had fetched me from Margaret Briody's but we had travelled in the car in silence. I could have taken my chance to tell him what he had to be told, but I had thought first I wanted to confront Brond.

'Or Muldoon,' Brond said. 'He was human enough surely.'

He got up and went over to the window. A restlessness flowed out of him I had not sensed before. Staring down as if watching something below, he asked, 'You like Irish jokes? I remember. What about this one?' He put a finger to his forehead in a parody of recollection and then tapped it on the air like a schoolmaster. 'What do you call a man who sticks his finger up an Irishman's arse? . . . No? A brain surgeon.'

He turned and came back to the bed.

'Isn't that the kind of joke you like?'

I picked up the newspaper.

'Primo killed him – or you did,' I said. 'Primo was there though. He had to be to pull open the safety door. I've never met anyone else who could do that.'

Brond, not at all upset, looked on kindly.

'You know, it's silly to make yourself unhappy about that woman – the not so young woman – you called her . . .'

'Jackie.' Primo rumbled the single word.

'We've all been foolish about some woman. It's of no significance. Be grateful that you're normal.' His mesmerist's hands formed a circle from which the abnormal were excluded. His hands made a language more absolute than speech. 'It's good to have feelings like that. You're at a lucky age. It's sad that she has to think of you as her husband's murderer.'

I winced from the ugly word.

'It was an accident.'

Brond smiled his kind smile and waited.

'I want to see her. I could make her understand.' The same fatal urge to accuse them came over me more recklessly. 'If you won't let me explain to her, I can explain to the police.'

'An odd choice of a Lonely Hearts Bureau.' Brond's laughter sounded easy and genuine. I had felt that kind of release into laughter after finishing a diet of examinations or coming to the end of a visit home.

'It was Primo and you at Riggs Lodge. You killed the old man there. You killed him and tied him with the same rope you used on Peter Kilpatrick.'

'We never touched the boy Kilpatrick. Not when he was alive.' It was Primo who thought that was worth denying. 'Leaving him in that shed was a right Fenian trick.'

'It was Kennedy who did it, don't doubt that,' Brond added. 'And for the same motive that made him attack you. Unfairly in your case, of course – you don't seem ever to have succeeded in getting his wife to bed.'

He dirtied the pity I felt for Jackie. I wanted to tell him what I felt for her – that I had never wanted to – he made everything confused.

'No,' I said. 'They were tied with the same rope. The police told me that. Why use the same rope on the old man?'

'The people I work for,' Brond said, sounding unctuous, 'wanted an act of terrorism that would make the public detest those who were accused of it. In any case, the old party in question,' he tapped the newspaper with its images of a hearse and dignitaries and nodding plumes, 'had become a confounded nuisance. Rash committments to business friends in Africa that were threatening to find their way out into the light . . . There's an economy in such matters. His death solved one problem, and if it could be made to forestall another – the risk, however remote, of the natives here getting restless – so much the better.'

What was it the Canadian strategist at Professor Gracemount's party had called Scotland? A valuable piece of real estate . . .

'I understand,' I said, but then I looked at Primo who was listening, and I didn't understand at all. How could he accept this?

'Do you?' Brond asked. 'I wonder if you really do. Those people I work for wanted a mischief, you know. If I hadn't arranged it, there are others who would have managed something . . . not so elegant, perhaps. But that length of rope which worries you so much cleared away all our difficulties. I saw it at once, and Sawney agreed with me.' He nodded at the big man, and, as late as that, I learned Primo's real name. 'We would give them the assasination they were demanding. We would let them break their scandal. We would even let them produce some poor misguided devils of dupes for a trial. But then, when all three rings of the circus are performing beyond recall, the defence will receive evidence which ties their murder case to that of a young man called Kilpatrick.' He smiled disquietingly. 'It's possible at that point you might find yourself briefly the centre of attention. But don't worry – the next stir of the pot will be to provide the defence with proof that *both* murders were committed by an obscure bookie's clerk and lodging-house keeper called Kennedy. They'll search for him – but he's hidden where they'll never dig to find him.'

I could see it all falling out as he described. He made it so easy to believe in him, even for me who knew better.

'The damage then will be entirely the other way. All kinds of questions – about the preparation of the trial, about the prosecution's carefully marshalled evidence – come next.' But then I heard his tone alter, the subtlest of changes, as he said, 'We could even provide the information that he was really Michael Dart – an Irish terrorist. A sleeper. This man who has disappeared – presumably gone on the run again. Sawney thinks that information wouldn't help what we want to do. He's right, but it's there to be used. Anyway, the result is going to be very different from what my employers anticipated. Sawney and I see a little victory coming.'

As Sawney-Primo's breath sighed in the silence, I heard that false note in Brond's voice so clearly, like a secret he wanted me to share. He stood up, buttoning the black coat to his throat. I realised he intended to leave and that I would be alone with Primo.

'As far as you are concerned, it's over,' he said smiling. 'I make you that promise.'

No prison, no trial, no disgrace; not again that desolate time of going through bright streets as a prisoner? Had he that power? It came into my head that when a piece was taken *en passant* in the game of chess, the piece that took it was only another pawn like itself. In the old black overcoat, hesitating at the door, Brond dwindled. I would have passed him in the street without a glance as an elderly man down on his luck.

'All good things come to an end. I've been a long time in this place,' he said. 'I stayed in Chicago once. I went to the airport to meet professional contacts from Sweden. They came off the plane jittering with nerves for they had seen too many movies about tommy guns and Al Capone and gangland killings. I laughed and told them I'd never heard a gun fired in anger in that city. People I knew who had been born there had never heard one. We walked out the front entrance and a car hurtled towards us, police units followed on both sides blocking its escape, men piled out firing from behind walls and opened car doors. Screams, yells, curses, everyone running for shelter, throwing themselves down. I stood there alone among the bullets, too astonished to react. My Swedes stayed in their hotel room doing business until it was time for their plane home . . . They didn't believe a word I said after that.'

It was a story you would tell to make people laugh, but he went out without a backward glance. His steps limped away through the flat's stillness.

'I don't hear your wife,' I said. 'Your little girl is very quiet.'

He would not look at me and that frightened me. To avoid me he went to the picture over the bed. The photograph had been taken in a battery chicken factory. The chickens hung upside down, stripped and obscene, a line of them hooked by the feet to a moving belt. Two large smiling women stood behind them, their hands reaching out. Very human, naked and detestable.

'Beth's always hated coming in here.' He put out a massive hand and tried to straighten the picture. It resisted and the bottom splintered off under his fingers. The magazine photograph had been stuck on the wall and four strips of wood glued round it to give the appearance of a frame. 'I've broken it.'

'Primo . . . Primo? Are you going to kill me?

'I took you back to the farm to your mammy,' he said bitterly, looking at the broken picture. 'I decided that myself. But you couldn't stay there.'

'You should've let that wardrobe kill me. It would have been easier.'

'Ya poor bloody clown,' he said without anger.

'Brond was lying. He'll let them have their trial. Just the way they want it. Couldn't you hear that he was lying?'

'Don't whine,' he said. 'Keep your dignity. That way it'll be easier for both of us.'

I crossed to the closed window, though I knew we were too high for that escape to be possible. From so high, it took a moment to realise what I was seeing. This room must be at the front of the building we had entered from the rear. I looked down on a curve of river and a bridge. Sodden heavy rain was threshing down after the days of heat. Primo had learned to kill in Malaya, giant hands choking tiny men in blue pyjamas. 'If you had information we needed – that might save a mate's life, like – sure Ah'd torture ye,' an uncle said one night, reminiscing. A man you could rely on, like Primo. Little men like children in pyjamas. A child might be killed for seeing something he was not meant to see, for overhearing something he should not have heard.

'I saw Brond murder a boy down there.' I knew I was talking of Primo's son. 'I can give you the day and the date. I was down there and saw the boy pull himself up on the rail. Brond – but I didn't know his name then – came over the bridge.' I spoke slowly and clearly, giving evidence in a matter of life and death. 'Brond put his hand under the boy and lifted him over. I can still hear the noise he made when he fell on the platform underneath.'

Behind me was utterly still. Why should a man not kill someone who had even seen such a thing?

'I'll never forget it. I looked over – I could see he was dead. There was nothing I could do. And then afterwards I was ill.'

When I found the courage to turn, the room was empty. I went through the deserted flat. Just after I had seen them the woman and child must have left taking the suitcases with them. In the tiny living room the ornaments still sat on the sideboard; a child's schoolbag was on the couch with books and an open jotter scattered beside it. I wondered where the family would go now; I wondered what organisation claimed Primo as a member, how Brond had infiltrated them, how he had become accepted. That he would come to dominate them I accepted as natural. I wondered how much the little girl understood and if she had liked the man who visited and stayed with them in their home.

A noise faint but persistent crept into my attention. I walked out of the open front door of the flat and stepped on to the factory's upper gallery. More clearly the sound came, drumming, rattling, going on without a pause as I came down the iron stair. After the second landing, the entire factory came in view as the stair carried me back and forward in front of three windows that went down from ceiling to floor. The floor was in shadow and the light was stained yellow by some chemical that had eaten into the glass. I moved cautiously across aisles of metal pillars until I saw Primo. In his fist the handle disappeared and as he shook the little door helplessly to and fro the whole frame of the exit trembled. He looked at me without seeming to know or care who I was. 'It won't open,' he said and stepped aside as if it was natural for me to try. When the handle did not turn normally, I reversed the direction and the lock released at once so that the door swung back on us letting Primo pass through the opening I had so easily accomplished.

Rain fell on the cobbled yard. Stepping under its drenched heaviness, sweat broke out on my sides. I walked through an echoing pend into a street of blank shopfronts and boarded windows that led me round two sides of the factory to the main road. When I stopped in the middle of the bridge, I could see high on the wall of the tenement opposite a row of windows. One of them must belong to the apartment. Behind me the downpour smoked on the river and beat against the crooked ladder on the gable wall.

I had turned Primo loose and it was time to search for what I had done.

Twice I passed the place. Just inside the park near a gate a column of undressed stone rose like a maned lion into the head of Carlyle: the second time I saw the body lying inside the low railing that surrounded the statue. Sprawled on the grass, it could have been an old man drunk on cheap wine or meths; but I recognised the long overcoat and he lay too still for bad dreams. Remembering Kilpatrick and the horror of Kennedy's death, I felt it unfair that he should lie so peacefully. I heard him saying: We see a victory coming. I couldn't stop the words, they ran over and over like a tune that drives you mad. There was no one in sight to help and I was afraid to touch him.

A long time later, a policeman came. I tried but I could not understand what he was asking. He was young like me but he stepped over the railing and touched what lay there. As the body was turned, the black coat which had only been thrown across it slipped off.

I thought it was a trick. I thought it was Brond but that he had put on a last disguise. I stepped over the rail and went down on my knees.

Nothing about him was certain.

Above me, the policeman prayed to the machine he held in his hand. I looked up at him from where I knelt. Watchfully, as he spoke, he took a careful step back.

What do you call someone who sticks his finger up a Scotsman's arse?

Wi the wig-wig-waggle o the kilt: another crazy tune.

'What do you call a man who sticks his finger up an Englishman's arse?' I asked aloud, but the constable stared back in dismay.

He did not realise that it was a joke. He was right, of course. You always spoiled a joke if you changed the ending.

Ah've been hurt masel.

Now the rain was heavy. It soaked the ground and turned it black. It streamed down the policeman's face. It ran in stone tears down the lion face of the prophet.

It fell like a judgement not on Brond but on Primo, the Scottish soldier, dead in the mud. But then when had it ever been Brond?